"Married! You don't seriously intend for me to marry you?"

Manda focused her gaze on Hunter. "You are so damn sure that once we announce our engagement, my secret admirer will make his move and you'll be able to catch him?" She pulled away from his arms. "By all means, let's follow through with this idiotic plan. Let's put both our lives in danger. Let's show everyone in Dearborn that we're fools in love, and to hell with the consequences."

Hunter grabbed her, cupping her chin as he stared into her eyes. "I don't think we'll have any trouble convincing everyone that we can't keep our hands off each other. Just pretend you feel about me now the way you did when you were sixteen."

Manda's face flushed. "And what are you going to pretend?"

"I'm a man, baby doll. With a woman who looks like you, I won't have to pretend."

Dear Reader,

This is officially "Get Caught Reading" month, so why not get caught reading one—or all!—of this month's Intimate Moments books? We've got six you won't be able to resist.

In *Whitelaw's Wedding,* Beverly Barton continues her popular miniseries THE PROTECTORS. Where does the Dundee Security Agency come up with such great guys—and where can I find one in real life? A YEAR OF LOVING DANGEROUSLY is almost over, but not before you read about *Cinderella's Secret Agent,* from Ingrid Weaver. Then come back next month, when Sharon Sala wraps things up in her signature compelling style.

Carla Cassidy offers a *Man on a Mission,* part of THE DELANEY HEIRS, her newest miniseries. Candace Irvin once again demonstrates her deft way with a military romance with *In Close Quarters,* while Claire King returns with a *Renegade with a Badge* who you won't be able to pass up. Finally, join Nina Bruhns for *Warrior's Bride,* a romance with a distinctly Native American feel.

And, of course, come back next month as the excitement continues in Intimate Moments, home of your favorite authors and the best in romantic reading.

Leslie J. Wainger
Executive Senior Editor

Please address questions and book requests to:
Silhouette Reader Service
U.S.: 3010 Walden Ave., P.O. Box 1325, Buffalo, NY 14269
Canadian: P.O. Box 609, Fort Erie, Ont. L2A 5X3

Whitelaw's Wedding

BEVERLY BARTON

INTIMATE MOMENTS™

Published by Silhouette Books

America's Publisher of Contemporary Romance

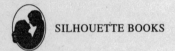

SILHOUETTE BOOKS

ISBN 0-373-27145-X

WHITELAW'S WEDDING

Copyright © 2001 by Beverly Beaver

This edition published by arrangement with Harlequin Books S.A.

Visit Silhouette at www.eHarlequin.com

Printed in U.S.A.

Books by Beverly Barton

BEVERLY BARTON

has been in love with romance since her grandfather gave her an illustrated book of *Beauty and the Beast.* An avid reader since childhood, Beverly wrote her first book at the age of nine. After marriage to her own "hero" and the births of her daughter and son, Beverly chose to be a full-time homemaker, aka wife, mother, friend and volunteer. The author of over thirty-five books, Beverly is a member of Romance Writers of America and helped found the Heart of Dixie chapter in Alabama. She has won numerous awards and made the Waldenbooks and *USA Today* bestseller lists.

To my fellow Heart of Dixie RWA chapter members, past and present, for the camaraderie, encouragement and support, but especially for all the good times we've shared over the years.

Prologue

Manda Munroe inspected her curves in the mirror. The woman she saw reflected there was one others referred to as beautiful. She supposed she was pretty, just as she was rich and pampered. At least that was what everyone told her. Her father, older brother and grandmother doted on her. And she loved them, too, which was why she would never tell them that all their smothering attention could never fill the void, never replace the gigantic hole created in her life by her mother's absence. Most of the time she didn't feel sorry for herself for being the only kid in her circle of friends who didn't have a mother. But for crying out loud, she had just turned sixteen and what she needed most was someone no one in her life could truly replace. A mother. Someone she could turn to for advice on being a woman. Grams was wonderful, but she was sixty and hardly up-to-date on the things today's teenage girls needed to know.

Manda pivoted slowly in front of the cherry cheval mirror in her bedroom. Grams wouldn't approve of the bikini she was wearing, even though some of her friends wore skimpier ones. But if she was ever going to make Hunter Whitelaw notice that she was no longer a little girl, she had to do something drastic. She'd decided letting him see her in next to nothing would open his eyes to the fact that she was all grown up. Now, maybe he'd stop thinking of her as nothing more than Perry's little sister. She'd had a crush on Hunter for as long as she could remember, since the first time Perry brought him to the house, about six years ago when the guys played high school football together. Of course, back then, she really had been just a kid. But even at ten, she'd somehow known that Hunter was the one and only boy on earth for her. And since that time, with each passing year, she had become more and more certain that he was destined to be the love of her life.

Now, all she had to do was convince him of that fact. And parading around in front of him in her bikini was a great way to start. She didn't have much time to accomplish her goal. Hunter was home in Dearborn for only two weeks, then he'd go back to the army.

Manda grabbed her waist-length hair, pulled it through a rubber band and secured it in a ponytail. She opened her bedroom door, peeked out into the hall for any sign of Grams, then rushed toward the back stairs. As she passed through the laundry room, she grabbed a huge white towel, then flew out the door and onto the patio. Seeing Hunter lying on one of the chaise longues by the pool, she skidded to a halt. He was all alone. Manda squared her shoulders, took a deep breath and sauntered in his direction. She probably had less than twenty minutes to make an impression on Hunter. Daddy was at work, Grams should be taking her afternoon nap and their housekeeper, Bobbie Rue, was enjoying her day off at her sister's house across town.

Manda had timed her arrival at the pool to coincide with Perry's trip to the store to pick up a couple of six-packs. He'd huffed about in the pantry, complaining that he couldn't understand where the hell the four six-packs he'd put in there this past weekend had gone. She'd hidden the beer under the sink in the kitchen, knowing her brother wouldn't spend a lazy summer afternoon without his favorite drink. Yuck. Manda had tried the nasty stuff and couldn't imagine anyone drinking such foul-tasting poison.

Hunter was stretched out to his full six-four height, his big, muscular arms thrown back and his hands resting above his head. He wore only a pair of loose black swim trunks, leaving most of his body bare. As she approached, she took inventory, scanning him from head to toe. Thick, dark brown hair, neatly trimmed. Sunglasses hooded his eyes, which she knew were a light blue-gray. Broad shoulders and wide chest, trim waist and hips. And long, long legs. Big hands. Big feet. And every inch of his flesh was tanned a golden brown. Curly dark hair covered his chest, as well as dusted his arms and legs.

Now, that's a man!

Manda paraded around in front of Hunter, who didn't seem to notice her. She cleared her throat. He eased the sunglasses down his nose and peered at her over the rim.

"Hi, there," she said, then tossed her towel on the chaise beside his, pulled back her shoulders and thrust forward her breasts, which were covered only by two triangles of shiny red material.

Hunter grunted and slid his shades back into place.

What was the matter with him? Manda wondered.

Couldn't he see that she was a gorgeous young woman? Everybody said so. All the guys her age drooled over her.

"Where's Perry?" she asked.

"He went to pick up some beer for us," Hunter replied, but didn't glance her way.

"Mind if I join you?"

He shrugged. "This is your house, your patio and your pool."

"So it is."

Doing her best to act alluring, Manda lay down on the chaise next to Hunter's and turned her head so that she faced him. She reached out, picked up the bottle of suntan lotion on the small table between them and flipped open the lid. After pouring a quarter-size amount of the white cream into the palm of her hand, she applied it to her arms, then repeated the process on her legs. She'd seen this seduction scene in a movie, so she figured it was worth a try.

"Do you mind doing my back?" she asked.

"Huh?"

"My back. Would you put some lotion on it for me? I can't reach my back and with this fair skin of mine, I burn easily."

Hunter barely suppressed the chuckle rising in his throat. Manda, Manda. What was he going to do with her? Perry had told him a couple of years ago that his little sister had a mad crush on her big brother's best friend. At the time, he'd thought it was cute and rather endearing. But for the past few days, while he'd been home on leave, Manda had been driving him crazy. She had done everything but strip off naked to gain his attention. And from the looks of that skimpy bikini she was wearing, she must have decided to use that tactic, as well. If Mrs. Munroe saw Manda in that scanty swimsuit, she would ground her granddaughter until she was thirty.

He had to admit that if he didn't know Manda was only sixteen—and if she weren't his buddy Perry's baby sister—he'd be tempted. Manda was just too damn pretty for her own good. Pretty? Hell, she was beautiful. And she knew it.

The girl was too pretty, too rich, too smart and too spoiled. He pitied the poor guy who wound up marrying her someday. She was growing up to be a high-maintenance lady.

"Sure, I'll do your back," Hunter said and took the bottle from her. "Turn around."

She obeyed instantly, but then she did the unexpected. She unhooked her bikini top, jerked it off and laid it on the chaise. Hunter hadn't been prepared for that particular move, but he supposed he should have been, considering the way Manda had been chasing him these past few days.

"That'll make it easier," she said.

Easier for what? Damn, this kid didn't know she was playing with fire. His guess was that she didn't understand how easily a guy could become sexually aroused. If she pulled this kind of stunt with another guy, she might get more than she bargained for. "Manda, I don't think that's a good idea."

"Why not?"

"A lady doesn't strip off her clothes that way and expose herself," Hunter said. "Your grams would be—"

"Grams is an old-fashioned prude who doesn't know the first thing about being a modern woman. It's been so long since she was young and in love that she's probably forgotten how it feels."

In love? Damn! He definitely wasn't prepared to handle that kind of complication. Even if Manda were older, there were too many things that separated them on every level imaginable. She was and always would be *off limits* to him.

"Damn it, Manda, put your top back on and act like a grown-up instead of a stupid kid."

"A stupid kid!"

She whirled around, anger flashing in her eyes, but before he could look away, he got an eyeful. God help him, the sight of her was enough to bring a strong man to his knees. Her breasts were large, firm and centered with pouting pink nipples.

Hunter jumped up, grabbed the red bikini top off the chaise and tossed it at Manda. "For heaven's sake, brat, put that on. Now!"

She ignored his command, flung the top on the patio floor and shot out of the chaise. "I'm not a stupid kid. I'm a grown woman. Damn it, will you look at me? Can't you see that I'm more than just Perry's little sister?"

Hunter tried his level best to keep his gaze focused on her face, but that wasn't an easy task. Not with her sweet, luscious body almost totally bare. He snatched the towel off the chaise and started to wrap it around her, but with another unexpected move, she flung herself at him and clung to him tenaciously. The towel slipped off and down to the floor. Her naked breasts pressed against his chest.

Hunter grabbed her shoulders, pulled her away from him and shook her soundly.

"What the hell's going on?" Perry Munroc stood at the back door, a beer in each hand.

Manda whirled around, gasped when she saw her brother, then glanced over her shoulder and glared malevolently at Hunter. "Your best friend here was putting the moves on me."

"Perry—"

"Damn it, Manda, put on some clothes, will you," Perry said. "And leave Hunter alone."

"You don't believe me?" Manda asked in a wounded, little-girl voice.

Perry walked onto the patio, handed Hunter a beer, set the other on the table, then picked up the towel off the floor and wrapped it around Manda, crossing it over her breasts. "Get upstairs and put on a decent bathing suit before Grams sees you. And for the rest of Hunter's stay with us, will you, please, leave him the hell alone?"

"You might not believe me, but we'll see what Grams and Daddy have to say." Manda scurried toward the house.

"Don't you dare repeat such a stupid accusation," Perry called after her, then turned to Hunter when Manda disappeared inside the house. "Sorry about that. She's spoiled rotten. We usually give her anything she wants and unfortunately the one thing she wants the most right now is you."

"She scares the hell out of me," Hunter admitted. "Manda's a stick of dynamite that's just about ready to go off. Y'all had better tighten the reins on that girl."

Perry laughed. "And think, she's only sixteen. Can you imagine what we'll have to deal with by the time she's eighteen? Heaven help us."

Hunter shook his head and laughed. "Heaven help the guy who marries her."

Chapter 1

Perry Munroe found his sister pacing the floor in Dearborn Memorial Hospital's ER waiting room. When she'd phoned him half an hour ago, she had been nearly hysterical. She'd kept repeating the same words. *It's happened again! The Manda Munroe Curse.* The best he could make out from their brief conversation was that her date had taken ill during dinner and she had rushed him to the hospital. Of all things to have happened to Manda, why this? She hadn't dated anyone in such a long time. Not since her fiancé Mike Farrar's death.

Perry had hoped that the nightmare she'd lived through in the past was over, that she could actually live a normal life, find a man to love, marry and have children. He knew that was what his sister wanted more than anything. He'd thought perhaps her colleague, Dr. Boyd Gipson, who worked with her at the clinic where she was a grief counselor, might turn out to be Mr. Right. But somehow, by a trick of fate, Boyd had fallen victim to the Manda Munroe Curse, the phrase an insensitive reporter for the local newspaper had coined five years ago when Mike Farrar's body had been found a week after his mysterious disappearance. At that time, the reporter had unearthed the tragic story of Manda's past and the death of her first fiancé when she'd been twenty-one.

The moment Manda saw him, she halted her frantic pacing and ran toward him. He opened his arms and embraced her. She trembled as she clung to him.

"Oh, Perry, it's happened again. Boyd and I were having dessert and coffee, when he suddenly became very ill. I don't know how it's possible, how anyone could have done it, but I know someone tried to kill him."

Perry grasped Manda's shoulders. "What does the ER doctor say?"

"He said it was food poisoning, but I know better." Manda glared at Perry, her eyes wild with fear. "I thought…I hoped and prayed that I could at least have a nice, comfortable friendship with a man, without—without—" She took in huge gulps of air. "We've had only three dates. Nothing serious. Just companionship. But then that's all there was between Mike and me. A marriage of two good friends, both who had lost a loved one in the past and… *He* won't let me have anyone else in my life, will he? Not even a friend."

Perry's stomach knotted painfully. "Look, brat, I honestly don't think that lunatic who might or might not have been responsible for Mike's death had anything to do with this. It's just a coincidence. It has to be. People get food poisoning fairly often. And you haven't gotten any notes predicting Boyd's demise, have you?"

She shook her head. "No, but… I'll have to tell Boyd that I can't see him again. Not socially. I can't take the risk. If anything happened to him, I'd never forgive myself."

"What do you plan to do, live the rest of your life like a nun? You deserve better. You're allowing some lunatic to dictate the terms of your life."

"Two men that I've cared for have died tragically," Manda said. "First Rodney and then Mike." She cupped her hands over her mouth and sighed in an effort to not cry again. "Someone killed them because he's obsessed with me and doesn't want me to marry anyone else. Whoever killed Rodney and Mike is probably still watching me, waiting for me to... I refuse to endanger another man's life. Not ever again!"

Perry knew that when she got like this there was no point in trying to reason with her. He felt certain that Boyd's food poisoning had been an accident, but Manda was bound and determined to blame herself. Poor girl. The woman standing before him bore little resemblance to the carefree, spoiled little hellion she'd once been. Rodney Austin's death in a car crash only a week before their wedding had devastated Manda. That had been twelve years ago. It had taken Manda years to get over that loss, but eventually she had become engaged to her good friend, Mike Farrar, who had lost his wife to cancer. When they became engaged, Manda had received a series of letters warning her to not marry Mike, that if she did, he would die, just as Rodney had. They had taken the letters to the police, but the local law enforcement had been unable to trace the letters to find the author. Only days before the wedding, Mike had disappeared. His body had been found in the Poloma River. He'd been shot in the back. His murderer was never found.

For the past five years, Manda hadn't dated. It had

taken him months to convince his sister to accept Boyd's pleas for a date.

Had he been wrong to encourage her to put the past to rest and move on with her life?

The letter arrived a week later. Manda had stopped by Perry's law office in downtown Dearborn and tossed the nondescript white envelope on his desk.

''Read it,'' she'd said.

The author of the printed missive had assured Manda that he was not responsible for Boyd's illness. But he had pointed out that even Fate didn't want Manda with another man. He had ended his letter with a warning.

You know that I'll never let you be happy with anyone else. If you ever try to marry another man, I'll kill him. And if you're foolish enough to allow it to happen again, I might have to kill you, too.

The letter was similar in tone and wording to the six letters that Manda had received in the weeks leading up to her wedding to Mike. A second wedding that never took place.

Perry had insisted Manda take the letter to the police, just as they'd done in the past. He had gone with her, of course, and as he had expected, the local authorities reluctantly admitted that there was little chance of apprehending the culprit, with nothing but the letters as evidence.

Damn it all, he wasn't going to allow his sister to crawl into a hole and pull the hole in after her. She was young—only thirty-three—and beautiful, with so much love and passion to give the right man. But out there somewhere was a nutcase determined to control Manda's love life.

There had to be a way to put an end to this craziness. He should have done something years ago, after Mike's death. But he'd known Manda needed time to heal and he had allowed the years to slip by without forming a plan of action.

What Manda needed was a fiancé capable of not only outwitting a would-be assassin, but one able to protect her, too. Perry grinned. He knew just the man. He'd call him tonight. And tomorrow he'd tell Manda that she was going to marry the man of her dreams—her teenage dreams.

Hunter Whitelaw propped his feet up on the rustic log coffee table, eased his weary shoulders into the back of the overstuffed sofa and groaned. He and his fellow Dundee agent Matt O'Brien had just completed a month-long assignment and agents Jack Parker and David Wolfe had also recently finished with a difficult job. Hunter and Matt's case had taken a toll on them and had dredged up some unpleasant memories for Hunter personally. An American billionaire had given his eighteen-year-old twins a trip to Europe as a high school graduation gift, but he'd wanted the two girls, Risa and Rhea, protected day and night. On the surface, it had seemed to be a plum assignment—a month in Europe, all expenses paid. At least that was what Matt had thought. Hunter could have warned them, but figured he would find out soon enough just how much trouble two cute little girls could be. Hunter had learned that lesson years ago.

The smell of frying fish wafted through the cabin. Jack Parker was cooking supper for them. Frying fish and hush puppies. Hunter closed his eyes and sighed. He could almost taste the delicious catfish they'd caught in the river this morning. He and Jack had persuaded Wolfe to go with them and the guy had turned out to be quite a fisherman. Apparently, Wolfe was good at whatever he did. But the man was too damn quiet, too reclusive. Hunter had actually been surprised that he'd accepted his offer to join them on their weekend trip.

Jack liked to fish as well as Hunter did. The gregarious Texan was a fellow who seemed to love just being alive. He was the exact opposite of Wolfe, a somber, solitary man, who seemed to carry the woes of the world on his shoulders. And then there was Matt, their movie-star-handsome buddy who had women swooning at his feet wherever they went. Hell, Risa and Rhea had been all over Matt, and the former Air Force Cowboy had been out of his league with the two nymphets. It had taken both of them working diligently to stay one step ahead of the twins and at the same time keep the girls out of their beds. If they'd been smart, they would have suggested Ellen, Dundee's CEO, take this job herself and enlist several female Dundee agents to help her.

Hunter chuckled. He hadn't been propositioned by a teenage girl since he'd been twenty-two and Perry Munroe's little sister had given him an eyeful that summer he'd been home in Dearborn on leave from the army. Her outraged grandmother, who had believed Manda's tale that Hunter had come on to her, had forbidden Hunter to set foot in the Munroe house ever again. Of course, Mr. Munroe and Perry had known the truth and assured Hunter he was always welcome.

"Supper's ready," Jack called from the kitchen. "Come and get it while it's hot."

After opening the front door, Hunter repeated Jack's invitation to Wolfe, who had escaped outside over an hour earlier. Then he walked halfway up the stairs to holler at Matt. Hunter waited for Wolfe to enter from the front porch and for Matt to emerge from the upstairs bedroom, where he'd been playing games on his laptop computer. Once the two men joined him in the living room, he followed them straight to the kitchen table. They all laughed when they saw Jack in a large floral apron, apparently left there by the last people who'd rented the cabin.

"Hey, don't laugh at my stylish attire." Jack plopped lightly breaded and browned catfish on each of the four plates. "You guys would starve if it wasn't for my culinary talents."

"Don't think you're indispensable," Matt said. "There's a steak house less than ten miles from here."

The four men gathered around the wooden table in the kitchen and quickly delved into the catfish meal. Three of them ate, talked and laughed. Wolfe just ate. Hunter couldn't figure the guy out, couldn't put his finger on exactly what it was about the man that bothered him. He had to be an okay kind of guy or he wouldn't be working for the Dundee agency. Sam Dundee, the agency's owner, had personally hired Wolfe. And no one was hired without a thorough background check. But Wolfe's former life was a mystery—to everyone at the agency, even the CEO, who usually did the hiring.

"So, are y'all interested in watching the Braves on TV tonight?" Matt asked.

"I thought we had satellite TV here," Jack said. "I wouldn't mind checking out the Playboy channel."

"Is that all you ever think about?" Hunter smiled. "If you don't slow down, Jackie boy, you're going to burn out before you're forty."

"That gives me two more years to burn the candle at both ends." Jack downed the last drops of coffee from the earthenware mug, then got up to pour himself another cup. "Anybody else want more coffee?"

''Only if you baked us an apple pie for dessert,'' Matt said.

The good-natured comradery between Hunter, Matt and Jack continued throughout the evening as they shared a couple of six-packs. Wolfe watched part of the Braves game with them, then excused himself to take a long walk. He returned after dark, said good-night and went upstairs to the bedroom he shared with Matt.

''What do you think it is?'' Matt asked.

''Huh?'' Jack stared quizzically at his buddy.

Matt nodded toward the stairs. ''Wolfe. What do you think his story is? Why is he such a mystery man?''

''Who knows?'' Jack shrugged.

''Whatever's going on with him, past or present, is none of our business,'' Hunter told them. ''The guy obviously has some demons chasing him, but if he wanted us to know, he'd tell us.''

''What about you Whitelaw—you got any demons on your tail?'' Matt asked.

Hunter chuckled. ''Sure. We all do, don't we? But it's not something any of us talk about, so why should Wolfe?''

Jack stood, stretched and then glanced at his companions. ''I think I'm going to go take a dip in the river. I sort of have a date to meet up with the gals staying in the cabin down the road. Either of you want to join us?''

''How many gals did you meet?'' Matt asked.

''Two,'' Jack replied. ''A brunette and a redhead.''

''I'll go.'' Matt stood. ''You don't mind, do you, Hunter? I know you have a thing for blondes, so—''

Motioning a get-out-of-here wave, Hunter said, ''Go on. I think I'll grab another beer and then read for a while.''

He did just as he'd said. Got himself another beer,

kicked back on the sofa and opened Tom Clancy's latest bestseller. But for some reason, he couldn't concentrate. The words on the page seemed to blur together. Hell, maybe he needed to have his eyesight checked. He was nearly forty. Bifocals were probably a part of his immediate future.

Forty in six months. Where had all the years gone? And just what did he have to show for his life? One marriage gone bad, ending in divorce ten years ago. No children. Not even a damn dog to call his own. However, he did have a job he liked and a fat bank account, and that wasn't bad for a poor Georgia boy who'd grown up on his grandparents' farm. From the age of sixteen when he'd first become friends with fellow Dearborn High football player Perry Munroe, Hunter had known that someday he wanted to be part of the privileged world in which the Munroes lived. A fine house on North Pine Street. A sleek sports car. Entree to the country club and the best homes in Georgia. But most of all he wanted a woman from that world, a lady who possessed a pedigree back to Adam.

Eventually, he had acquired everything he'd ever wanted. As a member of the top secret Delta Force, he had lived a life of excitement and danger. With some shrewd investments, he had acquired enough money to buy that big house and the sports car. And he had married Selina Lewis, a Virginia debutante. His wife had been a spoiled heiress to whom marriage vows meant nothing. Her affair with one of his Delta Force comrades had ended their three years of trying to make their mismatched union work. In the end, he had admitted to himself that no amount of education, money or polishing could completely erase the redneck Georgia boy from his personality.

The phone rang. Hunter eyed the source of the insistent

ringing, wondering who would be calling any of them during their weekend getaway. No one from the agency would dare disturb them, not after Jack had given boss-lady Ellen fair warning that they weren't to be disturbed.

In no hurry, Hunter rose languidly from the sofa and made his way across the room to the wall telephone near the staircase. He lifted the receiver and said, "Whitelaw, here. This had damn well better be important."

"Hunter, this is Perry Munroe. And this *is* damn important."

"Perry, how did you know where to find me?"

"I contacted the Dundee agency and told them it was a family emergency."

"I don't have any family left since Granny's death two years ago, so it must be your family emergency and not mine."

"Look, old buddy, I have a huge favor to ask of you."

"Name it." Although he and Perry hadn't seen each other in a couple of years, Hunter still considered the man one of his best friends. And if for no other reason than the good times they'd shared in the past, he would always be there for Perry, if and when his old pal ever needed him.

"I have a job offer for you," Perry said. "A bodyguard job."

"You need a bodyguard?"

"Not me."

"Your wife?"

"No, not Gwen."

"Then who?"

"Manda."

"You want to hire me as Manda's bodyguard?"

"Sort of," Perry said. "Actually, there's more to the job than just acting as her bodyguard."

"Exactly what do you want me to do?" Hunter asked.

"I want you to marry my sister."

Chapter 2

Manda had no choice but to attend tonight's gala celebration. After all, how would it look to Dearborn society if she didn't show up for her sister-in-law's birthday party? Throughout high school and college, she had loved parties and had given her share of them. But that had been years ago. Before Rodney died. Before Mike was murdered. She could barely remember the person she'd been before tragedy had struck her life. Everything had been fun once. Lighthearted enjoyment. Boyfriends and parties and laughter. Manda realized that she would have been forced to grow up, sooner or later, and take on adult responsibilities. She had thought those duties would include being a wife and a mother. But the fulfillment of those long-ago dreams was as out of reach for her as grasping a distant star and holding it in the palm of her hand. As unlikely to come true as her teenage fantasy of Hunter Whitelaw loving her the way she had loved him.

"The birthday girl is beaming, isn't she?" Chris Austin

came up beside Manda and slipped his arm around her waist. "Just looking at her, no one would believe she's forty."

Manda smiled at Chris, Rodney's younger brother, with whom she had tried to remain friends for Rodney's mother's sake. Chris was Claire Austin's only child now, and she doted on him, despite the fact that he disappointed her on a regular basis. Although physically similar to Rodney, with the same golden hair, hazel eyes and lanky build, Chris didn't possess the brilliance or charm that had been such an integral part of his older brother. She supposed having grown up in the shadow of an overachiever had given Chris an excuse to do absolutely nothing with his life.

"Gwen is lovely," Manda agreed. "And she doesn't look a day over thirty."

"Living the good life doesn't put wrinkles on a face, does it?"

When Chris pulled Manda closer to his side, she glared at him. Chris had been making passes at her for years, and for years, she'd been giving him the brush-off. After all this time, it had almost become a game with them. He advanced; she retreated.

"What say we ditch this boring society gig and head over to the Blues Club for some real fun," Chris said.

Manda disengaged herself from his annoying hold. "I'm not going anywhere with you. Not tonight. Not ever. Go find yourself another playmate, while I go speak to my sister-in-law and wish her a happy birthday."

With a little-boy pout on his face, Chris released her. "How long are you going to fight it, honey? You know Mother would love to see us get together."

Manda laughed. "Claire would think I'd lost my mind

if I even gave you the time of day. Your mother knows, better than anyone, what a womanizing rascal you are.''

"If you'd be mine, I'd—''

Grady Alder, who was Perry's law partner, came up behind Chris, clamped his hand down on Chris's shoulder and said, "Austin, why the hell don't you leave Manda alone? She's been telling you no for ten years, hasn't she?''

Chris tensed and frowned, but when he glanced over his shoulder at Grady, he grinned broadly. "It seems I have several years on you, then, don't I, Grady? She's only been turning you down for how long now? Three or four years?''

Grady instantly released his hold on Chris and glowered at the younger man. "I think I heard your mother calling you. You'd better see what she wants or she might tighten the purse strings, and then where would you be?''

Chris smirked at Grady, then smiled at Manda. "I don't blame you for refusing to date this jerk.''

"Will you two stop,'' Manda said. "There are dozens of other women here for both of you to pester, so why don't you leave me alone?''

"How does it feel, Alder, being lumped together with me?'' Chris asked, a devilish twinkle in his eyes. "Both of us rejected suitors.''

Manda wished both men would go away and leave her alone. She tolerated Chris for Claire's sake, because she adored Rodney's mother. And although she genuinely like Grady, she had just about reached her limit of tolerance with him, too. The man had been persistently pursuing her since his divorce several years ago.

"Sorry, Manda, sugar.'' Grady epitomized the old-fashioned Southern gentleman, and she knew Grams

would approve of him as a husband for her. *He's our kind,*
Grams had once told her.

In her peripheral vision, Manda caught a glimpse of Dr.
Boyd Gipson heading in her direction. Another suitable
beau. Great, she thought, that's all she needed—one more
man vying for her attention. After Boyd's bout with food
poisoning, she had politely refused to see him socially,
but he, too, had difficulty accepting her refusals. He had
called her almost every day. *Please, Lord, help me escape,*
Manda prayed silently. But with the wall at her back,
flanked closely on each side by Grady and Chris, and with
Boyd closing in on her, she was trapped.

"Manda, honey, you look gorgeous tonight," Boyd
said as he joined her other two admirers. "Would you
care to dance?"

"Hey, I was here first," Chris said like the spoiled
child he was, despite the fact he was thirty-two years old.

"Austin, I believe Manda had already told you to get
lost, hadn't she?" Grady said.

"Remember, that request was for you as well as me,"
Chris reminded his rival.

Manda put her hands on her hips, huffed and glanced
from one man to another, taking in all three. "If I promise
a dance to each of you, will y'all stop making spectacles
of yourselves and of me?"

"Sorry, sugar," Grady said again.

"Honey, I apologize if I've embarrassed you," Boyd
said.

"So, who's going to get you first?" Chris asked.

She wanted to scream, *Leave me alone!* These men
were fools. Didn't they understand that she was a dangerous woman? Any man who cared for her risked his life
in doing so. Her affection was as deadly as that of a black
widow spider's.

*   *   *

Hunter entered the house where he'd spent some happy days as a teenager. The last time he'd been in this house was eleven years ago, for a wedding reception, when Perry had married Gwen Richman and he had served as Perry's best man. And that had been the last time he'd seen Manda, who had been one of Gwen's bridesmaids. Although she'd been breathtakingly beautiful, he'd sensed the sadness in Perry's little sister and had known taking part in the wedding had been difficult for her. It had been a little over a year since she had lost her fiancé in a car crash, only days before their wedding.

Making his way through the laughing, chatting congregation of Dearborn's elite, Hunter searched the crowd for Perry, but the person who caught his eye was Perry's sister. Manda stood across the room from him, a strained smile on her face as three men formed a crescent around her, all of them talking at the same time and directing their conversation at her. Some things never changed. Now, as in the past, Manda Munroe was surrounded by admirers, each hoping she would grant him the privilege of a dance, a date or any small crumbs of attention. Who could blame these poor fools? Manda was more beautiful now than she'd ever been. So beautiful that she could easily take a man's breath away.

However, Hunter noticed that she did nothing to accentuate that beauty. The exact opposite was true. She wore her long blond hair restrained in a neat bun at the nape of her neck, had applied only a minimum of makeup and dressed conservatively in a simple black sheath. But looks like hers couldn't be disguised. She possessed a to-die-for body and a face like an angel. Just looking at her was enough to give any man a hard-on.

And this was the woman Perry wanted him to marry!

Perry had given him a brief rundown of the problem,
telling him that he'd fill him in on the details once he
arrived in Dearborn. But the gist of the situation was that
Manda was convinced that any man she became emotionally involved with was destined to die. Apparently her
bevy of suitors was either unaware of the danger or each
was so enamored that he didn't care.

As he came nearer, he realized that the men were actually arguing over who was going to dance with Manda
first. God help them. Didn't they know a damn thing about
this woman? He hadn't seen her in eleven years, but he
figured some things about Manda hadn't changed since
she'd been the bane of his existence when she was a kid.
With a strong-willed, stubborn woman like Manda, you
didn't beg. She respected strength and decisiveness…and
always wanted what she couldn't have.

He dove through the partygoers like Moses parting the
Red Sea, and headed straight for the most popular woman
at Gwen Munroe's birthday party.

Manda saw him, then blinked her eyes and looked
again. She hadn't been imagining it. It was him. Hunter
Whitelaw. Big, bold and towering over the other men in
the room from his six-foot-four height. His shoulders were
so broad, his arms so huge that she assumed the tuxedo
he wore had been tailor-made for him. Except for a few
lines around his eyes and mouth and just a hint of gray
in his military-short hair, he had changed very little in the
past eleven years. He was now, as he'd been then, totally,
absolutely, devastatingly male.

She'd had the most gosh-awful crush on him when
she'd been a teenager and had thrown herself at him more
than once. But he had always rebuffed her—and wisely
so, since he'd been a grown man and she only a sixteen-

year-old girl. Of course, that last silly prank she'd pulled by the pool had curtailed Hunter's visits. Like a spoiled child, which she had most certainly been, she had lied to Grams and insisted that Hunter had made sexual advances. Although her father and Perry hadn't believed her, Grams had. Finally months later she had confessed her lie, but by then the damage had been done and Hunter seldom came to the house after that.

Suddenly she realized that Hunter was coming straight toward her, his gaze riveted to hers. An unbidden and uncontrollable fluttering began in the pit of her stomach, and the closer he came, the wilder the sensations inside her grew. She hadn't felt this crazy feminine yearning since the last time she'd seen Hunter. His presence always created the same idiotic havoc on her nerves. Even with Rodney, whom she'd loved with all her heart, the sexual stirrings had never been so strong. It was as if she related to Hunter on a purely physical level. Woman to man.

She stood there watching his approach, her gaze remaining locked with his as he cut a path between Grady and Boyd to reach her. Both men stepped back, mouths slightly agape, eyes widened in surprise, as they gazed up at the big man. Chris actually jumped back.

Without even a nod of acknowledgment to the men surrounding her, Hunter reached out, took her hand in his and said, "I believe this is our dance."

She went with him, moving past her trio of admirers, who grumbled among themselves. Hunter led; she followed. When they joined the other dancers, he took her into his arms and began moving with an amazing agility for a man so huge. He held her close, but not too close, a hairbreadth between their bodies. He didn't speak, only continued staring into her eyes, as if he thought he would be able to see some profound truth revealed there. *Speak, damn it,* she told herself. *Say something to him. Say, it's been a long time. Or how about asking him what the hell he's doing here?*

"They can't help themselves, you know," Hunter said, no trace of humor in his voice or show of emotion on his face.

"What?"

"Your men." He nodded toward where the threesome stood on the sideline and watched. "They can't help being infatuated with you. When a woman looks the way you do, men can't resist."

When she stiffened in his arms, he eased her just a little closer, enough so that her breasts brushed his chest. "You certainly never had any trouble resisting me, did you?"

That's it, Manda, dredge up the past. Remind him of what a scandalous little hussy you were at sixteen. Remind him of why he felt unwelcome in this house for so many years.

"That's what you think," Hunter replied, a grin lifting the corners of his mouth.

Manda gasped. "You certainly could have fooled me. You acted like I was poison."

"Baby doll, you *were* poison. You were jailbait."

She quivered when his large, hard hand spread out across her back, his fingertips resting against the base of her spine. "I didn't stay sixteen forever. If you'd been interested, you could have made your move when I turned eighteen."

"I could have," he said. "But by then you had dozens of guys buzzing around you, ones far more suitable for you than I was. You and I both know that your grams wouldn't have approved of me. Besides, I've never liked the idea of being part of a male harem."

"A male harem?" Manda laughed. "This from a guy who can snap his fingers and have any woman he wants."

Hunter grinned. "You overestimate my charm. I'm just a good ole boy who does his best to remember the gentlemanly manners his grandparents taught him."

Enough idle chitchat, Manda thought. Time to get down to the crux of the matter. "What are you doing here tonight?"

"Perry invited me to Gwen's birthday party."

"Why accept this particular invitation? He's been inviting you to family events for the past ten years and you've never shown up before tonight."

"Let's just say that Perry's invitation intrigued me."

"How's that?" Manda asked.

"He made me a business proposition that I found interesting. He suggested I come to the party and then afterward, we'd talk to the other person involved in the deal and the three of us would come to an agreement."

"I must say that I'm intrigued now. I can't imagine what sort of business deal a former army major would have with a small-town lawyer."

"It's personal business."

"Is that so? Mind telling me who the third person is?"

The music ended. Hunter stopped, but continued holding Manda. He looked at her point-blank and said, "You're the other person."

"What?"

"I take it that Perry hasn't discussed his plan with you."

She shook her head. "No, he hasn't. But since I'm involved, why don't you fill me in on the details?" When the people around them began milling about, she realized that she was still in Hunter's arms. She tried to pull away from him, but he grasped her hand and led her toward the double set of French doors that opened to the backyard.

She didn't balk when he practically forced her onto the patio. What was it about this man that made her accept his caveman tactics? Just because she had always responded to him sexually, on a purely primitive level, didn't mean she wanted him to drag her around by her hair.

A dozen or so people meandered about on the patio, most of them smokers who had escaped for a nicotine fix. Hunter led her to the far side of the patio and into the shadows formed by the centuries-old oak tree at the edge of the house. A shiver of apprehension rippled up her spine. Once out of earshot of the others and with their bodies partially hidden in the jutting curve of the house, Hunter settled his hands on her shoulders, his touch gentle. She stared up at him. He was a good foot taller than she and his size alone was intimidating. But on some instinctive level she knew that he would never hurt her.

"Perry filled me in on your decision to never date again."

"How dare he discuss my personal business— Oh, my God! He called you here to be my protector, didn't he? I didn't think he was serious when he said that what I needed was a man who could defend me against the crazy person who killed Rodney and Mike."

"There was never any proof that Rodney was murdered," Hunter said. "Perry pointed out that before Rodney died in a car crash, you hadn't received any threatening letters, the way you did when you became engaged to Mike."

"What difference does that make? Both of the men I planned to marry met untimely deaths. Because of me."

Hunter tightened his grasp on her shoulders. "Manda, what happened to you is tragic, but if you stop living…if you give up and give in to this lunatic who's trying to control your life, then you're not the feisty, headstrong, determined girl I once knew. Sixteen-year-old Manda Munroe would have spit in the devil's eye.''

A shudder of remembrance passed through her as she looked at Hunter. ''That girl doesn't exist anymore. She was silly and spoiled and had no idea how unbearably cruel life could be. That Manda Munroe died, slowly and painfully, after being responsible for the deaths of two good men.''

''Damn it, you were not responsible for either of those deaths.'' Hunter slid one hand upward to grasp the nape of her neck and the other around to cradle her back. ''Perry was right. It's past time to put an end to this madness. We're going to bring your monster out into the light of day and drive a stake through his heart.''

Manda gulped in air. ''Whatever plan Perry has cooked up, I won't allow you to risk your life to—''

Hunter leaned over and lowered his head, bringing his mouth to hers. Shocked by his actions, she had no time to respond before he kissed her. Soft and languid in the beginning, but quickly escalating to a full-fledged, tongue-thrusting passionate kiss. Sizzling sensation radiated from the core of her femininity throughout her entire body. She had been kissed many times before, but never like this. This was a teenage girl's fantasy kiss. An all-consuming, curl-your-toes, Me-Tarzan-You-Jane kiss.

She found herself unable to resist. Passion had become a negative word in her vocabulary. She had willed herself to not succumb to any attraction she'd felt for various men over the past five years, but with Hunter she had no control. She suddenly felt sixteen again and her big brother's best friend was making her dreams come true.

Hunter ended the long, lingering kiss with tender nips on her bottom lip and a sweet trail made by his moist lips along her neck. She sighed as her body melted into his.

Breathless, Manda gazed at him and one word formed on her lips.

"Why?"

He glanced over her shoulder, across the patio and whispered in her ear, "To begin the charade. This was Act One for our audience."

"What audience?" She turned her head just enough to follow his gaze and saw Chris, Boyd and Grady on the far side of the patio, stunned expressions on their faces.

Damn. Had Hunter kissed her to prove a point to her three overzealous admirers? Was he thumbing his nose at them, showing them that he'd already gotten to first base with the woman they wanted?

Seething with anger, she went rigid in his arms. "I hope you enjoyed this," she said quietly, her jaw tight. "Because it will be the only time you ever use me to—"

He kissed her again. Nothing more than a silencing maneuver. Then he explained. "Don't you realize that one of those three could be your letter-writing menace? If we're going to draw him out into the open and force him to take action, then we will have to convince him that we're serious about each other."

"Is that why you kissed me? Just what sort of scheme did you and Perry cook up behind my back?"

"A pretty good scheme," he replied. "But I think we should wait until Perry has a free minute, so the three of us can discuss this plan together."

"I agree. Perry had no right to drag you into this mess without my consent."

"I'm sure he thought that you'd never agree," Hunter told her. "Some things about you may have changed, Manda, but one thing hasn't—you're still as stubborn as a mule."

"Hunter?"

"Yes, dear?"

"Go to hell!"

She pulled out of his embrace, marched across the patio, glared at the wide-eyed threesome and went into the house. If Hunter Whitelaw thought he was going to play hero for her, then he'd better think again. He might be a tough guy, but he wasn't invincible. He could be killed just like any ordinary man. He could die because of her. Just as Rodney and Mike had died.

Hunter watched Manda as she nervously tapped her foot on the floor in Perry's study. Apparently she hadn't cooled off much in the past hour. She was practically foaming at the mouth.

"You had no right to call Hunter and ask him to pretend to be my new boyfriend!" Manda glared at Perry. "You're asking him to risk his life and for what? Tell me that—for what?"

"How can you ask me such a question?" Perry slammed his fist down on top of his antique desk. "I've stood around and done nothing for the past twelve years, except watch you suffer. I thought that given time after Rodney's death, you'd find love again, and you did, with Mike. But then when he was murdered, you cut yourself off from men entirely. And just when you ventured back into the dating arena, you let a freak accident—a damn food poisoning incident—determine the rest of your life."

"It's my life, isn't it? I have a right to decide how to live it. And if I choose to spend the rest of my life alone, then—"

"I think there's something you're overlooking," Hunter said.

Settling her gaze on Hunter, she all but snarled at him. "And just what would that be?"

"The fact that no matter what you choose to do, men aren't going to stop coming on to you." His lips twitched with an almost smile. "A woman who looks the way you do is always going to have men chasing after her. This nutcase who's so determined to see that you never marry could eventually start eliminating any man who shows an interest in you."

"Oh, good Lord. Do you actually think that…" She shook her head as if trying to erase his words from her mind. "Oh, all right. Let me hear the rest of your plan." She pointed her finger first at Hunter and then at Perry. "But if I don't agree, then the whole thing is off. Is that understood?"

A response from Manda, but not exactly an agreement. Perry nodded. Hunter grunted. After what Perry had told him, all the details of Manda's life and the death of her second fiancé, Hunter realized that Manda could never live a normal life until the person behind the threats was exposed and ultimately, stopped.

"I called Hunter not only because he's an old friend and someone you knew in the past, someone you actually had a teenage crush on, but because of his background." Perry reached out and clasped Manda's hands in his. "For a number of years, Hunter was a member of the Delta Force, a special operations military unit. And now he's an agent for the top security and investigation agency in the country. He's qualified to not only protect you, but to take care of himself under fire."

"All right, I agree Hunter is highly qualified," Manda said. "But that doesn't tell me exactly what you intend for him to do. Are we supposed to date and see what happens?"

"You'll date," Perry said. "Y'all will have a whirl-wind courtship. Hunter's going to sweep you off your feet.

You two are going to fall madly in love and within a few weeks, we'll be putting together the quickest planned and executed wedding in history.''

"Wedding?" Manda's face paled.

"Hmm—mm." Perry placed Manda's hand in Hunter's. "You two are going to get married."

"Married!" Manda screamed. "You can't seriously intend for me to marry him." She focused her gaze on Hunter. "You're going to use yourself as bait to catch this guy. I won't allow you to risk your life for me. Don't you realize that— Oh, I get it. You're so damn sure of yourself that you think once we announce our engagement, my secret admirer will make his move and you'll not only be able protect me and yourself, but you'll catch him, too." She pulled away from Hunter and paced around the room. "By all means, let's follow through with this idiotic plan. Let's put both of our lives in danger. Let's show everyone in Dearborn that we're fools in love, and to hell with the consequences."

Hunter grabbed her, cupping her chin as he stared into her eyes. "No one outside this room is to know that we're only pretending. As far as anyone else is concerned—your grandmother, Gwen, Mrs. Austin—this thing between us is real. We're going to convince everyone that we can't keep our hands off each other."

"I'm not sure I'm that good an actress."

"Just pretend you feel about me now the way you did when you were sixteen and performed your little striptease for me out by the pool."

Manda's face flushed as she huffed loudly, "And what are you going to pretend?"

"I'm a man, baby doll. With a woman who looks like you, I won't have to pretend."

Chapter 3

Barbara Finch Munroe didn't bother to knock before she entered her grandson's study; she swept into the room like the queen she was. Mrs. Munroe had held the title of Dearborn society's grand dame for the past twenty-five years, and despite the fact she had to be close to eighty, Hunter would lay odds she'd be around to keep her crown for another twenty-five years. There was spirit in her step and determination in her eyes—eyes the exact same shade of blue as Manda's. She glanced from person to person, her gaze lingering on Hunter. A barely discernable change in her facial expression warned him that she remembered who he was.

"What are y'all doing hiding away in here when it's time to bring out Gwen's birthday cake? I was ready to give the caterers the nod when I noticed that you—" she glared at Perry "—were nowhere to be seen. It just so happened that Bobbie Rue saw you and Manda come into the study with a…gentleman."

"Grams, you remember Hunter Whitelaw, don't you?" Perry said, a quirky grin on his face.

Always the cordial lady, Mrs. Munroe offered Hunter a pleasant smile and nod. "Mr. Whitelaw, we haven't seen you in a number of years. Are you in town visiting family?"

"No, ma'am, I'm afraid I don't have any family left in Dearborn. I drove down from Atlanta for Gwen's birthday party, and I'm certainly glad that I accepted Perry's invitation." Hunter looked point-blank at Manda and grinned like a lovesick fool.

Manda's cheeks flushed. "I'm sorry you had to come looking for us." Manda walked over and laced her arm through her grandmother's. "Hunter and Perry and I were just talking over old times. And Hunter and I were laughing about that silly teenage crush I had on him when I was sixteen. Remember, Grams? I told you and Daddy the most awful fib about Hunter."

Mrs. Munroe focused her gaze directly on Hunter. She pursed her lips in a disapproving manner.

"Believe me, Mrs. Munroe, if she comes to you with that same story tomorrow, it will be true," Hunter said, his voice light, his tone humorous.

Manda gasped. "Hunter! Don't tease Grams." She tightened her hold on her grandmother and tried to maneuver the old woman toward the open door. "We'd better get back to the party, hadn't we?" She stared at Perry as she inclined her head toward the door. "Come on. We don't want to hold up the big production. I'm sure Gwen's getting anxious about the presentation of her cake."

Mrs. Munroe held her ground and pinned Hunter with her disapproving glare. "Young man, was that your rather vulgar way of saying that you're interested in my grand-daughter?"

"Yes, ma'am," Hunter said. "And I apologize, if my comment offended you. I'm afraid you're going to have to get used to seeing me with Manda. I've asked her out for tomorrow night and she's accepted."

Mrs. Munroe turned her attention to her granddaughter. "Manda, is this true? Do you intend to—"

"Grams, don't you think it's wonderful that these two have finally connected?" Perry rushed across the room and took his grandmother's hand. "I think it was practically love at first sight for both of them tonight."

"Hardly." Mrs. Munroe huffed in a delicate, ladylike way. "Manda and Hunter have known each other for years."

"That was just a figure of speech," Manda said. "What Perry was trying to say is that after seeing each other again tonight, Hunter and I find that we're attracted to each other and…and we're going to go with what we're feeling and see what happens. Right?" She looked to Hunter for affirmation.

"That's right. I plan to take some vacation time and stay in Dearborn so Manda and I can become reacquainted."

"Are you sure that's wise, my dear?" Mrs. Munroe asked. "After all… Does he know?"

"Yes, he knows," Perry said.

Mrs. Munroe nodded her head. "Very well. Then I see no harm in their dating." She grasped Manda's hand. "It'll do you good to have a social life again, even if…" She looked right at Hunter. "I'm an old-fashioned woman, Mr. Whitelaw. Anyone who knows me will tell you that I'm a snob, and they'd be right. I'm going to be honest with you—under normal circumstances, I wouldn't approve of your escorting Manda around, but if you can bring her back to life and make her happy, then you have my blessings.''

''Thank you. I'm sure your approval means a great deal to Manda,'' Hunter said, implying that her approval didn't mean a damn to him. ''And I promise that I intend to do everything I can to put a smile on her face.''

Manda's gaze connected momentarily with Hunter's and she caught the teasing gleam in his eyes. She just hoped that Grams hadn't comprehended the sexual connotation of his comment. Before she realized his intentions, Perry whisked Grams away from her and out the door.

Perry called out as he glanced over his shoulder. ''You two hurry along. You don't want to miss the birthday cake.''

Manda started to follow, but Hunter grabbed her arm, detaining her. ''Wait up a minute.''

She turned to face him. ''What?''

''We should go back into the party together and make sure everyone sees us being…infatuated with each other.''

''Before we begin this charade, I need to know if you're—''

''I'm sure,'' Hunter said. ''No one should live the way you're living. Afraid to care about anyone. Scared to even date a man because you think dating him might put him at risk. Whoever's out there, determined to keep you alone and miserable, needs to be exposed and dealt with so you can have a life of your choosing, not his.''

''I'm not sure we're doing the right thing.'' Manda took a deep breath. ''Two men are already dead because of me. I couldn't bear it if something happened to you.''

Hunter gently grasped her chin, cradling it between his

thumb and forefinger. "Nothing will happen to me. Or to you. I'm going to protect you and keep us both safe."

She nodded. More than anything she wanted to believe Hunter Whitelaw. He was so confident, so self-assured. She almost believed that he really could protect himself and her from an unknown enemy.

"Ready?" he asked.

"Yes."

He draped her arm over his and led her out of the den, but paused momentarily in the hallway. "Go along with whatever I say and whatever I do. And just remember that everything between us is an act, a performance staged to make your secret admirer jealous enough to expose himself."

"I'll do my best."

"That's all anyone can ask of you."

He led her back to the party. They arrived just in time to sing happy birthday along with the sixty other guests. She made no protest when he kept his arm around her waist, and whenever he nuzzled the side of her face or kissed her temple, she smiled and pretended that she loved Hunter's ardent attention. While cake was served and Gwen opened her stack of presents, Hunter escorted Manda past her three suitors—Grady, Boyd and Chris—leaving the men without any doubts about his claim on Manda. He had walked in and snatched her right out from under their noses. And it was apparent by the stunned, hurt and even angry expressions on their faces that they couldn't understand what had happened. Why had the reclusive, reluctant Manda suddenly thrown caution to the wind and succumbed to this big, dark stranger?

"If looks could kill, I'd be a dead man," Hunter whispered. "I think we should put those three at the top of our suspects list."

"You're kidding? Those guys are harmless. They wouldn't—"

"Never assume anything about anyone. It never pays to trust too easily. Professionally or personally. People are seldom what they seem. And putting your trust in the wrong person is a sure way to get your heart broken."

"Speaking from personal experience?" she asked.

"Definitely." He took her in his arms and joined the other couples dancing to the slow, sensual beat of a cool jazz tune.

She found that she liked the feel of his strong arms around her. It had been such a long time since she had allowed a man to hold her, even to simply dance with her. Hunter was so big that she should have felt dwarfed by his size, but somehow she felt protected and comforted. And even cherished. Damn, but he was a good actor.

"So, tell me, who did you trust that wound up breaking your heart?" She gazed into his stormy gray eyes and noted a hint of pain. Someone had hurt him. Maybe his ex-wife had broken his heart.

"I don't make a habit of talking about my personal life."

"No fair. If you get to know all the intimate details of my life, then I should at least be allowed to know something about yours."

He brought her closer until their bodies pressed intimately against each other, then he gazed down at her as if he were going to kiss her. Not here, she thought. Not in front of all these people. That would be taking the act a little too far and a little too fast.

"Do you remember meeting my ex-wife, Selina, at Perry and Gwen's wedding?" Hunter asked.

"Yes. She was a lovely woman." Manda remembered that several people at the wedding had mentioned the similarity between Selina Whitelaw and herself. Both blue-eyed blondes, about the same age. And she had later learned that Selina came from the same type of background—a respected, blue-blooded Southern family with old money.

"She was a spoiled, selfish, promiscuous hellcat," Hunter said, his smile never wavering.

He'd thought the same of her once. At least the spoiled, selfish hellcat part. At sixteen she might have been daring and determined where pursuing Hunter was concerned, but she hadn't been promiscuous. Actually, she'd still been a virgin. *And you still are!* No one would believe it. Sometimes she had a hard time explaining to herself how a thirty-three-year-old woman could still be a virgin. As a teenager, she'd been rebellious and self-centered, but had drawn the line at experimenting sexually with any of the guys she dated. She and Rodney had been very much in love, but both had agreed to wait for their wedding night. But that wedding night had never come. And her relationship with Mike hadn't been sexual. They had been friends, drawn to each other out of mutual admiration and similar interests. They had been affectionate with each other, and had they married, she didn't doubt that they would have been compatible sexually. But they had never married.

"I take it that Selina was unfaithful to you," Manda said.

"Mmm... I caught her in bed with one of my friends. Later, I found out that he wasn't the first."

"And you've never trusted another woman since. If that's true, then you're probably as afraid of forming a new relationship as I am."

"There's a difference. You want and need a husband and a houseful of kids. Or at least that's what Perry told me." He paused, as if waiting for her to deny his statement, which she didn't. "I, on the other hand, have no desire to remarry. And I date as much as I want to, have as many women in my life as I need."

"*Need* being the operative word?" Manda asked. "Need, as in physical need? You're afraid of an emotional relationship, but you don't have a problem having physical relationships. Am I right?"

"Are you inquiring for a personal reason?" Hunter nuzzled her neck.

Manda gasped as pure sensation shot through her. "What...what—"

"If you're wondering if after we get married, I'd be willing to screw you even though we won't be emotionally involved, then the answer is yes."

She tensed in his arms, then stopped dead-still. "Grams is right—you can be very vulgar."

When she tried to pull away from him, he refused to release her. "If you don't want to dance any longer, then why don't we go through the buffet line and get some cake? After all, we don't want anyone thinking that we're having an argument. Not when we're supposed to be falling in love."

Manda resigned herself to accept his smothering attention. Every glance, every hug, every kiss as phony as a three-dollar bill. But necessary, she reminded herself. If they were going to pull off this dangerous charade, she couldn't allow herself to be affected by anything Hunter said or did. Or by her own unwanted feelings for him. Crazy as it might seem, she found herself as strongly attracted to him now as she'd been at sixteen.

Don't you dare fall for this guy, she cautioned herself. Caring about Hunter would be dangerous—for him and for you. Even if there was no external danger, no lunatic watching and waiting for her to choose a new mate, she didn't dare risk losing her heart to Hunter Whitelaw, a man who still saw her as spoiled and selfish, the way his ex-wife had been.

As they made their way to the buffet table, Manda noticed Gwen heading in their direction. The birthday girl herself, all smiles, but with unmistakable curiosity in her eyes. She and Gwen had known each other most of their lives and had at one time been friends. But that was before they'd both fallen in love with Rodney Austin. Manda didn't think her sister-in-law had ever quite forgiven her for being the one Rodney had loved and wanted. Even though Gwen had married Perry only a year after Rodney's death, Manda wondered if her sister-in-law had ever truly loved Perry. They seemed to have a stable marriage. Gwen was the ideal wife for an up-and-coming lawyer with political aspirations. And she thought Perry was content, if not genuinely happy. He doted on Gwen, gave her anything her heart desired and had even accepted her decision for them to not adopt a child after she had found out that she couldn't have a baby of her own.

Before Gwen reached them, Claire Austin stopped Gwen to give her a hug. Hunter urged Manda into the line at the buffet table and as they waited their turn, he kept his arm around her shoulders and occasionally rubbed his hand up and down her arm in a gesture of affection. As Manda picked up a plate holding a piece of birthday cake, prepared by Atlanta's renowned Chef Maurice Claude, she cast a quick glimpse over her shoulder and saw that Gwen and Claire, talking happily to each other, were heading their way.

Manda tried to hurry Hunter along, but he insisted on acquiring flutes of champagne for them. By the time they had cake and champagne in hand, Gwen closed in on them.

"Manda," she called, and waved. "There you are. I haven't had a chance to even say hello." Moving nearer with each step, Gwen brought Claire with her. "I just had to postpone opening the rest of my gifts so that I could mix and mingle more with my guests."

Gwen sized up Hunter, her gaze traveling from the top of his head to the tips of his shoes. "Hunter Whitelaw, we haven't seen you in ages. I'm simply delighted that you'd drive down from Atlanta just for my birthday party."

"Happy birthday, Gwen," Hunter said. "You don't know how glad I am that I accepted Perry's invitation. Manda and I are getting to know each other all over again, and I must say that I'm finding myself intrigued by your beautiful sister-in-law. So much so that I'm staying over a few days, since I've persuaded Manda to go out to dinner with me tomorrow night."

"How wonderful," Claire said, a warm smile on her face. She reached out to clasp Manda's hand. "Sweet girl, I'm so glad to see that you didn't let that silly incident with Boyd Gipson keep you from accepting this young man's invitation."

"Claire, I'd like for you to meet Hunter Whitelaw," Manda said. "Hunter is an old and dear friend of Perry's. Hunter, this is Claire Austin. Rodney's mother."

"Ma'am." Hunter nodded

"Hunter was Perry's best man at our wedding." Gwen laughed, the sound hollow and brittle. "And he was Manda's first love, wasn't he, Manda?" Gwen skewered Manda with her cold black eyes.

"Is that right?" Claire asked, her gaze resting on Hunter.

"She had a teenage crush on me, ma'am," Hunter explained. "At the time she was a bit too young for me, but now six years difference in our ages doesn't matter."

"Of course, it doesn't." Claire patted Manda's arm, then leaned over and whispered to her, "I do so want you to be happy."

"Thank you." Manda kissed Claire's cheek.

"Manda and I were headed out to the patio to find a table. Would you ladies care to join us?" Hunter asked.

Gwen opened her mouth to reply, but Claire spoke first. "Nonsense. You two want to be alone…to talk. Besides, Gwen must spend more time with her guests, mustn't you, dear."

Manda took the opportunity Claire had given her to head toward the French doors. Hunter followed her along the escape route, through the open doors and onto the patio. The only empty table was in the garden, on the far side of the swimming pool. She halted immediately.

"Keep going," Hunter said. "We'll be out of earshot over there, but we can still put on quite a show for anyone watching us."

"Do we have something more we need to discuss in private?"

"We have a great deal more to discuss," he told her. "If we're going to walk down the aisle in a couple of weeks, we need to plan a whirlwind courtship and get started on it right away."

"A couple of weeks? You're kidding. You expect us to get married in two weeks?"

"Keep walking." He nudged her in the back with his plate. "And two weeks is my limit at playing adoring suitor. If our engagement doesn't bring out Mr. Lunatic, then we'll follow through with the wedding. That's sure to bring him out. He's not going to allow you to be happily married to another man.''

Manda set her plate and crystal flute on the wrought-iron table, then Hunter did the same. He pulled out a chair and with gentlemanly good manners assisted her. Once seated, she lifted the glass to her lips and sipped the champagne.

Hunter pulled a chair up beside her, so that when he sat, their arms brushed against each other. Quivers fluttered through her body. She hadn't been this aware of a man in years. This won't do, she told herself. She couldn't let her emotions come into play during their game of pretense.

''So, the way I see it, we need to become a constant twosome,'' he said. ''Dinner tomorrow night. And afterward, you'll invite me in and I'll stay for at least an hour.''

''An hour?''

''Just in case Mr. Lunatic is watching your house.''

''Oh.''

''Then day after tomorrow, we'll start having lunch and dinner together every day and by the end of the week, we'll be inseparable.''

''I don't know if I can stand that much of a good thing,'' she said sarcastically.

''Force yourself. After all, it's for your own good.''

''Okay, after we've shown the world how nauseatingly in love we are, what do we do next?''

''I move in with you—twenty-four hours a day.''

''No way!''

''Manda, that's what people do when they fall madly, passionately in love.'' Using his fork, Hunter sliced through his piece of cake, lifted the bite and brought it to Manda's mouth.

When she opened her mouth on a startled gasp, Hunter slid the cake inside and grinned as she glared at him. She chewed and swallowed. "And I assume you know that we won't be sharing a bed or even a bedroom."

"We'll work out the details later. As long as we give the appearance of being lovers, we don't actually have to be. Unless you'd like—"

"I wouldn't like," she told him.

"How do you know you wouldn't like it unless you try it?"

"I think you have me confused with your ex-wife. I don't sleep around. I believe that love and sex go together in a relationship and that the best sexual relationships are created as part of the lifelong commitment two people make to each other."

"Your grandmother did a good job of brainwashing you with her old-fashioned morals, didn't she?" Hunter chuckled

"I think more and more people these days are seeing the wisdom in waiting until—"

"Okay." He grabbed her hand, brought it to his mouth and kissed it. "I have no problem waiting until after we're married. It should make for an interesting wedding night."

"Hunter Whitelaw, if you think that I'm going to—"

He kissed her, adeptly silencing her tirade. She struggled for just a minute, then ceased her resistance, but refused to participate in the kiss.

When he lifted his head, he grinned and said, "Baby doll, if we're going to convince people that we're in love, you're going to have to put a little more into it. You're not doing a very good acting job."

Keeping her voice low and smiling at him as she spoke, she laid her hand on his shoulder and gazed dreamily into his eyes. "If you call me 'baby doll' one more time, I'm going to emasculate you. Do I make myself clear?"

Chuckling softly, he caressed her hand that lay on his shoulder.

"I've noticed that lovesick fools usually have pet names for their lady loves, so if you don't like 'baby doll,' would you prefer honey or sweetie or sugar or darling or—"

"I don't think a pet name is necessary. I have no intention of calling you anything other than Hunter."

He slid his arm around the back of her chair, effectively encompassing her shoulders. "Manda Munroe, you're still a stubborn, hardheaded brat. You want it all your way or— Hey, that's it. I'll call you 'brat,' the way Perry and I used to when you were a kid. People will find that endearing and amusing."

"Brat? Oh, that's just great."

"Take your pick—baby doll or brat?"

"Go to hell," she said through clenched teeth.

"I have a feeling that's where I'm headed. When I told Perry years ago that I pitied the poor guy who married you, I had no idea that I'd wind up being that guy. Or at least the first guy to marry you. Once we nab Mr. Lunatic and you and I get an annulment, I'm sure it won't take you long to find a real groom."

"I'm sure you're right." She glanced away, unable to continue meeting his gaze. Had he really told Perry that he pitied the guy who married her? Had he disliked her that much all those years ago? If she'd had even one silly little notion in her mind that Hunter might actually be attracted to her, that he might genuinely care about her, his comment had vanquished that thought. For the next few weeks she was going to have to accomplish a difficult task—pretending to fall madly in love with Hunter, without him ever realizing that he still held the power to affect her sexually and emotionally, more so than anyone she'd ever known.

Chapter 4

Manda was glad this was a Saturday morning and she didn't have to go to work today. She had slept fitfully last night, waking often between erotic dreams about Hunter Whitelaw and frightening dreams about a faceless killer pursuing them. In retrospect, she wondered if she was out of her mind for agreeing to go along with Perry's plan to trap her tormentor. What if something went wrong and Hunter was killed? She knew she couldn't survive another loss. It had taken her years to recover after losing Rodney, but at least when he died, she hadn't been eaten alive with guilt that his death had been her fault. No one, not even the police, had suspected that his car crash was anything other than an accident. Even now, Perry insisted that all the evidence showed that, after one of his long intern shifts at the hospital, Rodney had been driving too fast when he had probably fallen asleep at the wheel and careered over a steep embankment. More than anything, she wanted to believe that was true.

She would never forget Rodney. A part of her heart would always belong to him. Except for her teenage infatuation with Hunter, Rodney had been her first love. Until they met at the hospital where he'd been an intern when her father had been a chemotherapy patient, she had gone systematically through young men as if they were disposable tissues. From the age of sixteen until she met Rodney, she had dated dozens of guys, but not one of them had been special to her. By the time young Dr. Austin came along, she was accustomed to being the center of attention. And she had to admit that she had loved being pursued by countless lovesick boys. What a silly, foolish girl she'd been.

Falling in love with Rodney had been a good thing for her. Everyone had said so. And her entire family had not only approved her choice, but had adored Rodney as much as his mother had adored her. It had been considered an ideal match. After dating exclusively for eight months, during her senior year of college, Rodney had proposed and their families had combined efforts to plan an elaborate autumn wedding. A wedding that was supposed to be the beginning of a perfect life together.

Although they had come close to giving in to temptation, she and Rodney had stopped their lovemaking time and again before it progressed to the final act. They had agreed that since Manda was a virgin they would wait to consummate their love on their wedding night. An old-fashioned notion for people of their generation, but Rodney had been an old-fashioned kind of guy. She supposed that was one reason Grams had thought the world of him.

Manda had once believed that the day Rodney died was the worst day of her life. She had never known such agony. And it had been a pain that stayed with her, that was even now a part of her. Losing her father six months later, when he finally succumbed to cancer, had only added to her misery. But she hadn't know what true suffering was until someone killed Mike Farrar, a dear, kind man who had been murdered because he dared to care about her enough to ask her to marry him. Realizing that she had quite possibly been the cause of two men's deaths had almost destroyed her. If it hadn't been for Perry and Grams and the support of the other grief counselors at the clinic where she worked, she might have done something stupid. For several weeks after Mike's murder, she had been so distraught that she'd actually contemplated suicide.

What was it about her, she wondered, that brought death to those she loved? Except for Grams and Perry, she had lost everyone who had ever been important to her. Her mother had died in childbirth, something practically unheard of at the time. And then Hunter had rejected her foolish advances and walked out of her life. He'd been the only man who'd ever broken her heart. And then she had lost Rodney, followed by her father's death and then finally Mike's murder. She could not risk ever caring about another person. Others had to be aware of the horrible truth—loving Manda put your life in danger. She supposed on a subconscious level she had steered clear of even close friendships with other women, fearing that the Manda Munroe Curse would strike again.

For the past five years she had kept all of her relationships, with men and women alike, on a strictly casual basis. By doing this, she had held the curse at bay. But now she was planning to tempt fate by announcing to the world that in two weeks she was going to marry Hunter Whitelaw.

Although Perry had insisted that he be their guest at the Munroe home on North Pine Street, Hunter had opted

to stay at his grandmother's old house out on Mulberry
Lane. He supposed he should have sold the place after
Granny died, but he hadn't been able to bring himself to
sell a property that had been in his family for several
generations. His grandfather had been born in this old
house, and so had his great-grandfather, in the first month
of the first year of the twentieth century—January 1, 1900.

When he'd been a young idiot, Hunter had thought that
what he wanted more than anything was to get away from
the farm, to figure out a way to become a part of the social
set to which his good buddy Perry Munroe belonged. As
a young man he had been overly impressed with the fine
homes on North Pine Street, with the sleek sports cars the
rich boys drove and with the snobbish little debutantes
who wouldn't give him the time of day because he was
poor. Of course, there was one girl who'd been different.
But at the time, Manda had been years too young for him.

Odd that what was so important to a guy when he was
twenty wasn't what mattered to him when he was forty.

In the best of all possible worlds, he would come back
home, renovate the old house and either raise cattle or
rebuild the once thriving fruit orchard. Maybe he'd do
both. And in that fantasy life, there was always a woman
and a couple of kids living here on the farm with him.
But after his experience with Selina, he hadn't found a
woman he wanted to be his wife. Of course, he hadn't
been looking. Actually, he'd been doing the exact opposite. He steered clear of any woman who possessed the
qualities he now wanted in a mate. Loyalty. Compassion.
A desire to live a simple life, to build a home and have
children.

He'd told himself more than once this past year that
when he retired from the Dundee agency, he'd return to

Dearborn. Maybe while he was in town on this job for Perry, he could see about hiring a contractor and getting some work done on the old place. He had enough money to turn the family farmhouse into a showplace. Once he and Manda announced their engagement, him renovating the house would create speculation among her acquaintances as to whether he would dare to bring Manda out here to live.

Hunter laughed. After they married, maybe he should bring her here to stay for a while. She'd be miserable. The place was terribly rundown and still decorated with his grandmother's old furniture that had already seen better days when he'd been a child. No, there wasn't any need to make things worse for Manda than they already were. If the nutcase who wanted to control her life came out in the open with threats and maybe an attempt on his or Manda's life, she would have enough to deal with. But a part of him couldn't help wondering how Miss Manda would cope with life on the farm.

Hunter poured himself a cup of coffee from the old metal percolator his granny had used as far back as he could remember. Taking his coffee mug with him, he shoved open the kitchen door and walked out onto the back porch. The sun had just begun its ascent from the eastern horizon, but already at seven o'clock in the morning, the day was warm, predicting the accuracy of the weatherman's forecast that the temperature would climb into the high eighties by midafternoon. Barefoot and barechested, he strolled out into the yard. Weeds infested Granny's once picture-perfect flower beds that surrounded the ramshackle old house. His feet touched the dew-laden grass as he ventured past the wire clothesline and toward the small orchard of pear trees his great-grandfather had planted decades ago.

There was a sense of homecoming in being here, in setting foot on land that had been possessed by his ancestors for close to a hundred and fifty years. Strange how when he'd been a teenager, he had longed to get away from this place, from the daily chores that went along with being a farm kid.

Now, he wished that Granny and Pop were still alive so that he could tell them how wrong he'd been about wanting to escape the peace and solitude of the farm to live in a big city.

Had that been how his mother had felt when she'd run away at seventeen? Had she wanted to escape? But what she'd done was get herself pregnant. Unmarried and abandoned by her boyfriend, Tina Whitelaw had been forced to come home to her parents. Hunter had never known his father, didn't even know who the man was. No name. No description. Nothing. His mother had returned to the farm, dumped him on her parents and before his first birthday, had left again. They hadn't heard from her in years when they received a phone call ten years later telling them that she'd died from a drug overdose. She'd been living with her fourth husband in Los Angeles.

Hunter breathed deeply, savoring the smell of the earth and the abundance of verdant life surrounding him. Had his mother realized too late that what she had run away from was far better than anything she'd ever found?

Manda drank her morning tea on the patio of the house she had purchased eight years ago, shortly after acquiring her masters of education degree in community counseling. After Rodney's death and her father's six months later, Perry had sent her and Grams on a year-long trip through Europe. After the time she spent far away from Dearborn, her mind occupied with the wonders of the world, she had returned home to Georgia with a purpose. With love, comfort and support, she had survived the deaths of two people she dearly loved. She had wanted to spend her life helping others who were lost in the hopelessness of grief, as she had been. After acquiring her degree, she'd begun work as a counselor at the Hickory Hills Clinic. That's where she'd met Boyd, who was also a counselor.

Oxford came bounding across the yard, wagging his tail and panting madly, after retrieving his favorite red ball Manda had tossed. The black-and-white springer spaniel had been a gift from Grady Alders last year on her birthday. Oxford, whom she'd named in honor of the saddle oxfords she's worn as child because the dog's oddly striped front feet bore a striking resemblance to the shoes, had become her beloved friend and confidant. She found herself often talking to him as if he were a person. Of course, he had no idea that he wasn't. He slept at the foot of her bed on his own oversize, cedar-chips-stuffed pillow and had free reign of the house and yard. He ate table scraps along with choice cuts of meat she prepared especially for him. And she kept a supply of every dog treat product on the market, as well as an endless variety of toys. Oxford was probably one of the most pampered pets in the world, but why shouldn't she lavish her love and attention on the animal? Unless Perry's plan worked, she would never have the chance to become a mother and give all the love in her heart to a child of her own.

When the telephone rang, she made a mad dash into the kitchen, Oxford at her heels. Who would be calling her at seven on a Saturday morning? She lifted the receiver off the wall base.

"Hello?"

"Manda, dear, it's Claire. I hope I didn't waken you."

"I've been up for a good half hour," she said. "Oxford

and I were outside soaking up some of this great spring-time sunshine.''

"Well, I'm calling to see if you want to go shopping this morning."

"I hadn't planned on it, but if you'd like to go, I'll be happy to go with you."

"I thought perhaps you'd like to buy a new dress for tonight. After all, a date with an old boyfriend is a special occasion, and you want to look just right."

Manda smiled. Claire Austin was a clotheshorse. The woman spent a fortune on her clothes and accessories. Her bedroom boasted a closet twice the size of most bath-rooms. She had at least seventy pairs of shoes, over half with matching handbags. She wasn't surprised that Claire was concerned about what she would wear on a date. It was so like Claire to care about her and to show that affection by suggesting a shopping trip.

"The way everyone is acting, you'd think I've never had a date," Manda said. "Besides, I have more than enough clothes. I'm sure I can find something suitable for tonight."

"Nonsense. A woman never has enough clothes. Be-sides, dear girl, your clothes are all dark and drab and do nothing to accentuate that marvelous figure of yours. You need something smashing," Claire insisted. "Be ready by nine-thirty and we'll go straight to the mall. I'm thinking new dress, shoes and—"

"I'll agree to a new dress, but that's it."

"We'll see."

Manda sighed. She knew that Claire longed for her to be happy and that Claire worried about her lack of a love life almost as much as Perry and Grams did. Several years after Rodney's death, when Chris had begun pursuing her relentlessly, she had worried that her repeated rejections of Chris's proposals might affect her close relationship with Claire. But when she'd brought up the subject, Claire had said, "Don't be silly. Chris is my child and I love him. But he's not nearly good enough for you, dear girl. You keep looking until you find someone as worthy of you as my Rodney was."

"I'm off to take a shower," Manda told Oxford. "Do you want to take a nap or go back outside?"

The spaniel scratched at the back door. Manda opened the door to let him out, then turned and headed toward the bathroom. She hoped that Claire wouldn't expect her to buy something sexy and alluring for her date with Hunter. She hadn't dressed to attract male attention in twelve years, and she had no intention of changing her modest style for Hunter Whitelaw's benefit.

In the end she and Claire had compromised. She'd bought a simple, slightly fitted dress, with a straight skirt and short sleeves. And to pacify Claire, she had chosen a bright spring color. A brilliant blue that Claire said matched her eyes to perfection. And despite her determination not to do so, she also purchased a pair of shoes and a purse that matched the dress. She had adorned the outfit with the pearls her grandmother had given her for her eighteenth birthday.

Hunter inspected her thoroughly when he arrived on her doorstep promptly at seven, then grinned and let out a long, low whistle. She hated herself for reacting in a purely feminine way to that appreciative wolf whistle. Despite herself, she was immensely pleased that her appearance had more than met with his approval. It shouldn't matter what Hunter thought of her. But it did.

He took her to Dean's for dinner. Right before they arrived at the reservations-only restaurant, he'd pulled a tie from his jacket pocket and hurriedly closed the top button of his shirt and slipped the tie into place. A suit and tie wasn't Hunter's style. He was a casual kind of guy, more comfortable in khakis or jeans and shirts that didn't require ties. After they ate dinner and indulged in idle chitchat, he drove them across the Poloma River to the hottest spot in town. The Blues Club. Over the years, she had driven by the notorious club, but she'd never been inside, had never considered it a suitable place for her to go alone.

As they entered the dark, smoky interior, Hunter kept his hand at her back, a protective gesture that she found reassuring. Loud, brash jazz colored the atmosphere with a sultry, heated sound. Red and rich. Dripping with vibrant purple and gold. The mournful wail of a saxophone wrapped around them. Trickling piano keys blended with the seductive kiss of brushes against drums.

They found a table and Hunter ordered drinks. As her vision adjusted to the dimness, she noticed the club was crowded, overflowing with couples clinging to each other on the dance floor and single men and women at the bar. Searching. Longing. Hoping. One tune ended and another began, a soft, sad rendition of a tune called "My Romance."

The waitress brought their drinks, a peach daiquiri for her and a beer for him. She hated beer, but liked the taste of mixed drinks, especially anything sweet. He'd guessed right when he'd ordered a daiquiri for her.

"I've never been here," she admitted.

"Not exactly a classy place," he said as he glanced at their surroundings. "But I figured since it's such a popular watering hole for the elite and the peons alike, this was the place to go if we wanted to be seen together."

Don't be offended by his remark, she warned herself.

You didn't actually think he brought you here for any other reason. This entire date is a staged event. If necessary, remind yourself of the fact that every moment you spend with Hunter is part of an elaborate hoax, part of a dangerous scheme to coerce a madman out into the open.

Just as the pianist set the beat for a bluesy rendition of the old standard "One For My Baby," Hunter downed the last drops of his beer, scooted back his chair and stood. "We're more likely to be noticed on the dance floor."

He held out his hand. She eased back her chair and stood. Why was it that some ridiculously sentimental part of her heart wished that this was a real date, wished that Hunter truly wanted to hold her in his arms and whisper sweet nothings into her ear? She took his hand and went with him, as if she longed to press her body against his and feel the beating of his heart.

He held her close. Too close. He's pretending, she reminded herself. Just play along. It's all part of the act you two will be performing for a couple of weeks. She felt small and vulnerable next to a man so large, and yet at the same time she couldn't deny the pleasure of being enveloped by such raw, masculine strength. By some cruel trick of fate, she was a woman who loved men, but possessed the kiss of death for any man who dared claim her as his own.

They moved with the music's slow, languid tempo, their bodies touching, rubbing together. She could not resist the urge to cling to him. Her arms draped his neck. She rested her head on his broad chest. He cradled her buttocks with his big hands and laid his jaw against her temple. Such an intimate act. Arousal more profound than she'd known in years surged to life within her, tightening her nipples and moistening the folds of her femininity. And regardless of the motivation for this dance, Hunter was not any more immune to the seduction than she was. His sex grew hard and pressed against her belly. The moment she realized how aroused he was, her knees went weak and she clung to him all the more.

"Suspect to our right," Hunter whispered in her ear.

"What?"

"Chris Austin is dancing with some woman, only a few couples over from us. On the right. Take a look and if he sees you, smile and nod."

She obeyed his instructions. When her gaze met Chris's, he glared at her, despite the fact that some bosomy redhead was wrapped around him. Forcing herself, she smiled and nodded. Chris nodded, but he didn't return the smile.

"Can we go now?" Manda asked. "I think I've had about as much pretending as I can stand for one night."

"Not yet. Suspect Number Two just walked in."

"Who?"

"Boyd Gipson."

"Does he have a date?"

"Nope. Looks like he's headed for the bar. Who knows, he might get lucky."

"Boyd isn't the type to—"

"All men are the type," Hunter corrected.

"Do you want me to smile and nod to Boyd on our way out?"

"Why don't we just stop by the bar and say hello? Then, you should look at me as if you could eat me with a spoon and suggest we go home. If you put enough emotion into it, Gipson will believe that you can't wait to get me to your house so you can jump my bones."

Manda huffed. "All right. Let's get this over with. I'm more than ready to call it a night."

He guided her toward the bar. The moment Boyd saw

them, he stopped talking to the woman on the bar stool next to him. His gaze lingered on them as they approached.

"Hello, Boyd," Manda said, then leaned over to give him a brotherly kiss on the cheek. "You remember Hunter Whitelaw, don't you?"

"Certainly," Boyd said. "Nice to see you again, Mr. Whitelaw."

"Call me Hunter." He tightened his hold around her waist and pulled her closer to him. "Any friend of my Manda's is a friend of mine."

"Yes, of course." Boyd managed a tight-lipped smile.

"I'll see you at the clinic Monday," Manda said.

Before Boyd could reply, Chris came barreling through the crowd, dragging the sex-kitten redhead with him. He released his hold on the woman when he stopped beside Hunter. With the first words out of his mouth, Manda realized Chris was drunk.

Chris glared at her. "You wouldn't come here with me, but *he* obviously didn't have a problem getting you here." Chris pointed his finger in Manda's face. "What I want to know is why him?" Chris directed his gaze toward Boyd. "Aren't you curious? Don't you want to know why she prefers this big ape to you or me?"

"You're drunk, Austin," Boyd said. "Otherwise, I'd have to demand that you apologize to Manda immediately."

"Apologize?" Chris cackled with inebriated glee. "All right. Manda, let me apologize for asking you if your taste in men has drastically changed. My brother was a gentleman of the highest degree. Hell, even ole Boyd here and Grady Alders are gentlemen. But this—" Chris tapped Hunter in the center of his chest "—uncouth, white trash, farm boy has nothing to recommend him to a lady, unless

that lady has discovered what they say about big feet being a indication of a big—''

Hunter grasped Chris's arm, folded it against his back
and with quiet but deadly force shoved him against the
bar. ''Take your girlfriend and get the hell out of here
before I'm compelled to go against my better judgment
and kick your ass.''

Manda held her breath as Chris's eyes widened in
shock that quickly turned to fear. When he nodded nervously, Hunter released him. Chris staggered away from
the bar and grabbed the redhead, who was looking appre-
ciatively at Hunter, and hauled her back onto the dance
floor. Manda released her breath. She had forgotten her
lines, couldn't remember what she was supposed to say.

''The man's an idiot,'' Boyd said.

''On that, we agree,'' Hunter said, then reached out and
pulled Manda to his side. ''Ready to get out of here,
brat?''

She forced a smile, but when Hunter nuzzled her neck,
the quiver that raced along her nerve endings was real.
''Let's go to my house,'' she told him, finally remembering part of what she was supposed to say.

They bid a quick good-night to Boyd, then linked together like lovers headed straight for home and bed,
Hunter and Manda left the Blues Club. Hunter had parked
his Lexus in the second row of a large, well-lit parking
area to the left of the building. They maintained their arm-
in-arm walk all the way to the car. Just in case someone
was watching them.

''Damn!'' Hunter groaned as he stopped suddenly.
''Son of a bitch.''

At first Manda didn't understand what was wrong, why
he was cursing. But when she glanced at Hunter and then
followed his line of vision, she gasped. It was starting

already, and this was only her first date with Hunter. She stood frozen to the spot, trembling from head to toe as her mind processed the fact that all four tires on Hunter's Lexus had been slashed.

Chapter 5

Hunter called the police and then a tow truck to haul his Lexus to the garage. Officer McDowell told him that this was the third time in the past two weeks that a patron of the Blues Club had had their tires slashed. The suspects were a group of teenage boys, not exactly an organized gang, but well on their way to becoming one. So far, the police hadn't been able to catch the boys in the act and had no proof against them that would hold up in court.

While he dealt with the situation, Manda remained unnaturally quiet. When she'd first realized the tires had been slashed, she had gasped and stared at the tires as if in a trance. He'd given her a gentle shake and she'd snapped out of it quickly.

"It's already started," she had said. "He did this. It's his first warning." Her voice had been deceptively calm, despite the fact that her hands had been shaking and her face void of color.

"We don't know that this has anything to do with your nutcase. It could be a coincidence."

"Just like Boyd's food poisoning was a coincidence."

He hadn't been able to convince her she was wrong, not even after the police mentioned that this wasn't the first incident of tire slashing here at the club.

Later, on the cab ride to her house, Manda sat beside him, ramrod-straight, chin lifted and a somber expression on her face. He sensed that she was struggling to control her emotions, to prove to herself—and perhaps to him—that she was strong and brave and in control.

The cab pulled up in front of Manda's house on Bermuda Road, a meandering street that followed the Poloma River's path. The houses in this area were all new and sat on five-acre plots, each with access to the river. In doing his research on Manda, as he did on each client when he took a new case, he had discovered she'd had this house built eight years ago. After she and her grandmother had returned from their year in Europe, Grams had moved into the family home on North Pine Street, with Perry and Gwen. But Manda had rented an apartment, and several years later moved into this metal-roofed cottage, which was reminiscent of small tropical island homes.

Hunter paid the driver, then assisted Manda in getting out of the cab. Once on her feet, she pulled away from him. He followed her up the sidewalk, up the steps and onto the large, wraparound front porch. She removed a set of keys from her purse and quickly unlocked the door. Pausing in the doorway, she turned to face him.

"Why didn't you have the cab wait for you? I'm all right. I don't need baby-sitting."

He placed his left hand on the door post and leaned toward her. "I'm not staying to baby-sit. I'm staying because any man who cared about a woman wouldn't walk

her to her door and leave her. Especially not when she's
upset and on the verge of tears.''

"Damn it, I'm not on the verge of tears.''

"Let's not argue,'' he said. "Just be a good girl and
let me come inside for a while.''

As if all the fight had suddenly drained out of her,
Manda slumped her shoulders, sighed and turned around.
She left the door open behind her as she entered the house
and flipped on the overhead lighting in the foyer. From
out of nowhere a springer spaniel came galloping toward
Manda. He halted in front of her, his tongue panting, his
tail wagging.

"Did you miss me, you big baby?'' Manda leaned
down to scratch behind the dog's ears. "Have you been
a good boy? Huh? Want to go outside for a while?''

As if suddenly realizing that Manda wasn't alone, the
dog zeroed in on Hunter. He sniffed the air, then bared
his teeth and growled.

"No, no,'' Manda said. "Oxford, this is Hunter. He's
our friend.'' She patted the dog tenderly, then looked at
Hunter. "Say something to him and hold out the back of
your hand so he'll know you don't pose a threat to me.''

"Hey there, fellow. You sure are a good watchdog for
your mommy, aren't you?'' Hunter stuck out his hand.
Oxford sniffed, then wagged his tail, prompting Hunter to
pet the dog. "Are we friends now?''

"I believe he likes you.'' Manda offered Hunter a fragile smile. "Come on in and make yourself at home, while
I let my little monster outside.''

She led him into the great room, which appeared to be
a multi-functional area. The walls were painted some odd
color that reminded him of Dijon mustard. There were
two sitting areas, one clustered around the fireplace, which
was flanked by floor-to-ceiling bookshelves, and the other

apparently set up as an entertainment center with a wide-screen TV, VCR and audio equipment.

"If you're planning on staying, then I'll make us some coffee," she said. "Is decaf all right? I don't drink regular at this time of night."

"Don't go to any trouble."

"If I don't do something, I'm going to start screaming," she admitted. "Sit down. I won't be long."

He remained standing. "Why don't I help you? We can talk while you fix the coffee."

"What's there to talk about? Your first date with me ended on a real bang, didn't it? I'll bet you can't wait to see what happens on our second date."

She wasn't crying. And he figured she wouldn't cry. Not in front of him. Perhaps not even later when she was alone. He suspected that she had cried all her tears years ago. But she was hurting. He could see the pain in her eyes, could sense the uneasiness she was experiencing.

"If you want to scream, then go ahead and scream," he told her.

Pressing her lips together, she shook her head.

"It might make you feel better," he said.

"No, it won't help," Manda said. "Tell me something, are you really convinced that your slashed tires had nothing to do with our being on a date tonight?"

"I'm not one hundred percent sure. Maybe seventy-five percent to eighty percent sure. There's always the off chance that it was a copycat crime, done by your Mr. Maniac, as Perry calls him."

"Thanks for admitting that there is a chance it was him and not the teenagers the police suspect of similar crimes." She took a deep breath. "Come on out to the kitchen with me, if you'd like."

The big modern kitchen was a hybrid, with every up-to-date appliance imaginable, but decorated in an old-fashioned country style, with warm woodwork, yellow walls and upholstered chairs at the antique wooden table. A set of French doors opened up onto a screened back porch.

She opened the door and shooed Oxford outside, then walked over to the refrigerator. When she removed the sealed bowl in which the coffee beans were stored, her hands shook so much that she almost dropped the container. Hunter rushed toward her, grabbed the bowl and set it on the counter.

He clasped her hands in his. She glanced down at the floor, obviously trying to avoid eye contact with him. "Why don't you sit down and let me fix the coffee?" he said.

Her gaze shot straight to his face. "I don't want any coffee." She jerked her hands out of his and stormed across the room. With her back to him, she said, "I don't know if I can go through with this. Wondering what's going to happen next…when he'll make his next move. Afraid you'll wind up getting hurt, maybe even killed."

He came up behind her, wrapped his arms around her and lowered his head to nuzzle the side of her face. "Trust me, Manda. I'm not going to wind up dead. And neither are you."

"How can you be so sure?" She closed her eyes and leaned back into him.

He kissed her left temple. "From everything Perry has told me, I had some experts who work for the Dundee agency compile a profile of our Mr. Maniac. He's not going to act until we announce our engagement. He's not threatened by your casually dating other men. He's just determined to make sure you never marry anyone else."

"So you're saying that we're safe until we tell the world that we're getting married."

"Which will be next weekend. In a few days, I'll be seen at the local jewelry store picking out a ring, but I won't pop the question to you until next Saturday night."

Manda shivered. "Then the letters will start, the way they did when I became engaged to Mike."

He hugged her to him. "I'm sorry I couldn't make it to Mike's funeral. I was out of the country and didn't know about what had happened until weeks afterward."

"I know." She clutched his arms where they criss-crossed her waist. "I received your note and the flowers."

"You'll never have to go through that again. The next time you love a man and plan to marry him, everything will come off the way it should and you'll live happily ever after." Keeping her confined in his embrace, he eased her around so that she faced him. "If you start questioning yourself, if it begins to seem like too much of a risk, just remind yourself of why we're doing this."

"So I can live happily ever after with the man of my dreams?" A tentative smile quivered on her lips.

"Right." Hunter grinned. "By the way, did I mention that I'm meeting you for lunch tomorrow?"

"But I'm having lunch with Perry and— Oh. You're coming to the house for lunch with the family?"

"Perry set it up with Gwen today. Think what an interesting group we'll make. Perry and Gwen. You and me. Grams."

"You do realize that Grams is going to stir a stink when we tell her that we're getting married. She'd going to think I've lost my mind. And if this were a real romance, then she'd be right."

"But it's not real," Hunter said. "And remember this—no matter how much you want to tell Grams the truth, you can't. It's not that I don't trust her, but if she told anyone—Bobbie Rue, Gwen, Mrs. Austin, one of her bridge buddies—they might tell someone else."

"I understand. It's just that I hate the thought of lying to her. I've lied to her only one time in my life. That's why she believed me when I told her that you'd come on to me that day when Perry caught me doing my seduction routine by the pool. You must have been laughing yourself silly. How did you manage to keep a straight face when I—"

"I wasn't laughing." Hunter slid his hands up and down her arms. "You don't know how tempted I was. I had to keep reminding myself that not only were you Perry's kid sister, but that you were only sixteen."

"Are you saying that you were attracted to me?"

"Do you want me to be completely honest with you?"

She nodded.

"I've never forgotten the way you looked standing there in nothing but the bottom half of your bikini. You were the most beautiful thing I'd ever seen. And if you'd been eighteen instead of sixteen… Well, let's just say that it wouldn't have mattered if you were my best friend's kid sister."

"And all this time I thought…"

She stared at him and for a split second he saw that same hungry look that had been in her eyes all those years ago.

Without thought of the consequences, he cradled her face with his hands, lowered his head and kissed her. Her lips were warm and soft. Moist and yielding. She complied with the demands of his mouth, mimicking his marauding movements, accepting every thrust, every nip and giving as good as she got. While he held her face, she flattened her open palms across his chest, whether to push him away or to brace herself, he wasn't sure. But she made no move to withdraw, so he continued the kiss, deepening it until every nerve in his body came to full alert. He ached with the need to take her. Here. Now. His sex hardened and throbbed. If he didn't stop immediately, he'd find it difficult to walk away and leave her tonight. He was ready. But despite the needy way she was responding, she wasn't ready. She was reacting to the memory of a hot summer day seventeen years ago when she had wanted to experiment with sex and he had been her chosen partner.

He ended the kiss. She gasped for air and gazed up at him, her eyes filled with passion. For a couple of minutes they simply looked at each other, each of them slowly gaining control over themselves and the moment.

"Well," she said as she took a step away from him. "That certainly got out of hand fast, didn't it?"

"Yes, it did. Just goes to show that we shouldn't have too much trouble faking being in love. After all, in the beginning of a relationship passion is pretty much the driving force, and you and I seem to have more than enough passion."

"Was that the way it was with you and your ex-wife? A lot of passion in the beginning and then love after—"

"I don't think there was ever any love. Not on her part." Hunter grimaced. "And probably not much love on my part, either. I made a big mistake with Selina. She married me to piss off her old man and prove him wrong about us. I married a type, not a woman. I thought she was exactly what I wanted and she thought I was what she needed. We were both wrong."

"Then she didn't leave you with a broken heart?"

He thumped on his chest. "My heart's still intact. My pride took a beating. And trusting another woman won't

ever be easy for me.'' The one thing he could never tell
Manda was that when he first met Selina, she had reminded him of her. She'd been a gorgeous blonde, surrounded by drooling admirers. Her father was filthy rich
and she was daddy's darling. But Selina hadn't been a
sixteen-year-old virgin, so she hadn't been off limits.
''What about you, brat? You've been deeply in love twice
and lost both men. Has that made you afraid to ever love
again?''

''You don't pull any punches, do you?''

''I don't see any need. I've always thought that getting
straight to the point was the best way.''

Manda opened the French doors, walked across the
screened-in porch and outside. Hunter followed. She sat
down on the back steps. He sat beside her. Oxford came
running up to them for some more petting and then raced
back out into the yard to chase a squirrel.

''I met Rodney when Daddy was in the hospital,''
Manda said. ''He was an intern. All the nurses had a crush
on him. I suppose he was my male counterpart. Fair,
blond and blue-eyed. We had so much fun together. Had
so much in common. I guess it was inevitable that we fell
in love. His mother and Grams were delighted. They belonged to several of the same organizations and were already acquainted.''

''I'm so sorry, Manda. I can't imagine what you went
through when he died.''

''I thought I'd lose my mind. It took me nearly two
years to start living again.'' She rubbed her hands up and
down her legs, then cupped her knees as she stared out at
the moonlit river behind her house. ''Six years after Rodney died, I met Mike. Actually Boyd introduced us. Boyd
was Mike's grief counselor. You see, Mike's wife had
died the year before and he hadn't come to grips with that

loss. With Mike, I could talk about Rodney and he could talk about his wife, Chassie. We became dear friends and after we'd been dating for about a year, we decided that we should get married. We weren't in love, but we did love each other and we both wanted a home and children and… If only I'd known that someone would kill him because of me.''

Hunter slipped his arm around her shoulders. They sat there on the back steps for quite some time. They didn't talk anymore. Words weren't necessary. An odd sense of calm settled over them and Hunter thought how good it was to be able to share solitude with another human being.

Hunter and Manda became the talk of Dearborn, Georgia. They were seen together everywhere. At local restaurants. At her brother's home. At Mrs. Austin's home. At the mall. They had dinner together every night and lunch every day. Sometimes he picked her up at the clinic and other days he brought lunch to her. They were seen arm-in-arm, cuddling, kissing, laughing and gazing longingly into one another's eyes. And rumor was that Hunter had been spotted at Somerville Jewelers over on Fifth Street.

Manda knew that tonight was the night. Hunter was going to propose, just as he'd said he would. Saturday night. She had prepared dinner here at the house and told everyone who'd listen to her that she knew tonight would be special. Both Gwen and Grams had warned her that she was rushing foolhardily into trouble. Even Claire suggested that she might want to slow down just a bit and make sure about her feelings for Hunter. Boyd had stopped by her office to ask if she was sure she knew what she doing. Grady had phoned her to inquire about the rumors he'd heard. And Chris had been sitting on her front porch waiting for her yesterday evening.

"You can't be serious about this Whitelaw guy," Chris had said. "He's nothing but a big, macho jock. He's not one of our kind."

Her discussion with Chris had turned into an argument and she'd been forced to ask him to leave. He had left, but not before he warned her that she'd be sorry if she married Hunter. A cool shiver of apprehension had spiraled through her and for the first time since she'd known Chris, she wondered if he was capable of murder.

Manda brushed aside her doubts and concerns. She had to get through tonight first, which shouldn't be too difficult. After all, it wasn't as if Hunter was really proposing or that they were really in love. But heaven help her, sometimes she had to remind herself that this was all a ruse, all a grand scheme to trap a killer. She couldn't deny the attraction she felt for Hunter. They were drawn to each other on a primitive level that had nothing to do with compatibility or shared hopes and dreams. The magnetism that drew them together wasn't rational or logical, but had everything to do with basic human needs.

Hunter had been right when he'd said that it wouldn't be difficult for them to fool the world with their lovebirds act. Every time he touched her, she trembled with desire. And every time she looked at him, he seemed compelled to touch her. If she didn't know better, she would think that they *were* falling in love.

Lust isn't love, she kept reminding herself.

Dinner was ready to be served. She had spent hours preparing the meal. She loved to cook, but seldom had the opportunity to use her culinary expertise. She had set the table with her best china, silver and crystal. All that was left to do was light the candles just before they sat down to eat.

The doorbell rang. Manda jumped. Chill out, she told

herself. But how could she stay calm and cool when, come morning, everyone would know that she was engaged to Hunter? Perry had arranged to have Reverend Titus make the announcement at church tomorrow.

As she passed the mirror in the foyer, she paused to take a quick look at herself. Nothing spectacular. Just simple tan slacks and white blouse. A little makeup. She had given in to her vanity on only one point. She'd left her hair loose for a change…because Hunter had asked her to.

When she opened the door, she couldn't see Hunter for the enormous bouquet of lilies, roses and baby's breath that he held in front of him.

"What did you do, buy out the florist?" she asked.

He handed her the massive bouquet, then entered the foyer. "I told Mrs. Brownfield that I wanted something impressive because I planned to propose to you tonight."

Manda laughed as she carried the flowers through the great room and into the kitchen. She called out to Hunter. "That was a stroke of genius. Mrs. Brownfield is the biggest gossip in town. Sometimes I think the only reason she opened a florist shop was so that she could interrogate her customers about their private lives."

Hunter came into the kitchen and watched her as she separated the flowers into two bouquets and placed each into tall glass vases.

"I had to show her the ring." Hunter grinned. "She insisted."

"No fair. Another woman saw my engagement ring before I did." Manda placed one vase in the middle of the kitchen table, then handed the other to Hunter. "Put this in the center of the dining room table, while I check on our dinner."

He took the vase. "Half the town will know we're engaged before Reverend Titus makes the announcement in the morning.''

"Don't forget to pick me up at ten-thirty," Manda reminded him as she lifted the lid on the skillet containing the stuffed pork chops. "Church starts promptly at eleven.''

"I guess you know that I haven't been inside a church in years. The Good Lord sure is going to be surprised to see me there.''

"I doubt it," Manda said. "I'm pretty sure the Good Lord already knows your intentions.''

"Mmm-hmm... Want me to light the candles?" he asked, deftly changing the subject.

An hour later, with the meal enjoyed, the dishwasher loaded and the kitchen tidied, Hunter led Manda into the great room. Oxford lay sleeping on a handwoven rug in front of the fireplace. When Manda sat on the sofa as Hunter instructed her to do, he knelt down in front of her, pulled a tiny box from his pants' pocket and smiled when he looked directly at her.

"What on earth are you doing?" she asked, tiny giggles tittering in her throat.

"I'm assuming the correct position," he replied, a wide grin on his face. "Miss Manda, will you do me the great honor of giving me your hand in marriage? I very much want you to be my wife.''

Suddenly, without any warning, tears sprang into Manda's eyes. Why? she asked herself. What had prompted such an emotional reaction to a phony proposal? If he just hadn't added on that last sentence. *I very much want you to be my wife.* Get hold of yourself, Manda. Right this minute, she scolded herself.

"Ah, brat...don't." Hunter's big hand lifted, but before

his fingertips made contact with her cheek, she pulled back, letting him know she wouldn't welcome his touch.

"I'm all right," she assured him.

"Sure you are." He snapped open the box lid and held out the velvet case.

The ring inside wasn't a diamond solitaire. It was a blue, square-cut, three-carat sapphire flanked by a half-carat diamond on either side. Manda sucked in her breath. The ring was incredibly beautiful and quite unique. If she didn't know better she would think that Hunter had put a great deal of thought into its choice. The sapphire was not only her birthstone, but it was her favorite gem. Had Perry given Hunter that tidbit of information? she wondered.

"It's perfect," Manda said.

"Here, let's try it on and see if it fits." He lifted her hand from her lap and slipped the ring on the third finger of her left hand.

"It fits." She lifted her hand and gazed at the ring. Rodney had given her the traditional diamond solitaire. She and Mike had decided on a wedding band alone, but he had surprised her with a diamond heart pendant.

"Don't think about the other times," Hunter said, his voice slightly gruff. He cleared his throat. "I don't want you to be unhappy. Okay?"

"I'm not. But—"

He placed his right index finger across her lips. "What we're doing, what we will accomplish with this phony engagement and even fake marriage, if necessary, is to lay the past to rest. No more unhappiness. We're going to destroy the Manda Munroe Curse once and for all."

Manda clasped her hands together in a prayer-like gesture. "I want that more than anything. To be free to love again." She noted a slight change in Hunter's expression, as if he had tasted something unpleasant. "Once this is over, I'll owe you more than I'll ever be able to repay."

Hunter rose from his kneeling position, held out his hand to her and said, "On to the next act. Time to head over to the Munroe house to tell your brother and sister-in-law and Grams the good news."

"Maybe we'd better stop by the drugstore and pick up some smelling salts for Grams. I have a feeling she's going to keel over in a faint."

Chapter 6

This morning, everyone at the Hickory Hills Clinic—personnel and clients alike—had admired, gushed and gooed over and ogled Manda's ring. All the sincere congratulations had been difficult to accept since she knew the engagement was a farce and that even if the wedding, which Gwen and Claire were planning, came to be, it, too, would be only a staged production. Knowing in advance that everyone, except Perry, would question the hasty marriage, Manda and Hunter decided that she would tell everyone that the decision had been hers. After all, wasn't it understandable that having had two lengthy engagements end with the deaths of her fiancés that she wouldn't want to wait, wouldn't risk another wedding that would never happen? Her sister-in-law had been surprised by the news that she planned to wed Hunter, but had quickly offered her a hug and best wishes. Tears had sprung to Claire's eyes immediately, but her smile hadn't wavered as she wished them much happiness. Grams had voiced her opinion, stating the reasons why Manda would regret a hasty marriage to anyone, but especially to Hunter. No one had been surprised when Grams had pointed out the vast difference in Hunter's and Manda's backgrounds.

Despite Grams objections, the wedding was set for the following Saturday. A small, close-friends-and-family affair at the Munroe home. At six in the evening. While Grams had fussed and fumed, Gwen and Claire had gone into action mode and began bustling about helping Manda make a list of all that had to be done to pull off a *socially acceptable* wedding in less than a week.

"Leave it to us, dear girl," Claire had said. "Barbara, Gwen and I will make sure everything is perfect for you."

"Leave me out of this," Grams had told them. "I do not approve."

Gwen had assured Manda that Grams would come around—eventually. And Claire's biggest concern had been that Manda would have to purchase a bridal gown off the rack, instead of having one designed especially for her. Manda had pointed out that she'd had two other wedding dresses designed for her and neither dress had ever been worn.

During her morning break, Manda went straight to Boyd's office. He was the clinic's administrator and would be the one responsible for granting her vacation time for her honeymoon. She felt like a fraud, sitting here pretending to be the blushing bride-to-be. Although he didn't seem pleased about her upcoming nuptials, Boyd maintained a cordial expression.

"Of course, I wish you well, Manda." He splayed his palms atop his desk, then curled his hands into loose fists. "I must admit that I'm shocked. I never thought you were the type of woman who would act on impulse. After all, you hardly know Mr. Whitelaw.''

"I've known Hunter since I was ten," she said. "He and Perry have been best friends since high school.''

"That was years ago. What do you know about the man now?''

"I know that we love each other," she lied. "And Hunter isn't afraid of some lunatic who might try to prevent us from marrying. I feel confident that if any problems come up, Hunter can deal with them. You do know that he was a member of the Delta Force, don't you?''

Hunter had told her to mention that bit of information to their three top suspects. She had agreed, although she still didn't believe that Boyd or Grady or Chris was capable of murder. She knew these three men so well…or at least she thought she did.

"If you're determined to go through with this marriage, then I hope you'll include me on the guest list for the wedding,'' Boyd said.

"Yes, of course you'll be invited," Manda replied. Hunter had insisted that the three top suspects head the guest list. "Gwen is going to have the invitations delivered Wednesday. We're inviting only two dozen or so close friends and the immediate family.''

"Yes, yes. I understand. You've planned two larger, more elaborate weddings before, so naturally, you'd want this one to be more discreet. Very wise of you. Less gossip that way. People will talk, won't they?''

"Yes, you're right. That's exactly what we thought.'' Manda wondered why she'd never noticed what a stuffed shirt Boyd was. An uptight, judgmental snob. "I've asked Lisa to reschedule my afternoon appointments so I can shop for a wedding dress today. And I'll need next week off for a honeymoon.''

"Certainly. Certainly. Where will you two be going on your honeymoon?"

"I don't know. Hunter wants it to be a surprise." The truth was that they hadn't planned that far ahead. She assumed that if they were forced to go through with the wedding, Hunter would come up with a plan for a romantic honeymoon. Everything possible had to be done to make this engagement seem like the real McCoy.

When Manda stood, Boyd jumped up and rushed forward to open the door for her. As she started to walk away, he reached out and grasped her wrist. When she looked at him, she was startled by the intensity of his gaze. His facial muscles tensed as his fingers bit into her flesh.

"Is something wrong?" she asked, a sense of uncertainty tightening her stomach muscles.

"I only wish that things had worked out for us." Boyd cleared his throat. "If ever there's anything… Well, you must know that I'd do anything for you. All you have to do is ask."

Let go of me, Manda wanted to scream. *Please, Boyd, you're frightening me.* But instead she said, "That's very sweet of you. Thank you." Forcing herself to stay calm, she tugged on her wrist. At first, he held fast, but when she tugged a second time, he released her.

She exited his office as quickly as she could and practically ran down the hall to her own office. The thud of her heartbeat drummed in her ears as she approached her secretary's desk.

Lisa glanced up and smiled, but the warm greeting died instantly. "What's wrong, Manda? You look like you've just seen a ghost."

Manda released a breath that was part huff and part

sigh. "I'm fine. Really." She eyed the fifteen-inch-square white box on Lisa's desk. "What's that?"

"Oh, it must be a wedding gift," Lisa said.

"From whom?"

"I don't know. Someone must have dropped it off while I was getting a cup of coffee." She jerked off the small white envelope attached. "Here. Read the card and find out who it's from."

Manda took the envelope, lifted the flap and pulled out the enclosed card, then read the message out loud. "'Third time's the charm.'" No signature. Just the cryptic statement. Nausea rose in Manda's throat as a sinking feeling hit her in the belly.

"What sort of person would write something so crass?" Lisa glowered at the box.

"I don't know." But Manda suspected she did know who had sent her her first wedding gift. The proof's in the pudding, she reminded herself. Open the damn thing and see what's inside.

Manda stared at the big white bow atop the present, then hurriedly ripped off the ribbon, removed the lid and lifted the tissue paper. Nestled inside was a beautiful white leather "Memories of Our Wedding" album.

"At least the gift is a nice one, even if the note was rather odd," Lisa said as she visually inspected the album.

With shaky hands, Manda lifted the book out of the box and laid it on Lisa's desk. She had to force herself to look inside. Do it now and get it over with, she told herself.

She opened the album and turned over the first page. Name of bride: Manda Munroe. Name of groom: Rodney Austin, Michael Farrar and Hunter Whitelaw. Rodney's name and Mike's had been crossed out with large, black X marks.

"This has got to be somebody's idea of a sick joke," Lisa said.

Manda forced herself to turn to the next page. She gasped. This gift was a sick joke all right, one planned and executed by a sick mind. Manda's unsteady fingers traced the headlines of first one and then another obituary that had been cut from the local *Dearborn Daily* years ago and recently pasted into the wedding album, side-by-side, on facing pages. She quickly turned the page again only to be confronted by more newspaper clippings. Articles about Rodney's death in the car crash and even more articles about Mike's disappearance and murder.

"Oh, Manda, I'm so sorry," Lisa said. "You should call the police right away."

"No." Manda shook her head. "I'll call Hunter. He'll know what to do."

She closed the album, placed it back in the box and gathered up the ribbons and bow. "When Hunter gets here, let me know. And, please, see if one of the other counselors can take the next session with my group therapy patients."

"I'll take care of everything."

"Thanks."

When Manda opened her office door, Lisa called to her, "How about a cup of coffee?"

"No, thank you."

Manda closed the door behind her, walked across the room and laid the gift box on her desk. Then she took a deep breath before she picked up the receiver and dialed Hunter's cellular phone number.

Two hours later the ominous box lay on the back seat of Hunter's Lexus, which sported a set of new tires. He pulled the car into a parking space in front of Lady

Leona's Bridal Shoppe. The box and its contents wouldn't be thrown away, just on the off chance that they might at some future time be used for evidence. However, there wasn't much chance of tracing the gift-giver. As Hunter escorted her into the boutique, Manda tried to forget about the disturbing gift.

He cupped her elbow as they entered the only store in Dearborn that catered solely to brides. The interior was a Pepto-Bismol pink, with gold-framed portraits of their happy customers lining the walls, each woman wearing a gown purchased at Lady Leona's. Two burgundy velvet Victorian sofas and four matching chairs formed a sitting area in the middle of the store. Floor-to-ceiling mirrors covered the entire back wall. Hundreds of white, ecru and pastel wedding gowns, encased in zippered bags, lined the sides of the walls to the right and left. White and pink silk roses twined about the winding metal staircase that led to a mezzanine level. From where she stood, just inside the front door, Manda could see that the second level was filled with colorful dresses that she assumed were costumes for the bride's attendants.

A middle-aged brunette wearing a pink smock came rushing forward to greet them. "Hello. I'm Sylvie. Welcome to Lady Leona's Bridal Shoppe. How may I help you?"

"I'm looking for a bridal gown," Manda said.

"But of course you are." Sylvie smiled at Hunter. "But if you're the groom, it's highly inappropriate for you to be here. Mustn't see the bride in her gown before the wedding. It's bad luck, you know."

"We'll risk it," Hunter said.

The woman's eyes widened, but sensing a sale, she managed to keep her smile in place. "Yes, well…yes."

She looked straight at Manda. "Do you have something in particular in mind?"

"No, not really. Just something simple."

"Is this a second wedding for you? In that case you might want a gown in one of our pastels."

"No," Hunter replied for Manda. "It's her first wedding. She wants something in white. Something understated, classic and elegant, like the lady herself."

"My, my, he's certainly smitten with you, isn't he?" Sylvie all but tittered. "I have several gowns that fill the bill. But I'll warn you, they're rather expensive."

"Money is no object," Manda said. "But I need to find something today and have it altered and ready by this coming Saturday."

Sylvie gasped. "This Saturday." The woman's gaze went directly to Manda's stomach, checking for any signs of pregnancy.

"What about bridesmaids and a maid of honor and tuxedos for the groom?" She surveyed Hunter and shook her head. "We might have to special order something large enough to fit you. Are your best man and groomsmen big fellows like you?"

"My fiancé and his best man own tuxedos," Manda said. "And I'm having only one attendant, a matron of honor. My sister-in-law. She already owns something appropriate for the ceremony."

"I see." Sylvie's tone said plainly that she didn't approve. "Very well. Follow me. What you want is back this way." She glanced at Hunter. "If you'd like, you may sit here and wait."

Hunter eyed the Victorian settees and chairs, then shook his head. "I'll stand."

"Yes, that's probably a good idea. Our furniture is antique and rather delicate. I do apologize for any inconvenience, but we aren't accustomed to fiancés accompanying their brides-to-be.''

Manda followed the salesclerk to a row of gowns near the back of the room. She would rather be anywhere than here, doing anything other than this. The gown for her wedding to Rodney, an elaborate, beaded, white satin with a ten-foot train, had been designed especially for her by Rosemary Marcuse, who had been an up-and-coming young New York designer twelve years ago. And the dress for her wedding to Mike had been designed by Rosemary, also, who by that time was a renowned couturiere. That dress had been a cream Venetian lace, as was her bridal veil.

"What size are you?" Sylvie asked. "A six?"

"An eight," Manda said.

"Mmm-hmm…let me see."

Sylvie looked through the rack of eights, then pulled out a clear bag, unzipped and removed the cover to reveal a gown that matched Hunter's request. Understated. Classic. Elegant.

"Why don't you take this one into the dressing room to try on?" Sylvie suggested as she handed the gown to Manda. "And while you're doing that, I'll find you a veil."

"No veil," Manda said. Wearing a veil would make the wedding seem more real. Silly notion, but one she couldn't shake.

"No veil? Very well. Flowers then, or perhaps a headband."

"A headband."

Sylvie snapped her fingers. "I know just the one. It's an almost perfect match to the bodice of this gown."

Manda nodded, then entered the dressing room. As she stripped off her street clothes and stood in front of the

mirror wearing only her bra, panties, knee-highs—and a
pair of two-inch black heels, she prayed for the strength
to see her through this next week.

*Please, God, please, let this plan to trap a madman be
over and done with before next Saturday. Don't make me
go through with this wedding farce. I can't bear the
thought that my first marriage won't be a real union of
love and a promise of forever.*

Hunter waited patiently while Sylvie knocked on the
dressing room door, then went inside to assist her cus-
tomer. How Manda must hate going through this ordeal,
he thought. Choosing a bridal gown had to bring back so
many memories—both pleasant and terrifying. But if they
were lucky, the lunatic threatening her would reveal himself before the big wedding day. Sending that outrageous
wedding album so quickly after their engagement had
been announced had to mean that their nutcase would es-
calate his tactics once he saw that nothing he did would
stop the wedding. With each day that passed, the danger
would increase. He had to be on guard constantly, always
aware that a strike could come at any time and from any
direction. And what made it even more frightening was
that it could come from anyone.

Hunter had told Manda about only three suspects—the
three most obvious ones being the men who had been
pursuing her. But Hunter had secretly added two more to
the list. Gwen Munroe, who had once been in love with
Rodney Austin. Whenever they were around Gwen, he
could sense an underlying tension in her. His guess was
that she both loved and hated Manda. And his other suspect was Claire Austin. Despite the woman's motherly
affection for Manda, it was possible that she didn't really
want to see her dead son's former fiancée happy with

another man. Of course, neither woman had ever done anything that was suspect, but Hunter's gut instincts warned him to not rule out anyone.

Except perhaps Perry and Grams.

Of course, it was conceivable that Mr. Maniac was someone unknown to Manda. A secret admirer who had been lurking in the shadows for over twelve years. Hunter had heard of crazier scenarios. When it came to obsession, anything and everything was possible.

The dressing room door opened and Manda emerged. God Almighty, she was ravishing. Like a golden-haired angel. Odd, he thought, but that was what had come to mind the first time he'd seen her. She'd been ten and looked like a plump, blond cherub. But she was no longer plump nor was she ten years old. But she still looked like an angel.

Manda glided across the room to stand in front of the long mirrors across the back wall. Hunter studied her, enjoying the sight more than he should. The sleeveless gown had an arched beaded bodice, a rounded neckline, a fitted waist and flowed to a full, floor-length skirt of shimmering white silk. As classically elegant as anything he'd ever seen. Her only other adornment aside from white, elbow-length gloves was a beaded headband. A really stupid thought crossed his mind—he wished this beautiful creature *was* his bride, the woman he could claim for a lifetime—but as quickly as the idea hit him, he banished it. He sure as hell couldn't allow himself to get emotionally involved with Manda.

"Isn't she lovely?" Sylvie beamed with pride for having made an excellent choice.

"Yes, she is," Hunter said.

"I like this one," Manda told Sylvie, then glanced at Hunter. "I don't see any need to look at others, do you?"

He shook his head. "That one's perfect."

Sylvie clapped her hands. "It will require only minor alterations. We'll have to take it up about half an inch in the waist and let it out about the same in the bust."

"Fine," Manda said. "I'll write you a check today. I want it delivered to my brother's house Saturday morning. I'll give you the address."

Fifteen minutes later Hunter escorted Manda outside to his Lexus. Once in the car, she sat quietly as he pulled into traffic and headed toward the Poloma River.

"Would you like to stop somewhere on the way for a bite of lunch?" he asked.

"Why don't we just go to the house? I can fix us some sandwiches. I'm not really in the mood to sit in a restaurant and put on a show of lovesick happiness."

Hunter grunted. Was it necessary for her to remind him every chance she got how difficult it was for her to keep up the pretense that they were lovers? Maybe he should take care of that problem as soon as possible. If they actually were lovers, she would probably be more at ease with the charade that they had to enact for the benefit of everyone around them. What would she say, he wondered, if he suggested they share a bed tonight? After all, they were both consenting adults, both experienced and capable of a sexual relationship without love. And there was no doubt they desired one another. He could tell by the hungry look in her eyes every time he got too close.

Manda picked up the mail from the decorative brass box attached to the wall by the front door, then unlocked the dead bolt. Before she entered her house, she sifted through the envelopes lying on top of three magazines. She could tell without opening each item what most were. Two bills, two requests for charity donations, one credit card application and one... Her heartbeat accelerated as she inspected the final missive. A plain white envelope, her name and address typed plainly on front, but no return address. Mailed yesterday, here in Dearborn.

''What is it?'' Carrying a black vinyl carry-all and the box containing the wedding album, Hunter bounded onto the front porch.

Ignoring his question, she shoved open the front door and walked into the house, straight through the foyer and into the great room. She flung the mail onto the table— all except the mysterious white envelope. With the letter in her hand, she turned and pointed it at Hunter as if it were a gun.

''I think this is our first warning letter,'' she said.

Hunter dropped the carry-all on the floor and tossed the box onto the nearby sofa. Manda glared at his vinyl bag as if it were a slithering snake.

''I just brought what I'd need for a couple of days,'' he said. ''I left the rest of my stuff out at the farm.''

''I'd almost forgotten that you were moving in with me this afternoon.'' Manda walked over to him and handed him the letter. ''Why don't you open it and read it? I've already had my fun for the day.'' She glanced meaningfully at the gift box on the sofa. ''I put Oxford on the back porch this morning, so he could go in and out through the doggie door and enjoy the backyard. Once he hears me, he'll start scratching at the kitchen door.''

''Oxford can wait for a few minutes. Let's check out this letter and see if it's what we think it is.'' Hunter ripped off the end of the envelope and pulled out the single sheet of unlined paper. He spread it apart and scanned the message. His big hand crumpled the edge where he held it tightly.

''It's from *him*, isn't it?'' she asked

"Yes, it is."

When Hunter started to fold the letter, Manda held out her hand. "Wait. I want to know what he said."

"Pretty much what we were expecting. Something to the effect that if you don't call off your engagement to me immediately, I'm a dead man. And that if you even try to go through with the wedding, he'll kill both of us."

"God!" Manda tensed. Her heartbeat accelerated. Anger rushed through her like a tidal wave devouring a shoreline.

Hunter laid the letter and envelope on the table, then reached for Manda, who sidestepped him and began pacing frantically. She felt like running and screaming. She had thought she was prepared to go through this nightmare again, but she wasn't. When she'd been engaged to Mike and the letters began, even she hadn't taken them too seriously. Mike and Perry had convinced her to ignore them, saying they were just a stupid prank or perhaps the tirade of a rejected old boyfriend. But Mike and Perry had been wrong. Dead wrong. The person who had written those letters had followed through with his threats and killed Mike.

"He's going to try to kill you," Manda said, stopping to glare at Hunter. "Our engagement may be a pretense, but his threats are real. If you're having any second thoughts about going through with this, we can call off the engagement."

"No second thoughts," Hunter told her. "We're going to see this thing through to the end."

"I just don't want it to be the end of your life."

He came toward her. A part of her wanted to run, to get as far away from him as she possibly could. But another part of her wanted to rush into his arms and find not only solace, but comfort and caring. As her mind struggled with the decision, Hunter grasped her shoulders. She forced herself to look right at him.

"That box—" he inclined his head toward the sofa "—and that letter are only the beginning. Things will get worse. Once he realizes that we're going through with the wedding, he'll have to make a move. He's going to come after me. And maybe you, too."

She nodded, the truth of his words ripping through her like the blade of a sharp knife, cutting to shreds what little was left of her composure.

"From now on, until he's caught, we're going to be together twenty-four hours a day." Hunter ran his hands down her arms and encircled her wrists. "I'm going to be at your side day and night. And when he makes his move, we'll be ready for him. Do you understand what I'm saying?"

"I think so. You're staying here at the house with me. You'll take me to work every day, come back to the clinic to have lunch with me and then pick me up in the evening."

"You're partially right," he said. "I'm going in to work with you and staying there all day. It'll be easy enough to explain my presence since we'll tell everyone about the letter and make it clear that our wedding plans haven't changed. I doubt anyone will question my wanting to protect you."

"What you're saying is that from this moment on, you'll not only be my fiancé, but you'll be my bodyguard."

"That's right. You're never going to be more than a few feet away from me."

"Except at night, when you're in my guest bedroom."

"Wrong."

"Wrong? Surely you're not implying that we're going to sleep together."

"I'm not implying anything," he said. "I'm telling you."

Chapter 7

Fury brightened her sky-blue eyes as she glared at Hunter. "If you think for one minute that we're going to—"

"Share the same bed," Hunter said. "That's all. You on your side of the bed and me on my side."

Manda shook her head. Was he out of his mind? Did he honestly think that she was going to allow him to sleep in the bed with her? Regardless of what he said, she knew damn well that he wasn't any more immune to the attraction between them than she was. She might not be very experienced, but she wasn't some naive kid, either. Every time their bodies touched, Hunter became aroused. Okay, so maybe it was only a physical reaction, but that's all it took for a man. And she had a feeling that what Hunter wanted, he usually got. She doubted very many women had turned him down. But she couldn't—wouldn't—allow herself to become emotionally involved with him. If she made love with Hunter, it would mean more to her than only the release of sexual tension. If they made love, she would care too much, want too much.

"I have two bedrooms." Manda held up two fingers. "Mine and yours. You can make it easily from one bedroom to the other in a minute flat."

"Someone could smother you in your sleep, slit your throat or blow your brains out in a minute flat." Hunter looked at her point-blank as he issued his warning.

"I have a security system," she reminded him, not daunted by his dire predictions. "Before anyone could get to my bedroom from either the front or back door, you'd hear the alarm and—"

"Is the security system hooked up to all the windows in this house?" he asked.

"What?"

"I said are all the windows connected to—"

"No. No, they're not. When I had the system put in, I was told that ninety percent of all break-ins are through doors, not windows."

"That's probably true if the culprit is breaking in to rob you, but our perpetrator wouldn't be trying to get inside to rob you, would he? So, how many windows are there in this house? How many potential ways could he get inside?"

"Damn it, Hunter, if someone broke out a window to get in, we'd both hear him."

"If he's an amateur, sure. But not if he's a professional."

"What do you mean, a professional?"

"Maybe Mr. Maniac will play it smart and hire a professional killer to do the job for him. It's a possibility we have to consider."

Manda slumped down on the sofa, cupped her face with her open palms and sighed. A professional killer? The idea had never crossed her mind. But that was the difference between Hunter and her, between Hunter and any untrained person. In his job as a Dundee agent, he dealt with situations like this all the time. He knew every possible scenario and planned ahead to be prepared for whatever might happen.

Standing over Manda, Hunter gazed down at her. "I'm not going to be an easy kill. Our nutcase has got to know that. If he's done his homework on me, which he probably has, he'll know my background. If he's smart, he'll realize he needs a professional to fight a professional."

She nodded her head. "It makes sense."

"It will make things easier for both of us, if you don't question my orders. I know what I'm doing. That's why Perry hired me."

"I know." But regardless of that fact, she couldn't share a bed with Hunter. "I can call the security people and have them come out tomorrow and connect all the windows to the alarm system."

"You could do that." Hunter nodded. "But it might take them several days or even a week to get to the job and when they do, it'll cost you a small fortune with as many windows as you have in the house." He studied her face, then chuckled. "If you're that afraid to have me in your bed, then I'll sleep on a pallet on the floor beside your bed."

Her relief was quickly followed by guilt. She couldn't let him sleep on the floor. "No, I can't ask you to do that. I have a big bed. But I'm warning you right now that you'd better stay on your side."

"I'll stay on my side as long as you stay on yours."

She gasped. He laughed.

They had prepared dinner together, cleaned up the kitchen together and shared popcorn while they watched a movie on satellite. Neither had been talkative. Hunter figured Manda was as tense about their sharing a bed as he was. He'd been a fool to insist that they sleep together. She'd been right—he could have made it out of the other bedroom and into hers in a minute flat. But he'd been right, too. In an emergency situation, even seconds counted.

He had brushed his teeth and put on a pair of pajama bottoms. While on an assignment he didn't sleep in his boxer shorts the way he did at home. When he came out of the bathroom, Manda hurried inside and closed the door. Since there were no windows in the room and no other way in or out, he knew she was safe.

Her bed was king-size with big, heavy wooden posts connected by a headboard and footboard of metal fashioned into an intricate pattern of flowers and leaves. The bedding was white, except for the spread, which was a light green and matched the color of the walls. The room was feminine, but not frilly. Classic. Understated. Elegant.

A large round pillow covered in a green plaid material rested at the foot of the bed. After sniffing his bed, Oxford scratched the surface as if digging for bones, then circled the pillow several times. Once finished with the ritual, he flopped down and curled into a ball.

Hunter placed his Ruger P-95 on the nightstand. He turned back the spread and top sheet, then stood there staring at the bed. Manda's bed. He had to be out of his mind to put himself in such a position. He should do what he'd done before in situations like this and slept on the floor or even in a chair. Never in his career as a Dundee agent had he slept in the bed with a client. But Manda was no ordinary client. And that posed a major problem. She was his best friend's sister. And she was a woman whose image had haunted him over the years. He'd even married a Manda look-alike. Manda had once represented all he thought he wanted. Even now, knowing how hollow and meaningless money and social position were if they were all you had, he couldn't shake the notion that Manda was the ideal woman. Beautiful. Smart. Classy. And loving.

Idiot! Hunter berated himself. You don't know the real Manda. How could you, since you've been with her for only a week. You thought you knew Selina, too, didn't you? Boy, did she have you fooled. Don't let Manda's pretty facade trick you into thinking she's so damn perfect.

Hunter turned off the overhead light, but left both bedside lamps burning; then he got into bed, rested his head on the large, fluffy pillow and pulled the covers up to mid-chest. If he were lucky, he might get a little sleep tonight. But it was damn difficult to sleep with a hard-on, and he knew that the minute Manda crawled into bed beside him, he wouldn't be able to prevent the inevitable. Suddenly he heard water running into the garden tub and the image of a naked Manda flashed through his mind. Damn! He'd never forgotten the sight of her standing in front of him that day by the pool, her large, firm breasts a temptation no mortal man should have been asked to resist.

His sex grew hard and heavy. She wasn't even in bed with him yet, and he was already fully aroused. Just thinking about her had been enough to get him primed and ready.

Hunter tossed and turned. Think about something else. Baseball. Cars. Fishing. Anything but Manda and the fact that she's going to come through that door, walk across the room and get into bed with you.

* * *

Manda stayed in the tub until the water turned cold and her fingers and toes wrinkled like prunes. She couldn't stay in the bathroom all night, but the alternative unnerved her. The very thought of sleeping in the same bed as Hunter conjured up all sorts of sexual images. And every one of them involved him being totally naked. Shivers rippled through her, and she wasn't quite sure if they were caused by the cool bathwater or the vision inside her head of a nude Hunter.

Damn! Enough procrastinating. You know Hunter isn't lying there in your bed naked and aroused, just waiting to jump on you.

Hunter was wearing pajamas, and since she'd stayed in the bathroom for such a long time, it was possible that he was already asleep. And the bed was large, very large. So there was absolutely no reason why the two of them should brush up against each other during the night. But what if they did? What if she accidently rolled over and into him? What if he flung one of his big arms over her while he slept?

She was borrowing trouble and there was no need to do that. She had enough real problems without dreaming up more. Hunter wasn't here in Dearborn, in her house—in her bed!—to destroy her, but to save her. He was part of Perry's grand "Save Manda" scheme. And if she hadn't had that silly teenage crush on Hunter, if he wasn't the man by which she had measured all other men since she was sixteen, then lying beside him tonight would be a lot easier. But this was Hunter. Her Hunter. The guy she'd mooned over, fantasized about, tried to seduce and sworn to God that she would love until the day she died. How many women got to go to bed with the object of their first teenage infatuation?

Manda forced herself to get out of the tub. After drying off, she followed her nightly ritual and covered her skin with a scented lotion and dusted herself lightly with scented powder. As she turned to lift her gown from the back of the vanity chair, she caught a glimpse of herself in the wall-wide mirror. Her face was faintly flushed and her nipples were slightly puckered. A tingling sensation radiated upward from the core of her femininity. Thinking about Hunter had always aroused her, even when she'd been a teenager and knew very little about sexual reaction to an attractive, desirable man.

Stop thinking about Hunter that way. Not now, not tonight. She grabbed her gown, slipped in over her head and slid her feet into her house slippers. Reaching up, she removed the clip from her hair and let it fall down and around her shoulders. After taking a deep breath, she squared her shoulders, grabbed the doorknob and turned off the bathroom light. When she emerged from the safe haven of her bath, she found both bedside lamps burning and Hunter fighting with his pillow. His big fist thrust into the downy softness, then he doubled the pillow and burrowed his head into it. The sheet and spread covered him from his feet to just below his waist, but his chest and arms were bare. Manda stopped and stared at him while he wasn't aware of her presence. Or was he? He'd suddenly stopped moving and lay on his back, still and quiet, his gaze focused on the ceiling.

The man was huge. Built like the linebacker he'd been in high school and college. Massive shoulders and arms. Broad chest. Washboard-lean belly. And impressive muscles. His skin was naturally dark, as if he had a perpetual tan. All of her feminine instincts urged her on, telling her that this was a prime specimen, an alpha male with whom she should mate. The primitive part of her nature recognized him as a male who was capable of taking care of her and any children she might bear him.

Get a grip, girl, Manda warned herself. *You're teetering on the edge and if you don't hang on tight, you're going to fall hard.*

"Are you coming to bed or are you going to stand there staring at me all night?" Hunter asked, but he didn't move a muscle.

"Oh. Sorry." She walked over to the bed, kicked off her slippers, shoved back the covers and got in. "I'm not accustomed to having a man in my bed. You'll have to excuse me for taking a few minutes to get used to the idea." She reached over and switched off the lamp. "Are you planning on reading?"

"Huh?"

"You've left your lamp on."

Without replying, he turned off the lamp.

Manda pulled up the covers all the way to her chin. She remained as close to the edge of the wide bed as she could without toppling off, but even with more than an arm's length between them, she felt uncomfortable. Go to sleep, she told herself. All she had to do was close her eyes and pretend he wasn't lying on the other side of the bed. She needed to think about something that didn't involve Hunter. But what? He seemed to have invaded every aspect of her life. Think about work. In the morning she had individual appointments until noon, then after lunch she had two group therapy sessions. And Hunter would drive her to the clinic, spend the day there and drive her home tomorrow night. Even at work, she wouldn't be free of him. Until this plan to capture her tormentor came to a conclusion, she and Hunter were figuratively "joined at the hip."

He certainly was quiet and still. He hadn't so much as

twitched since she'd joined him in bed, and she couldn't even hear him breathing. Her first instinct was to turn over and look at him, to see if he was still lying on his back, staring up at the ceiling. But common sense warned her to do nothing to arouse the beast.

Minutes ticked by as she lay there, her eyes closed, her mind repeatedly telling her to go to sleep. But the harder she tried to rest, the more tense she became. And her body ached from lying in one position for so long. Sooner or later she would have to move. But she'd make it later, when she felt more certain that Hunter was asleep.

Suddenly he moved. He flopped over onto his side, shaking the bed with the turn. She held her breath, wondering if he had turned toward her and was now lying closer. If she reached for him, would she be able to touch him? Her fingers itched to find out. Common sense won out over curiosity. Instead of reaching for him, she opened her eyes. The room lay in darkness, except for the faint moonlight that shimmered through the widows facing the river. She saw the shadowed outline of his big body. He lay with his back to her. She sighed with relief. Now that he had made the first move and turned away from her, she could move, too. She promptly turned her back to him.

She cuddled into the pillow, then bent her knees and curled into a fetal position. Sleep, damn it, she told herself. But sleep wouldn't come. Time passed. How much she wasn't sure. Finally she stole a glance at the lighted digital clock on her nightstand. Eleven forty-five. She'd been in bed nearly an hour and was still wide awake.

"What's wrong?" Hunter asked. "Can't you sleep?"

Manda jerked, gasped and clutched her chest, then shot straight up in bed. "My heavens, you scared me to death. I thought you were asleep."

He rolled over so that he faced her. "We have a problem, don't we?"

"Uh-huh."

"Neither of us is used to sleeping with someone else."

"I've never shared a bed with anyone in my entire life," she admitted.

"Never?"

"Never."

"What about with Rodney or with Mike?" he asked.

"Mike and I didn't have that sort of relationship," she said. "Naturally, once we were married, we would have slept together."

"Mmm-hmm. Surely you and Rodney—"

"I was away at college part of the time and when I was here in Dearborn, I lived at home. You know Grams would never have approved of a man staying over and sleeping in my bed."

"What about his place? Surely you stayed over with him occasionally, at least part of a night."

Her love life—or lack thereof—with her former fiancés was really none of Hunter's business. She certainly had no intention of telling him that she was, technically, still a virgin. He probably wouldn't believe her even if she did tell him. Not many people would believe that such a thing as a thirty-three-year-old virgin actually existed.

"Rodney lived at home with Claire and Chris," Manda said. "And Claire is as old-fashioned as Grams."

"You two must have gotten tired of making out in the back seat of his car."

"Mmm-hmm."

She and Rodney had made out in the front seat as well as the back. They had kissed, touched, fondled, petted and relieved their sexual tension in every way possible, except intercourse. After he'd been killed in the car crash, she had regretted that they had decided to wait until after they were married to consummate their love. If only she had known that they would never have a wedding night, that she would be left to live on without him.

After she had gone through the mourning process, through every stage of grieving, she hadn't dated much. Guilt had tormented her any time she had become the least bit interested in a man. Her heart had still belonged to Rodney. How could she betray him with someone else? The few occasions when she'd been sexually attracted to a man, she had felt disloyal to Rodney. She supposed that was one reason she had felt comfortable with Mike from the very beginning. She hadn't felt any strong sexual attraction to him. And they had discussed their mutual feelings of guilt and worked through them together. They would have married, been friends and he could have gone on loving Chassie and she Rodney.

She was a woman who wanted a man, needed a man. In her life and in her bed. She yearned for marriage and children, for the kind of life others took for granted. But this strong sexual chemistry between Hunter and her wasn't something she wanted. Nor was the renewed emotional attachment she had once felt for him. She could never love him. Never open herself up for that kind of pain again.

When Hunter reached out and clutched her arm, she gasped and jumped.

"Calm down. I'm not going to attack you."

"I know you aren't."

"I'll tell you what I think we should do."

"What?"

"I think we should give ourselves permission to relax." He ran his hand up her arm, stopping at her shoulder. "You're awfully tense." He massaged her shoulder. "I promise that I'm not going to do anything to you that you don't want me to do.''

That didn't soothe her rioting nerves at all. Doing what she wanted him to do would be enough to set the sheets on fire. Manda could not deny her desire to be with Hunter, to give herself to a man for whom she cared. And she did care for Hunter. She always had and probably always would. She didn't have to love him to have sex with him. And he didn't have to love her. There was no reason they couldn't be together without their relationship being some life-altering grand passion.

''What do you suggest we do?'' she asked, then held her breath, waiting for his answer.

''I think I should scoot a little closer.'' Which he did. ''And then I should slip my arm around you.'' Which he did. ''And you should cuddle up against me.'' Which she did. ''There. Isn't that better?''

''I guess so.''

''You're in my arms. We're in bed together. And you're perfectly safe. This is the most that's going to happen between us tonight, so you and I can both relax and get some sleep.''

''And that's all there is to it, huh?''

''Close your eyes, brat, and see what happens.''

Hunter lay there half awake and half asleep, partially aroused and yet strangely content to simply hold Manda in his arms. She had finally drifted off to sleep over an hour ago. He wondered what she had thought would happen between them. What had she wanted to happen? He believed that he understood women pretty well. Good women, bad women and all those in between. He knew when a woman wanted him. And Manda did want him.

But he sensed that she was afraid of that basic human need—sex.

Was she still in love with Rodney Austin, after all this time? In a way, the thought that she'd never gotten over her former fiancé bothered him, and yet in another way knowing her love and loyalty was that abiding made him wish that someone cared for him half as much.

Manda was a woman meant to be loved and cherished and adored. Fate had given her a raw deal. But once this person—whoever he was—made a mistake and revealed himself, then his hold over Manda's life would come to an end. She'd be free. Free to live as she chose. Free to love and marry and have children. She deserved to be happy, and he intended to do everything in his power to give her that chance.

Fifteen minutes later he drifted off to sleep still thinking about Manda.

The ringing telephone woke her. As she came awake, she realized that she was using Hunter's chest as a pillow and that their legs were entangled. When she pulled away from him and reached out for the phone, he roused and grumbled.

Still lying in bed, she lifted the receiver and put it to her ear. ''Hello?'' she mumbled drowsily.

''Manda, you're being a bad girl.'' The voice was slow and muffled. Disguised. As if the message had been recorded and was now being played back at low speed. ''I'll have to punish you. Unless you break your engagement, I'll be forced to kill Hunter.'' Manda jerked straight up into a sitting position. ''Is that what you want, to be responsible for the death of another man?''

As she clutched the phone with white-knuckled pressure, she gulped in a deep breath. Fear shook her, creating tremors through her body.

Hunter lunged up and over, grabbed the phone out of her hand and said, "Who the hell is this?"

Manda heard the hum of the dial tone as Hunter reached around her and laid the receiver back on its base. He grabbed her shoulders. She looked into his eyes. With her mouth sucking in air and shivers racking her body, she couldn't speak.

"Was it him?" Hunter asked.

She nodded her head.

"Did you recognize his voice?"

She shook her head.

"Was his voice disguised in some way?"

She nodded again, then began shaking harder and knew she was on the verge of hyperventilating. Hunter shook her soundly. She cried out, putting a voice to her pain and fear. Desperately needing Hunter's comfort and strength, she flung herself at him.

As if he understood what she wanted, he lifted her up and onto his lap. Then he wrapped his arms around her while whispering her name and caressing her back.

"Shh-hh, Manda. It's all right. I'm here. You're safe. I'm safe. He can't hurt either of us," Hunter assured her. "He was trying to frighten you, to make you bend to his will. But you aren't going to let him win. Not this time."

Hunter sounded so confident, so sure. She wanted to believe him.

And she did. Almost. "He said that unless I broke my engagement to you, he'd be forced to kill you."

"No one is going to kill me," Hunter told her, all the while holding her, caressing her, his lips brushing against her temple. "Remember that I'm the cavalry to the rescue.

We're going to catch that son of a bitch. Do you hear me?''

Manda nodded, but didn't reply. Fear clutched her heart. Just the thought that something might happen to Hunter was unbearable.

Continuing to hold Manda on his lap, Hunter reached over and lifted the phone. ''There's a number here on the caller ID. I'll call the police and have them run a check on it.''

A mixture of numbness and anxiety claimed Manda as she sat quietly while Hunter contacted the local authorities, but she sensed that her stalker was too smart to give himself away so easily. The police weren't going to be able to catch this man. And despite Hunter's self-confidence, all Manda could think about was the possibility that Hunter might die because of her. Just like Rodney and Mike had.

The minute Hunter ended his conversation with the police, he reached out to grasp Manda's face. But she pulled away and scooted out of his arms, then hopped out of bed.

She glared at him, then all but screamed, ''I will not be responsible for the death of another man I care about!''

When she ran out of the bedroom, Oxford at her heels, she sensed Hunter following her as she raced down the hall. She had no idea where she was going, barely knew what she was doing. All she understood was that she had to escape, had to get away from the guilt and the anger and the pain and the loss. Oh, God, the emptiness of loss, of having loved and then been left alone.

He reached out for her, but she kept running away. Suddenly he tackled her, sending them both flying toward the floor. He somehow managed to catch himself and come down on one knee, then yanked her into his arms before her body landed beneath him. He held her so tightly, with such fierce determination, that she couldn't move, could barely breathe. With her face pressed against the side of his neck, she cried and cried. She couldn't stop the racking sobs that came from her very soul. He didn't say anything else, just held her while she unraveled, inch by slow, tormented inch.

When her sobs subsided into an occasional gasp, he stood and lifted her up and into his arms. Then without a word, he carried her down the hall and into the living room. Oxford followed them, matching them step for step. She held on to Hunter for dear life, sensing that he was the only thing in the world that could keep her sane tonight. He sat in the large, overstuffed burgundy chair and brought her down onto his lap. Oxford plopped down beside the chair.

Quite suddenly she felt exhausted, as if all her strength had drained out of her body. But the fear that had prompted her irrational actions was gone, evaporated by the heat of Hunter's strength. She relaxed against him, limp as a rag doll, and accepted his tender care. Somehow he understood what she needed from him right now. Her eyelids drooped. She yawned. Hunter leaned over, grabbed a hand-knitted afghan off the ottoman and wrapped it around them, then kissed her gently on the forehead.

She sighed, a feeling of security and contentment unlike any she'd known since childhood cocooned her. She was safe. Safe in Hunter Whitelaw's arms.

Chapter 8

Manda had spent the morning doing her job and trying to not think about the eerie phone call she'd received last night. Or the way she'd fallen apart emotionally. Or the fact that she had spent the rest of the night sleeping in Hunter's arms. He'd been a gentleman this morning when she awoke and found herself in his lap. Realizing that he probably hadn't gotten much sleep sitting up in the living room chair for hours while she rested, she had apologized to him. He had grinned and said it had been his pleasure.

Lisa came through the open door and into Manda's office. "Mr. McCullough called and canceled. He's rescheduled for two weeks from today." Lisa handed Manda a cup of coffee, then nodded toward the outer office. "He's been on the phone most of the morning. I didn't mean to eavesdrop, but he was using my telephone."

"Are you trying to tell me something?" Manda set the coffee mug on her desk.

"He's amazing, isn't he? I mean, what woman wouldn't want a guy like that? I wouldn't be afraid of anybody or anything if I had somebody like Mr. Whitelaw protecting me," Lisa said. "Did you know that he's called his office and put them on alert? He told them he might need one or more agents as backup. And he's talked to the police chief twice. He told Chief Burgess that you had received another one of those threatening letters."

"Hunter is a professional security agent. He's handling the situation as he would if this were a job assignment. And as for him talking to Chief Burgess, even though there isn't much the police can do without any evidence against someone, they need to know what's going on."

"Don't you have caller ID?" Lisa asked. "I'd think that guy's number would have shown up."

"It did. He was using a pay phone in downtown Dearborn."

"In the middle of the night? And how did you know that—"

"Hunter spoke to Chief Burgess and to Perry before we left the house this morning," Manda explained. "The police ran a check on the phone number immediately."

"He's so efficient, isn't he? A real take-charge kind of man." Lisa sighed dreamily.

Hunter appeared in the doorway. "Would you like to go for an early lunch?"

Manda glanced at him and her stomach fluttered the way it used to do when she'd been a teenager mooning over her big brother's best friend. Despite all the warnings she had given herself, she seemed powerless to stop her body's purely instinctive reaction to Hunter, so she could hardly blame her secretary for drooling over him.

"I'd rather order in," she said. "With the honeymoon coming up and my taking off a week from work, I have a hundred and one things to do around here. Do you mind if we just have sandwiches?''

"I don't mind," he said. "We'll do whatever you want to do."

"Wow!" Lisa stared at Hunter, adoration in her eyes. "Mr. Whitelaw, you're too good to be true. You don't happen to have a brother who'd like to date a lowly secretary, do you?"

Hunter chuckled. "Sorry. I'm an only child."

"Figures," Lisa said, still staring at him.

"Lisa, would you order a couple of ham and cheese specials from Josie's Café?" Manda glanced at Hunter. "Want dessert? Josie makes the most delicious fried pies. Peach, apple and blueberry."

"Peach," Hunter said.

"Add two peach pies to that order."

Lisa nodded, then backed out of the office, her gaze still glued to Hunter. The moment she returned to her desk, Hunter closed the door and walked across the room toward Manda.

"Do you have a few minutes?" he asked.

"Of course. What's wrong? Has something happened that I don't know about? Please, don't keep anything from me. You probably think I'll turn into a basket case again, considering the way I acted when I received that stupid phone call. But I promise that I won't fall apart on you the way I did last night. I'm usually a tower of strength in a crisis. Just ask anyone who knows me."

His gaze settled on her face. "I'll take your word for it. Besides, everyone has a right to come unglued occasionally."

She offered him an appreciative smile.

"As to what's going on—nothing new has happened." He sat on the edge of her desk. "But Chief Burgess gave

me some information that might or might not have anything to do with our mystery caller.''

Manda looked directly at Hunter. "What sort of information?"

"It seems that Burgess checked with the officer who
patrolled the downtown area last night and early this
morning. The officer distinctly remembers seeing a couple
of our suspects downtown between two and three this
morning. An odd coincidence, don't you think?''

Her nerves tensed. "Who did the police officer see?"

"He gave Grady Alder a ticket for running the red light
at the intersection of Main Street and Seventh, which was
only two blocks from the pay telephone that our caller
used. This was around two o'clock this morning.''

"Grady? What was Grady doing out at two in the
morning?''

"He told the officer that he was driving home from
a lady friend's house and he was a bit preoccupied
with…er…romantic thoughts, and that's why he went
straight through the traffic light.''

"That's possible,'' Manda said. "Since his divorce,
Grady has been quite popular with the ladies.''

"His story is credible,'' Hunter admitted. "But whatever his reason for being downtown at that time of night,
it puts him in the vicinity of the telephone used by our
caller and puts him there at approximately the time you
answered the phone.''

A sour nausea rippled in Manda's stomach. She had
known and liked Grady for years. He and his ex-wife,
Eva, had belonged to the country club and attended the
same church as her family did. He and Eva had even
hosted an engagement party for Mike and her.

"Who was the other person the officer saw?'' Manda
asked.

''Well, he didn't actually see the other person, just his car.''

''Who's car?''

''A yellow Ferrari was parked in front of the Dearborn Museum, one block from the telephone our caller used,'' Hunter told her. ''The officer didn't see anyone in the car, but he remembers thinking it odd that Chris Austin would have left the Ferrari downtown overnight.''

''Have they questioned Chris?''

Hunter nodded. ''He says it wasn't his car. He and Claire swear he was home in bed. The officer had no reason to check the license plate number, so we have no proof that it actually was Chris's car. But what are the odds of another yellow Ferrari being in Dearborn?''

''Claire probably thought he was at home. She wouldn't lie for him. So, now Grady and Chris move up to the top your suspects list.''

''They were already at the top of the list. This just confirms my suspicions, and it should warn you that either man could be our nutcase.''

Manda shook her head. ''I can't believe...I don't want to believe that either of them is capable of making my life a living hell. Chris swears that he loves me. And Grady has always seemed genuinely fond of me. I've known both of them for ages.''

The outer door swung open and Lisa stood there with a stricken look on her face. Manda's heartbeat accelerated as she sensed the fear radiating from her secretary.

Lisa opened her mouth to speak, but she didn't make a sound.

Manda jumped up and rushed toward Lisa. ''What's wrong?''

Hunter approached the two women. ''Lisa, whatever it is, it'll be all right. Just tell us.''

Lisa swallowed hard. "Phone call." She gulped. "Just now. He said...he said we would all die."

"Dear God!" Manda gasped.

Hunter grabbed Lisa's shoulders gently and forced her to look directly at him. "Who called? And was that everything he said, that we would all die?"

Lisa shook her head. "I don't know who it was, but his voice sounded funny. You know, like it was recorded at low speed. And he said...he said that we would all die because he had to do something to make Manda listen to him. There's a bomb—" Lisa began huffing, sucking in air rapidly.

Hunter shook her soundly. "Where is there a bomb? Here, in the clinic?"

Lisa nodded her head repeatedly. "Do you think...he's bluffing? Is there really a bomb?"

"I don't know," Hunter said. "But we're going to have to work under the assumption that there is. We need to clear out the clinic fast, without alarming the personnel or the patients." He tightened his hold on Lisa's shoulders. "Can you pull yourself together and help us? We need you."

Lisa nodded. "I'll be okay. What—what do you want me to do?"

He glanced at Manda. "Call the police and tell them that we're fixing to set off a fire alarm, but there is no fire. We've had a bomb threat called in and we need to clear out the clinic as quickly as possible." He turned back to Lisa. "Do you know how to set off the fire alarm?"

"Yes."

"Then go do it. Now. And tell anyone who'll listen to you that it's simply an unannounced fire drill."

Manda dialed 9-1-1 and explained the situation. By the

time she got off the phone, the fire alarm sounded. Hunter grabbed her arm and together they fled her office. She couldn't believe this was happening. How could this person, this lunatic, put the lives of everyone in the clinic at risk because he was obsessed with her? If she'd had any doubts that she was doing the right thing by going along with Perry and Hunter's plan to bring this nutcase out into open, she no longer had any doubts. He had to be stopped before he harmed anyone else. It wasn't a matter of only her personal happiness at stake now.

When they passed Boyd's office, he came running toward them, a wild-eyed expression on his face. "What's going on? Is there a fire?"

"It's a fire drill," Hunter said, keeping Manda moving as he responded.

Boyd ran after them. "Who authorized a fire drill?"

"I did," Manda said and continued rushing toward the exit.

"Why would you do such a thing?" Boyd asked.

In the distance sirens wailed, alerting everyone that help was on the way. People milled around outside, in designated areas, far enough away from the building to be safe in case there actually was a fire inside the clinic. Hunter didn't allow Manda to stop until they were across the street, then he turned to face Boyd, who had followed them.

"Someone called in a bomb threat," Hunter said, his voice low. "We need to get everyone farther away from the clinic. Depending on what kind of bomb is inside the building, it could blow up one room or it could wipe out half a city block."

Boyd turned chalk white. "A bomb? But why? Who would—" He glowered at Manda. "This has something to do with you and this business with the person who killed Mike Farrar and… Do you realize that you've put everyone in my clinic at risk?''

"Shut up, Gipson.'' Hunter clamped his hand down on Boyd's shoulder. ''You have more important things to do right now than assign blame.''

"Yes, of course, you're right.'' Boyd glanced at Manda. ''I'm sorry. I didn't mean—''

"It's all right,'' she assured him. ''Hunter's right. We need to get everyone across the street and as far away from the clinic as possible.''

When the fire department, the police department and the paramedics arrived, the clinic's personnel and clients had been evacuated and two-thirds of them were already safely a block away. In his official capacity as the administrator of the Hickory Hills Clinic, Boyd remained with Chief Burgess while they waited for the bomb squad to search the building. Hunter stayed with Manda, though she realized he wanted to be in the middle of the action. He was a man accustomed to handling danger himself and not relying on others.

"It's been a good twenty minutes since Lisa received the call,'' Hunter said. ''Either this guy called us in plenty of time so that we could get everyone out or something went wrong with his bomb.''

Manda tugged on Hunter's arm. ''I don't think Chris or Grady or Boyd would know how to build a bomb.''

"A ten-year-old can build a bomb these days,'' Hunter told her. ''Anyone with access to a computer can get detailed instructions. But it's possible that our guy has already hired himself a professional. In that case, this was only a warning. If a professional had built and set that bomb, it would have already gone off.''

"Well, I know one thing for sure, it's not Boyd. You

can rule him out. He'd never do anything to destroy the clinic or harm the people here. This clinic is his life.''

"Maybe so, but I'll wait until we get a report from the bomb squad before I start ruling out suspects.''

Hunter and Manda watched the activity across the street as Dearborn's emergency teams combined their efforts, some in charge of crowd control, while others faced immediate danger and the rest were on standby, prepared to go into action at a moment's notice.

"You don't trust anyone, do you?" Manda's words were half question and half comment.

Hunter glanced over his shoulder, a solemn expression on his face. "That's not true." He turned toward her. "I trust people who have earned my trust, those who have shown me by their actions that they're trustworthy. People like my comrades in the Dundee agency. And I've always trusted Perry. He's never let me down.''

Manda wished she'd never brought up the issue of trust. She figured that Hunter would never quite forgive her for the lie she'd told Grams all those years ago. Although she had very little in common with the spoiled, pampered child she'd been then, she wasn't sure it mattered to Hunter. He seemed to be the type who didn't forgive easily and never forgot. He might be risking his life to help her, but he was doing it only as a favor to Perry.

"What's taking them so long?" Manda rubbed her hands together nervously, half expecting to hear a huge explosion at any moment. How would she feel if any lives were lost because of a bomb set by her twisted admirer? Would she be able to live with the guilt?

She heard them calling her name before she saw them shoving their way through the crowd, which was a mixture of clinic personnel and clients, as well as curiosity seekers who had gathered to check out the excitement.

Because he was the taller of the two, she saw Perry first when the sunlight glistened on his blond hair. The moment he caught a glimpse of her, his frown changed to a smile and he ran toward her. Grady Alder followed close behind and he, too, was smiling.

Perry grabbed her and hugged her close. "God, Manda, when I heard, I thought I'd go crazy until we got here and I saw for myself that you were all right."

"I broke the speed limit getting us here," Grady said. "I can't believe this is happening. Do you know for sure that there's a bomb in the clinic?"

"All we know is that he—the same person who wrote the two letters and made the phone call last night—called my office and told my secretary Lisa that he had put a bomb in the clinic and we would all die because he had to do something to make me listen to him."

"Oh, Manda…" Perry caressed her face. "Don't start blaming yourself for this. No matter what happens, it's not your fault."

"Of course it isn't her fault," Grady said as he moved closer and grasped Manda's hand. "I just hope that the police can do something to catch this guy. He must be insane."

"Not necessarily," Hunter said. "He may simply be deviously clever and only slightly unbalanced."

"What?" Grady glared at Hunter. "Are you saying a sane person would do the things this man has done?"

"All I'm saying is that he may not be clinically insane."

"I think we should take Manda home," Grady said. "She needs to get away from this madness." He gazed beseechingly at Manda. "Why don't you let Perry and me get you out of here?"

Hunter narrowed his gaze directly on Grady. "Manda goes nowhere without me."

"Now, see here, Whitelaw, I believe that Perry and I are capable of taking care of Manda until you finish up here." Thrusting out his chest, Grady's determined gaze issued Hunter a challenge.

"Manda stays with me." Hunter spoke the words slowly, his tone brooking no argument.

Grady curled his meaty hands into tight fists. Manda sensed he wanted to defy Hunter, but didn't quite have the courage to go up against a superior opponent. Even knowing that Hunter's reaction hadn't been personal, something totally primitive within her actually enjoyed the possessiveness he had displayed.

"I can't leave until they find the bomb and we know they've been able to disarm it," Manda said. "Perry, you should go over to the house and let Grams and Gwen know we're all right. Grady, maybe you can either call or go by to let Claire and Chris—"

"Chris is the one who called and told us about the situation," Perry said. "He had heard the news break on our local TV station. He and Claire are on their way here. They should arrive any minute now. It doesn't take more than ten minutes longer to get from their house here than from our office to here. And I'm sure Claire called Gwen, so I expect she and Grams will be showing up soon, too."

An hour later Chief Burgess approached Hunter. Manda, who was surrounded by family and friends, broke away from Grams's and Claire's smothering attention and reached for Hunter's arm. She gripped his biceps tenaciously, nervous tremors rioting inside her.

"We've gone over the clinic from top to bottom and found nothing," the chief said. "We're going to let everybody go home now, while we continue going over the place with a fine-tooth comb. But my guess is that your office received a prank call and there isn't a bomb and never was one. Ms. Munroe, I'd say somebody is trying their damnedest to scare the hell out of you.''

"I'd say they're succeeding," Manda said.

"Will you need us for any further questioning?'' Hunter asked.

"I think I've got all the information I need," the chief replied. "Go ahead and take Ms. Munroe home. If we need anything else, I'll get in touch with you." Chief Burgess turned to go, then stopped and glanced back over his shoulder. "If I were you, I wouldn't let her out of my sight.''

"Don't worry, I don't intend to." Hunter eased his arm around Manda's waist.

Manda's hair whipped about her face as the evening breeze bombarded her. She closed her eyes as Hunter raced the old Chevrolet convertible down the highway. The car had once belonged to his grandfather, purchased secondhand over forty years ago. Pop had given Hunter the car on his sixteenth birthday and he'd driven it during high school and college, then left it behind when he joined the army. Over the years, he'd kept the car in tip-top shape and stored it there at the farm, inside the barn. When they'd arrived at his grandparents' home place several hours ago, he had parked his Lexus beside the old farmhouse, then they had hopped into the convertible and taken off to parts unknown. At least unknown to her.

"Where are we going?'' she'd asked.

"As far away from Dearborn as we can get this afternoon," he had told her.

They had been traveling for at least four hours and had

stopped only once, to fill up with gas and to pick up fast food for supper. Neither of them had talked much, but Hunter had found a station that played nothing but classic country songs. Recordings by Eddy Arnold and Jim Reeves and Patsy Cline. Songs created to bring tears to the eyes and relief to the heart.

Manda could hardly believe that Hunter had whisked her away from everyone—Grams, Perry and Gwen, as well as Claire and Chris and Boyd. He'd told them that he would take care of Manda and she would call them in the morning. Everyone except Perry had protested, but Hunter had ignored them all. He had told Perry to go by Manda's and feed Oxford. Then when he'd held out his hand to her, she'd taken it and run away with him. The really crazy thing was that at that precise moment she would have gone anywhere with Hunter, even if he'd asked her to fly to the moon with him. In a very brief span of time she had come to rely on him, to think of him as her protector, her rescuer and hopefully her salvation.

While they had wolfed down greasy hamburgers and onion rings as they sat in the car outside the fast-food restaurant, she had asked Hunter why he hadn't just taken her home when they'd left the clinic.

"You need a few hours of living in the moment instead of the past or the future. For one evening I want you to forget about what's happening in your life."

"Before things get worse," she'd said.

"You can worry about that tomorrow. Tonight, pretend that you don't have a care in the world."

It had taken a while before she had actually given herself permission to put aside all her worries, to do as he'd asked and pretend for this one night that her life wasn't in utter chaos. Somewhere, back down the road an hour or so ago, she had, inside her mind, dumped her worries out of the old convertible and accepted these stolen hours of freedom from reality as a gift from Hunter.

They reached the coast at sunset. The first full moon of May shone brightly in the twilight sky and cast a shimmering wash of transparent gold across the occasional glimpses she caught of the Atlantic Ocean. Hunter pulled the car to a halt, got out and unlocked an impressive set of iron gates. After which he drove the car onto the gravel road beyond the gate, then got back out to close and lock the gates behind them.

"What is this place?" she asked.

"There used to be an old antebellum mansion here," he said. "It was burned to the ground during the Civil War. The property belongs to one of the Dundee agents. He inherited it from a great-aunt. He's thinking about building some condos here and he'd like several of us to invest in the idea. He gave us keys to the gate, so that whenever we wanted to we could check out the property. There's supposed to be an old beach house close by."

He drove over the bumpy, curving road for a good quarter of a mile before the ruins of the old mansion came into view. Eight massive columns stood like silent sentries, guarding the ghosts of the past. The scent of the sea was in the air. They couldn't be far from the ocean. About fifty yards past the ruins, the gravel road turned to a dirt pathway, no more than six feet wide. Within a few minutes, the beach came into view and the path came to an abrupt halt. To their right a ramshackle old beach house perched on the rise above the shoreline. He parked the car, then opened the driver's door and got out. He stretched, his big body a dark silhouette outlined by the moonlight.

"Want to take a walk on the beach?" he asked.

"Sure, why not."

Bracing himself against the convertible, Hunter removed his shoes and socks and rolled up his pant legs. Manda removed her shoes, then reached up under her skirt and grabbed the waistband of her panty hose. She quickly tugged them down her legs, then tossed them into the back seat. Hunter rounded the hood and opened the passenger door for her.

"I can't believe we're doing this," she said. "I haven't done something this spontaneous since I was a teenager."

Hand-in-hand, they walked to the beach. The sand retained some warmth from the day's sunshine, but the water lapping at their feet was icy cold. As they strolled along the beach, they darted in and out of the surf, laughing happily as if they didn't have a care in the world. Feeling almost giddy, Manda broke away from Hunter and ran, daring him to chase her. As he raced to catch up with her, he called her name. When she glanced over her shoulder to reply, he caught her off guard.

Hunter lifted her up and off the ground, then swung her around and around, until she squealed for him to put her down. When he lowered her to her feet, he brought her down slowly, languidly, sliding her body over his. When her toes burrowed into the sand, she lifted her arms and draped them around his neck.

"Are you enjoying yourself?" he asked.

"Yes." She sighed the word just as he brushed his lips over hers. She sucked in a deep breath. "Yes," she said again, knowing that he understood what she had given him permission to do.

Chapter 9

She looked at him with hungry eyes. Manda needed more than comfort and caring from a concerned friend. Hunter knew it had been a long time since she'd been with a man and understood that despite her hellion teenage years, Manda was a woman who took lovemaking seriously. Seeking release and fulfillment from casual relationships wasn't her style. Unlike his former wife. The more time he spent with Manda, the more he realized how completely different she was from Selina.

He could offer Manda a brief sexual liaison, and he could make it good for both of them. Situations that thrust a person into the middle of danger usually heightened the senses and added an intimacy to the bodyguard and client bond. He'd been attracted to female clients and they to him, but he had never allowed those associations to become personal. With Manda, things were different. She was more than a client. Not only was she his old pal Perry's sister, she was the golden girl he had always thought of as the ideal female. Making love to Manda would fulfill a long-time fantasy for him, and he suspected it would do the same for her.

How could he resist what she was offering? He'd have to go slow, take things nice and easy. It had been a long time for her and she would need gentle handling. No matter how difficult it would be for him to hold back, to wait, to deny himself, he wanted this night to be for Manda.

Then realization struck. *If you have unprotected sex with her, she could get pregnant.*

Why hadn't he picked up some condoms when they'd stopped for gas? Damn, he would have, if he'd known this was going to happen.

He brought her into his arms. Lifting her up on her tiptoes and lowering his head, he initiated a tender kiss. As soft, as luxuriously languid, as seductive as any kiss he'd ever shared with a woman. She eased one hand from his neck to grip his shoulder and lifted the other to caress the back of his head. Her body pressed against his. Full breasts to hard chest. Slowly, so as not to appear too eager, he slid his hands from her waist to her hips, then cupped her buttocks and lifted her so her feminine mound fit snugly against his rigid sex.

Lips connected with furious passion and tongues mated frantically. He couldn't get enough of her and she seemed to be as wild for him as he was for her. When he rubbed her butt in a circular motion, wadding a section of her skirt in his hand, she whimpered and spread her thighs apart just enough to capture his leg between her knees. He delved his hand beneath her skirt and slipped his searching fingers inside the leg band of her panties. While his grip bit into the flesh of one firm, fleshy cheek, he thrust his tongue into her mouth and claimed her with the excitement he could no longer contain.

He wanted her. Here. Now. And she wanted him. Overcome with the desire to take her, he dropped to his knees, bringing her down with him. She reached out to undo his shirt, popping buttons in her enthusiasm. He nuzzled her neck, then inched his way down to the first button on her V-necked blouse. A hint of her perfume lingered on her skin. He flicked out his tongue and tasted the damp, salty essence of her flesh. He longed to expose and explore, to bare her body and familiarize himself with every inch of luscious female flesh.

Despite his sex ruling him at that moment, a vestige of sanity remained, enough so that he realized a bed of sand wasn't the ideal place for them to make love. He had tried it once, when he'd been younger, and found it less than ideal. Quickly, with need riding him hard, he rose to his feet, bringing her with him. Then he swept her up into his arms and strode toward the old beach house.

"Hunter," she whispered his name against his neck, her warm breath arousing him all the more.

"Let's see if this place has a bed." He took the groaning, whining wooden steps two at a time and prayed they wouldn't give way beneath his feet.

She clung to him, her arm around his neck, her head resting against his shoulder. "I'm not sure...I—"

He paused on the porch long enough to kiss her again—his intention clear—to erase any doubts from her mind. If he gave her time to think, to hesitate for more than a moment, she might start questioning the wisdom of her actions. And he didn't want her to think; he wanted her to feel. If she would allow him to make love to her, he would give such sweet pleasure.

"I'll make it good for you," he told her. "And with what I have in mind, you'll be protected, if that's what concerns you."

She sucked in a deep breath, as if his words had both enticed and frightened her. But when he sought her lips again, she made no protest, simply gave herself over completely. With his mouth on hers, he moved forward, heading straight toward the door. If it was locked, he'd kick the damn thing open. If that didn't work, he would lower her to the wooden porch floor and after he'd brought her to fulfillment, he would ask her to pleasure him in return.

As he spread kisses along her neck, he felt for the doorknob. Finding the tarnished brass handle, he gave it a quick turn and the door creaked open. When he carried her over the threshold, she tensed in his arms.

Don't stop now, his body told him. *She may be having second thoughts, but if you don't hesitate, she'll give herself to you.*

His eyesight adjusted to the interior darkness in just a couple of minutes, but not before he had stumbled over what appeared to be the only piece of furniture in the room, a large, dusty table. Moonlight flowed in through the broken windowpanes and the series of wide cracks in the wooden exterior, as well as through the holes in the roof. The place was a dump. Hardly the setting for an unforgettable night of lovemaking.

Keeping Manda in his arms, he went from room to room—four in all—and found them empty. No bed. Not even a lumpy mattress. The floor would have to do. When he set Manda on her feet, she surprised him by reaching for his face. She cupped his cheeks with her palms and gazed straight into his eyes.

"It's all right," she told him. "All I need is to be with you."

"You should have candlelight and music and satin sheets. I'm sorry, Manda. This was a bad idea. I must have been out of my mind."

She smiled, and the sight of her, there in the shadows, took his breath away. He'd never seen anything as beautiful. Damn, how he wanted her!

She ran her hands over his chest, then down his arms to clasp his hands in hers. "I want to be with you," she admitted. "I've wanted to belong to you since I was sixteen. If you had wanted me then, I would have come to you without hesitation, with no doubts and uncertainties. And I would never have regretted your being my first lover. It's all I wanted."

He couldn't keep his hands off her. Did she have any idea how her declaration affected him? He'd already been aroused, but now he ached and throbbed.

"I wanted you," he told her. "But at least back then I had sense enough to know I had no right to take your innocence. I think maybe I'd forgotten that I still have no rights where you're concerned. You may be an adult now, but tonight you're vulnerable and I was about to take advantage of you. I'm sorry, Manda."

She squeezed his hands. "Don't be sorry. You didn't do anything I didn't want you to do." She lifted one of his hands to her lips.

The touch of her wet, hot mouth against his skin set off explosions inside him. Didn't she have any idea how seductive she was acting or how difficult she was making it for him to keep his hands off her? Her actions were an odd mixture of experience and naiveté. But how was that possible? Manda was no innocent. She'd had boys swarming around her since she'd gone from being a plump little girl to an alluring femme fatale when she'd filled out a D-cup bra at sixteen. No male who came into contact with her was immune to her beauty. A woman who attracted men the way she did had probably experimented with sex long before Rodney Austin came on the scene.

When Hunter grabbed her shoulders and shook her gently, she gasped and stared at him, a shocked expression on her face.

"You're still a tempting little brat," he said. "But you know that, don't you? I'm hurting something awful." He clutched her hand and dragged it to the fly of his pants, then laid her open palm over his erection. "You're giving me mixed signals. If the answer is no, then we're going to have to put some distance between us or I'm liable to explode."

"Oh, I'm sorry." Her hand at his crotch closed into a fist. "I didn't mean to... It's been a long time since I've been..." Suddenly she opened her hand and covered him intimately through the barrier of his slacks and briefs.

He was so stunned that he didn't say anything when she unzipped his pants and maneuvered her hand inside and through the opening in his boxer shorts. The moment her fingers surrounded him, he sucked in a deep, startled breath, then groaned when she began a slow, tantalizing rhythm. Her movements were awkward, not those of a woman who had done this sort of thing often or recently. But the more she pumped him, the less he cared that she didn't possess a practiced touch. He covered her hand with his and began an immediate tutorial. Using his other hand, he molded his palm to her breast and kneaded softly. Her jutting nipple and her ragged breath told him how aroused she was.

Hunter sensed that his release was only moments away. He stilled her hand and murmured, "Are you sure you want—"

She leaned into him, placing her lips on his. "I'm sure."

The moment he allowed her to continue, she kissed him. Her mouth open. Her teeth nibbling. When she thrust

her tongue inside, he climaxed. It was all he could do to
not bellow like a rutting animal, but he somehow managed
to keep his reaction down to a rumbling moan. When the
aftershocks of release subsided, he jerked a handkerchief
from his pocket and cleaned her hand and then his sex.
He tossed the soiled cloth on the floor, then pulled Manda
into his arms and kissed her, all the while backing her
toward the table in the center of the room.

She didn't protest when he ravaged her mouth nor when
he lifted her off the floor and onto the table. But when he
unbuttoned her blouse, she grabbed his hands.

"Didn't I satisfy you?" she asked.

He noticed the disappointed look in her eyes. "Of
course, you satisfied me. How could you doubt it? And
now, it's my turn to pleasure you."

"But I don't understand. How can you be ready to…to
do it again, so soon?"

"Believe me, I'm not ready." He chuckled. "Manda,
my love, I'm nearly forty. I don't bounce back quite as
fast as I once did. But I don't have to have an erection in
order to give you the kind of pleasure you gave me."

"Oh." The air rushed out of her lungs. "Do you mean,
you're going to…to…"

She acted as if no one had ever brought her to completion with his hand or mouth, as if the idea of reciprocal
pleasure was an alien concept to her. Hadn't Rodney or
any of the guys before him ever repaid her for the satisfaction she gave them? He could hardly ask her, could
he? Some women wouldn't be embarrassed by the question, and he had to admit that he was surprised that he
thought Manda would be. But instinctively he knew she
felt uncomfortable discussing sex. She'd been more lib-
erated when she was sixteen than she was now. How
could a thirty-three-year-old woman act and react like a

novice? Was it possible that she really hadn't been with a man in any way even remotely sexual since Rodney's death?

Talking about sex wasn't necessary. The less talk the better, he decided. Manda was a woman in need, whether she knew it or not.

Returning his hands to the task, he spread apart her blouse and removed it, then slipped his fingers around her to unhook her bra. After he eased the straps down her arms, her large, full breasts came into view. Hunter took a deep breath, the sight of her there in the moonlight arousing him anew. The stirrings of desire spiraled inside him, urging him to further action.

"You're a beauty, Manda Munroe," he said, his voice husky with emotion.

She smiled faintly, but he noted she was shivering.

"Will you touch me?" she asked. "My breasts are aching and I—"

When he cupped both breasts and flicked his thumbs across her nipples, she keened softly and trembled. "Let me make them stop aching."

He lowered his head to one breast and sucked, tenderly at first and then as he plucked at her other nipple, his mouth intensified its hold. She tossed back her head and gasped with pleasure. While his lips continued their attention on her breasts, going from one to the other, he placed his hands on her knees and began shoving up her skirt, inch by inch, until he had it bunched around her hips. Then he placed one hand on her belly and pushed her gently down on the table. She cried out in surprise, but cooperated with him when he pulled her toward him until her hips rested near the edge of the table. He lifted her hips and removed her panties. She lay before him, a magnificent woman in need of loving.

He spread her legs farther apart, then slipped a couple of his fingers between her feminine folds and found her most sensitive spot. When he stroked her, she whimpered and closed her thighs to trap his hand. As he petted her, she moved against his fingers, as if seeking more.

"Take it easy, babe. I'm going to give you just what you need."

All rational thought left her. Under Hunter's skillful hands, she had become a quivering mass of sexual longing, a woman desperate for satisfaction.

How had she let things get out of control so quickly? When she'd been engaged to Rodney, she had become accustomed to using her hand to bring him to a climax and he had often done his best to bring her relief in the same manner. A few times, it had happened. Like fireworks exploding inside her. He had been the only man who had ever touched her intimately, but now she wanted that from Hunter.

If she were completely honest with herself, she would have to admit that she wanted more—much more. Afterward, she wouldn't be able to think of him the same, wouldn't be able to keep him at arm's length. But heaven help her, she couldn't stop him. Didn't want to stop him. Not now. Not when she thought she'd die if he didn't give her the relief she needed.

His fingers stopped; she whimpered. When he slid his hand out from between her clenched thighs, she grabbed his hand. "Please, Hunter. Please."

He ignored her pleas. Then suddenly, he lifted her legs up and over his shoulders. The moment his mouth touched her, she bit down on her bottom lip in an effort to not scream. As he began the onslaught, she tensed and splayed her hands flat atop the table on either side of her hips. While his lips and tongue became intimately acquainted with her body, sensations so wild and hot that she felt as if she were on fire spread from the core of her femininity to every cell and nerve in her body.

As he increased the tempo and deepened the pressure, he reached up to caress her breasts, doubling the sensations bombarding her body. Within moments, she came apart and cried out her pleasure. He continued his assault on her senses until she completely shattered and went limp. Tiny, rippling aftershocks drifted through her.

Hunter lifted her off her back and brought her into his arms. His mouth covered hers in a demanding kiss. She could taste herself on his lips, reminding her of what they had only moments ago shared.

She responded, kissing him with equal passion. When they came up for air, he brushed flyaway tendrils of hair from her face.

"When I brought you here, I didn't plan on this," he said. "I'm not prepared. Maybe we should go back to the car and see if we can find a motel."

She shook her head. "No, please, Hunter, I don't want my first time to be in a roadside motel."

"Your first time?" He stared at her as if she'd shot him, totally dazed, his eyes filled with disbelief. "Are you trying to tell me that you've never…that you're still a… How is that possible? You're thirty-three years old!"

"I thought you knew," she said. "Didn't I explain that Mike and I didn't have sex and that Rodney and I…" No, she hadn't bothered to explain that she and Rodney had waited for a wedding night that had never happened. "Rodney and I did things…but not…we planned to wait for our wedding night."

"What about all the guys before Rodney? You had

more boyfriends than ten other girls put together. Are you
telling me that you never let a one of them—''

She shook her head. ''Never.''

Hunter burst into laughter. Manda stared at him,
stunned by his reaction.

''What's so damn funny?'' she demanded.

''Ah, brat, if you only knew how often I thought about
all those guys getting in your pants.''

She suddenly realized that she was practically naked,
was still sitting on the table and Hunter was still standing
between her spread thighs. She reached out and gave him
a shove. The moment he reeled backward, she slid off the
table and began searching for her bra, panties and blouse.
While she searched, Hunter continued laughing. By the
time she found the items, he had tapered off to an occasional chuckle.

She stepped into her panties, then put on her bra, fum-
bling as she tried to hook the back closure. Hunter whirled
her around, gripped the bra hooks and slipped them
through the catches. She stiffened when he clasped her
shoulders and leaned over to nuzzle her neck. ''I had no
idea that you'd been saving yourself for me all these
years.''

Manda gasped, then whipped around and glared at him.
She saw the humor in his eyes, the wide grin on his face
and knew he was joking with her. But anger rose inside
her, heating her temper to the boiling point. Damn infuriating man! The comment he'd made in jest had hit a
nerve. She hadn't intentionally saved herself for him, but
it seemed that Fate had done it for her.

She would be damned if she gave him her virginity.
Not when he didn't love her. She was so close to falling
for him again that if she allowed him to become her first
lover, she would be forever lost. And it would have been

nothing more than sex for him. She knew that only too well.

"I have no intention of making love...of having sex with anyone unless he's my husband," Manda told him.

"Okay, I can wait until Saturday night. It won't be easy, but if you'd rather—"

"What are you talking about?"

"We're getting married Saturday evening at six," he said. "Don't you remember? Saturday night, I'll be your husband and then there will be no reason for us not to finish what we started tonight."

Manda and Hunter arrived at the Hickory Hills Clinic fifteen minutes late the next day. They had driven home during the night, arrived on Bermuda Road around dawn, and had gone to sleep immediately after falling into bed. Manda had kept slamming the snooze button on the clock this morning, until Hunter had finally dragged her out of bed. By the time she'd showered and dressed, he had coffee and toast waiting for her. She'd wolfed down the buttered whole wheat toast and gulped the coffee.

All during the day, she'd kept catching Hunter watching her and when their gazes collided, he would smile at her as if they shared some naughty little secret. Perhaps they did. Maybe what they'd shared at the ramshackle beach house had been a bit naughty, but it had been wonderful. Whenever she thought about Hunter's reminder that come Saturday night, he would be her husband, she could not control the anticipation that heightened her senses. Their planned marriage would be one of convenience, a make-believe union to trap a killer. But legally, they would be husband and wife. The minister from her church, Reverend Titus, would officiate at their nuptials. Everyone who knew her would find it strange, if anyone other than Patrick Titus performed the ceremony. Because of this one fact alone, Perry had immediately ruled out the possibility of using a fake minister.

Everything was set for the big event. They had gone for their blood tests first thing Monday, before Hunter had driven her to work. And they had picked up their marriage license that same day, making a detour to the county courthouse on their way to Lady Leona's Bridal Shoppe. Gwen was sending all the invitations by special messenger today and Claire had assured her, when she'd phoned this morning, that the florist and caterers had promised nothing less than perfection.

If she were really marrying Hunter, she'd be the happiest woman in the world. She realized that despite all the dire warnings she had issued to herself, she'd gone and done something really stupid—she had fallen for Hunter again. Maybe a spark of that old attraction had never died. Maybe deep in her heart, she had never stopped loving him.

But she couldn't be in love with Hunter Whitelaw! What she felt had to be nothing more than a very strong sexual attraction. She had simply become infatuated with the man, just as she'd been years ago. Hunter was handsome and virile and possessed that certain something that made a woman feel like a woman. When he kissed her, she knew she'd been kissed by a man who wanted her. When he touched her, she became instantly aroused. When he brought her to fulfillment, she experienced pleasure beyond anything she'd ever known. She could only imagine what having sex with him would be like. The anticipation alone nearly brought her to the brink.

If she actually had to go through with this marriage and found herself legally wed, would she be able to resist Hunter? Heaven help her, she really didn't think she could deprive herself of knowing what it was like to belong to him completely.

"Gathering wool?" Hunter asked as he rose from the sofa where he'd been sitting, waiting for her to clear off her desk before they left for the day.

She smiled at him. "Something like that."

"Are you about ready to leave?"

She nodded. "Let me put away these folders and then we can go."

After unlocking the small file cabinet beside her desk, she slipped the folders into their designated slots, then closed and locked the cabinet. She removed her purse from inside the bottom desk drawer, stood and walked across the room to where Hunter waited.

The minute they emerged from her office, Lisa stopped them. "Manda, would you mind terribly going by the lounge? Dr. Pierce left a wedding present for you and I forgot to—"

"No problem," Manda assured her. "The lounge is on the way out."

Hunter escorted her down the hall, then when they reached the staff lounge, he halted and instead of opening the door for her, as was his usual custom, he leaned back against the wall and crossed his arms over his chest.

"I'll wait here for you," he said.

"You mean you're going to let me go in there all by myself," she said teasingly.

"Just scream if you need me."

Manda shoved open the door and the minute she did, a deafening shout of feminine voices rang out and a dozen women came rushing toward her. It took her a minute to realize that white streamers adorned with wedding bells draped across the ceiling and white helium balloon bouquets had been tied to every stick of furniture in the room.

A white linen tablecloth adorned the dining table used by the staff. Cake, punch, mints and nuts provided the refreshments and a floral arrangement of white roses overflowed from a crystal vase.

Just as Gwen reached out and hugged Manda, Lisa came barreling through the door.

"Were you surprised?" Lisa asked.

"Very surprised," Manda said.

"We couldn't let you get married without a bridal shower." Claire kissed Manda's cheek. "So, Gwen and Lisa contacted your friends and those of us who love you dearly…and here we are."

"This is so sweet of y'all." Tears misted Manda's eyes. She felt guilty. These dear people believed that her upcoming marriage to Hunter was a love match, one destined to last a lifetime.

Manda scanned the room and saw a compilation of family and friends. Another female grief counselor, with whom she'd worked for a number of years, as well as several other clinic employees. Two old college sorority sisters. Three cousins. A great-aunt. A number of ladies from church. And even Grams.

She made a beeline to her grandmother, who looked her up and down, then huffed before she said, "You know I don't approve of this hasty marriage, but…if you're determined to go through with it, I don't intend to be left out of the festivities."

Everyone within earshot of Barbara Munroe laughed. Manda hugged her grams, the woman who had been the only mother she'd ever known.

"I love you," Manda said.

Grams cleared her throat. "And I love you, my dearest child."

Gwen grabbed Manda's arm. "Come along. You have

a pile of presents to open. You get started, while I play hostess and make sure everyone is served.''

Manda sat in the seat of honor, Claire at her side, with pen and pad in hand, prepared to make a record of the gifts and the gift-givers. Manda ripped into the wrapping paper and tossed bows aside as she revealed gift after gift. Most were lingerie items that were sheer, luxurious and sexy. Everyone gushed with admiration over each newly opened present. Finally only two unopened gifts remained, each in large boxes, one tied with an enormous pink ribbon and the other sporting white lace ribbon decked with silk roses.

"Open this one next." Lisa brought the gift with the pink ribbon over to Manda. "This is from the clinic staff."

Manda untied the ribbon, then lifted the lid and tissue paper. She removed the matching robes—his and hers—in a lush white velour.

Underneath lay a pair of extra-large, men's white silk pajamas. She held them up, looked at Lisa and said, "Only one pair?"

Lisa giggled. "Sure. Top for you and bottoms for Hunter."

While the group laughed, nibbled on cake and sipped punch, Gwen brought the final gift to Manda. She removed the beautiful bow, lifted the lid and found another box inside. Everyone gathered around to see the gift. Manda opened the second box only to be faced with a third box, which was a rectangular-shaped item wrapped in black paper.

A shudder of apprehension forewarned Manda. She grasped Lisa's hand. "Please, go get Hunter."

"Is something wrong?" Lisa asked.

"I'm not sure, but I don't think any of you would give me a wedding present wrapped in black paper."

Chapter 10

The moment Hunter entered the room, the bevy of females who hovered around Manda moved away from her. Forming two rows flanking the chair in which Manda sat, the women watched him as he came near. What the hell was going on? he wondered. All Lisa had said was that Manda wanted to see him. He'd thought maybe the party was over and she wanted to make a big deal out of showing the gifts to her groom. Apparently that wasn't the case. Nobody was laughing. Heck, nobody was even smiling. His gut tightened.

He approached Manda, who looked up at him and held out a small black package. He noted first the fear in her eyes and then the quiver in her hand.

"What's wrong?" he asked.

"This," she replied, lifting the rectangular box toward him. "It was disguised as a wedding gift, but I hardly think anyone here would give me a present wrapped in black paper."

Hunter reached out and took the box from her. A bomb? Possibly. But somehow he doubted it. "Let me carry this outside and take a look."

Manda grabbed his arm. "Please, be careful."

He leaned down and kissed her, just an affectionate and reassuring peck. "Don't worry. You stay right here and don't leave this room until I get back."

She nodded.

Claire moved in behind Manda and laid her hand on Manda's shoulder. "Don't you worry. We'll take care of her."

Hunter went outside, far enough away from the building that he felt it safe to open the package. Only a thin strip of cellophane tape held down the lid, so it was easy enough to open. Lying inside was a folded sheet of paper. Another letter? Hunter wondered. Why the hell go to so much trouble to send another warning letter disguised as a gift? He examined the box, then slipped it into his sport coat pocket before he unfolded the piece of white stationery.

The message was brief, but straightforward. Damn! If that lunatic had done anything to hurt— Damn! He'd rather take a beating than go back into the lounge and tell Manda what he'd found. But he had no other choice. She would want to go home immediately, of course.

Please, God, please, let this be another hoax!

When Hunter returned to the lounge, Manda met him at the door, while the other ladies made a show of cleaning up and clearing away.

"What was in the box?" she asked.

"Another warning letter."

"Is that all?"

"This one was different from the others," he said. "He issued a specific warning."

She held out her hand. "Let me read it."

Reluctantly, he gave her the note, then waited for her reaction.

Manda scanned the brief message.

Why won't you listen to me? I do not want anyone else to die, but if you refuse to do as I say, then you leave me no choice. This is your last warning. This time, Oxford. Next time, Hunter Whitelaw.

"Oh, no. Please, no." Manda crumpled the note in her hand. "We have to go home right now."

"What is it, Manda?" Grams asked.

"I think this maniac has done something to Oxford."

Grams gasped. "Who would— Go, dear. See if that precious little dog is all right. And call to let us know, please."

"I'll gather up your gifts and take care of them for you," Gwen said. "Everyone here understands why you have to rush off."

Manda ran out of the lounge, down the hall and out to the parking lot. Hunter kept pace with her and when they reached his Lexus, he opened the door for her, then hurried to the driver's side and got in.

He broke the speed limit getting them through Dearborn and out of town toward the Poloma River. Manda sat tensely, her hands clasped together in her lap. A couple of times he stole a quick glimpse of her in his peripheral vision and saw that her eyes were closed. He knew she was praying—praying for the life of a sweet, innocent dog.

The moment he brought the car to a screeching halt, Manda unhooked her seat belt, shoved open the door and jumped out onto the driveway. She ran around to the back of the house to the screened-in porch. First she visually scanned the yard, then opened the unlocked screened door and cried out the dog's name. When Hunter came up behind her, he saw Oxford lying deadly still on the porch floor. Manda knelt over the dog to examine him.

"He's still breathing," she said.

"Let me check him." Hunter knelt on the other side and ran his hands over Oxford's body and limbs. "I can't find an injury of any kind. That probably means poison. We need to get him to the vet as soon as possible."

When Manda started to lift Oxford, Hunter handed her his car keys, then scooped the fifty-pound dog into his arms. "Open the car door, then get in and I'll put him in your lap. We'll call the vet on our way there."

She nodded, then ran off the porch and around to the driveway. Within minutes they were headed up Bermuda Road, back toward Dearborn.

Dr. Charlie, as everyone affectionately called Charles Henderson, the veterinarian who'd been tending to the animals in and around Dearborn for the past thirty-five years, patted Manda on the back as he handed her a tissue.

"Blow your nose, Manda. Everything is going to be all right."

A weight lifted from her heart. "Did you have to pump Oxford's stomach or what?"

"No need for that," Dr. Charlie said. "By the way, Oxford wasn't poisoned."

"He wasn't?"

"No. Somebody doped him up on sleeping pills." Charlie shook his head sadly. "Who'd do a thing like that to our Oxford? Luckily, he threw up all over the place, which got most of the pills out of his stomach, but he digested enough to keep him sound asleep for another hour or so. My guess is that he'd thrown up earlier, before y'all found him and that's what saved him.''

"Sleeping pills. Could those pills have killed him?" she asked.

"Sure could have, as many as he was given. Somebody didn't intend for Oxford to wake up," Dr. Charlie told them.

"Should we leave Oxford here or can we take him home?" Hunter asked.

"If y'all don't mind staying around here for a while, I'll let him go home as soon as he wakes up."

Two hours later they arrived at the Whitelaw farm—Manda, Hunter, Oxford and a huge picnic basket from a local restaurant that specialized in meals-to-go. Oxford was wide awake, if somewhat unsteady on his legs when Manda first lifted him out of the car and put him down on the ground. But he immediately began sniffing at nearby bushes. Hunter removed the basket from the back seat. After the ordeal with Oxford, he'd thought Manda needed a distraction, so he had suggested picking up dinner and brining Oxford out to the farm to run around until dark. Manda had readily agreed.

Quite a few prayers had been answered when Oxford survived. If they hadn't gotten the spaniel to the vet as quickly as they had, he would have died. Whoever drugged Oxford and managed to place a gift among the other presents at Manda's bridal shower had intended to kill her dog.

Warning letters, a phone call, a bomb threat and now drugging Oxford. Hunter knew what was next—an attempt on his life. Tonight. Tomorrow. Tomorrow night. Their Mr. Maniac was bound to attack before Manda's wedding day. Time was running out. The one thing

Hunter wished he knew was whether their nutcase had hired himself a professional or if he would try to handle the job himself. Going by his experience and his gut instincts, Hunter would bet on a professional, even if the guy turned out to be a two-bit hood who could be bought for a thousand bucks. And he figured the hit would come tomorrow night. Before, during or after the rehearsal dinner/engagement party.

While they'd been at the veterinary clinic, he had called the Dundee agency and requested a backup agent. Ellen had said that Wolfe was available and would drive down from Atlanta this evening and be available for as long as Hunter needed him. He trusted Wolfe, admired his finesse and expertise. The man seemed to be adept at just about everything, except sharing personal information about himself. He figured there was something pretty bad in Wolfe's past, some real heavy-duty crap. Otherwise, why all the mystery? Only a guy with secrets too deadly to be revealed became such an enigma.

And Ellen had told him that she'd be able to send Matt and Jack by tomorrow evening, since both were due in from assignments by noon. He'd accepted her offer, knowing that three extra sets of eyes and ears would help ensure the success of this mission. And tomorrow the prime focus of the mission would be to keep Hunter Whitelaw alive.

"You're doing a good job of rescuing me," Manda said to him as she watched Oxford exploring around the house, occasionally marking his territory. "Whenever things become overwhelming, you whisk me away like a white knight."

"That's my job." But what he did for Manda was more than any damn assignment. Knowing what he knew now, he would have taken this task on his own, without any inducement from Perry. In a short period of time, his estimation of Manda as a human being had drastically changed. He'd always thought of her as a golden girl, and in a way, she still was. She might be rich and pampered by those who loved her, but she was no longer a spoiled brat, no longer a little hellion who thought of no one except herself.

Her grateful smile wavered. "If you give all your clients this kind of special treatment, your services must be in high demand."

Hunter realized that he had inadvertently hurt her feelings, which was the last thing on earth he wanted to do. This woman had been hurt enough. More than enough.

After setting the picnic basket down on the porch steps, he walked over beside her, but didn't touch her. "This is more than an assignment to me. I think you know that."

She avoided eye contact, instead she surveyed her surroundings. "Yes, I know that you're doing this for Perry."

Sometimes she could still be an infuriating brat. Like right now. She was going to make him admit that he had feelings for her, that she was more to him than his best friend's little sister.

"I took the case because Perry asked me to," Hunter admitted. "But you know I care about you. And not because you're Perry's sister."

She looked at him then, a head-on collision of gazes. "You sound angry about it. You care about me, but you don't want to. Is that it?"

"Damn it, Manda, do we have to argue? Just believe me when I say that I care about you and will do everything in my power to help you."

"I believe you," she said.

"But?"

"No buts." She walked toward the porch. "So, where do we have our picnic?"

Just let it go, Whitelaw, he told himself. Don't delve too deeply into your emotions or hers. Either was dangerous territory. He figured that Manda was as confused about her feelings as he was, and now certainly wasn't the time for any major confessions.

"How about in the orchard?" he suggested. "It's a warm springtime evening and the orchard is beautiful this time of year. I can get a quilt from the house and a bowl for some water for Oxford. How does that sound?"

"It sounds nice. And restful. But is it safe?"

He came over to her, lifted the picnic basket and whistled for Oxford, who came running. "Looks like he's fine." He nodded toward the dog. "And yes, we should be safe here. No one knows where we are. Believe me, I kept an eye out for a tail. No one followed us. And if by some remote chance anyone shows up, I'm prepared."

"Then what are we waiting for? Believe it or not, I'm hungry."

They spread the old patchwork quilt out on the ground near the pear orchard. The trees were ripe with budding fruit. On the western horizon, the sun dipped low, and already myriad bold, brilliant colors coated the sky. A wispy evening breeze wafted about them, soft and warm. Hunter opened the bottle of zinfandel, while Manda spread out the array of delectable delights. Sandwiches, potato salad, pickles, cheese and fruit. Enough food to feed half a dozen people. They sat across from each other, the banquet between them. A chorus of nighttime insects sang, the music faint now, but after dark the serenade would grow louder.

Oxford chased a butterfly around for several minutes,

then when he smelled food, came lolloping toward them, his tail wagging and his tongue hanging out.

Even now, with Oxford safe, she couldn't quite let go of the tension that had painfully knotted her stomach when she'd thought she might lose her precious pet. Over the years she had lost too much. She didn't think she could bear another loss. She had thought that loving a dog would be a safe outlet for her affections, that she couldn't be hurt by loving an animal. But even Oxford wasn't immune to the Manda Munroe Curse.

What was she going to do about her feelings for Hunter? She couldn't let him know that she was falling in love with him. If he were in possession of that knowledge, it would make her much too vulnerable. More so than she already was. Although he wasn't the type of man who would take advantage of a woman, if he knew she loved him, he wouldn't hesitate to carry their relationship to the next level. And she couldn't deny that a part of her longed for that final act of physical intimacy. At sixteen, she had dreamed of Hunter being her first lover. She could easily make that dream come true now. All she had to do was say yes.

Even if Hunter was able to banish Mr. Maniac from her life, he wouldn't be able to protect her from himself. If she didn't stop this insanity, this headlong fall into loving him, she would find herself alone and brokenhearted when Hunter walked out of her life.

"Wine?" he asked as he held out one of the glass flutes that the restaurant provided with the basket.

She accepted the glass, but didn't sip the wine until he poured a drink for himself. He lifted the glass in a salute.

"Here's to a peaceful evening," he said.

"I'll definitely drink to that."

Oxford nudged Manda's arm. His cold, wet nose tickled

her skin. She set the glass between her knees, then petted her playful dog. "Are you hungry, boy? Want some cheese or a sandwich?"

"You've spoiled that dog rotten." Hunter grinned. "He thinks he's a baby instead of a dog."

"I like spoiling him," Manda admitted. "And in a way, he is my baby."

Hunter picked up a sandwich half and tossed it to Oxford. "I'm sorry, Manda. I realize that if either of your marriages had come off as planned, you'd have some kids by now. You have every right to lavish attention on Oxford."

She took one of the plastic plates, also provided by the restaurant, and dipped up potato salad, then added a sandwich and a pickle. "What about you, have you ever wanted a family? Do you want to have children someday?"

Hunter ate half a sandwich in two bites, then washed it down with a hefty swig of wine. "When I married Selina, I thought we'd have a baby right away. But she wasn't ready, so we waited." He tore a slice of cheese in half and tossed first one bite and then another to Oxford. "Good thing we waited. Selina would have made a terrible mother. She was too selfish and spoiled to have ever put the needs of a child before what she wanted."

"Do you think I'm like that?" The question popped out of her mouth before she had a chance to stop herself from being so blunt.

Hunter looked straight at her. "I thought you were a spoiled, pampered brat when you were sixteen, but you've grown up since then. Of course, I don't think you're like Selina."

"But you did, when you first agreed to take this assignment, didn't you? You've been comparing me to your ex-wife ever since you came back to Dearborn.''

"You're right on both counts. But I was wrong. Except for some superficial similarities, you and Selina are nothing alike.''

"I take that as a compliment.''

"It was meant as one,'' he said.

"So, what are the superficial similarities?''

Hunter chuckled. "You really want to know?''

She nodded. "Yes, I really want to know.''

"Well, you met her at Perry and Gwen's wedding, so you know she was blond and beautiful. And she came from a rich old Virginia family. She always had a swarm of men around her, vying for her favors. Those similarities alone were enough to intrigue me the first time I met her.''

Manda's heartbeat accelerated. Had Hunter realized what he'd said, what he had admitted by his choice of words? She had to ask him, had to make sure she had understood him correctly. "Are you saying that you were first attracted to Selina because she reminded you of me?''

As Hunter glanced away, his smile faded. "I didn't realize it at the time and even when Perry pointed it out to me, I denied it. But yeah—'' his gaze reverted to Manda and met headlong with hers ''—if I'm honest with myself and with you, I'll have to admit that I was attracted to Selina because I thought I'd found someone like you—only more my own age.''

"You really were attracted to me back then, when I was making a fool of myself over you. And all the time, I thought you didn't even like me, that you tolerated me only because I was Perry's silly little sister.''

Hunter chuckled. "Well, in a way, that's true. The only thing that kept me from breaking your spoiled-rotten, little neck was because you were Perry's sister. You drove me nuts. In every way a girl can drive a guy nuts.''

"You wanted me, even then, didn't you?"

"You know I did. But hell, Manda, I couldn't take you seriously, not when you were only sixteen. I had to pretend, even to myself, that I thought of you only as a pesky brat."

"Thank you, Hunter." She lifted the flute to her lips and sipped the wine.

"Thanks for what?"

"Thanks for being honest with me."

A clap of thunder echoed in the distance and a streak of faraway lightning slashed through the sky.

"If that rainstorm gets any closer, we'll be taking our picnic inside," Hunter said.

"I love it out here. Maybe the rain will either go around us or wait a couple of hours."

They ate and drank, talked and laughed, setting aside their worries for a few hours. Hunter possessed the ability to know what she needed and somehow provide it for her. After each new traumatic event, he had picked her up and carried her away to peace and sanity and safety. But they both knew they could avoid reality for only so long. Danger lurked out there, waiting for them, only a heartbeat away.

They cleared away the remnants of their meal, using the picnic basket as their garbage pail. Hunter shook the crumbs from the quilt and folded it, then put the quilt and the basket on the back porch steps. The sunset burst across the western sky, shooting out thick billows of vibrant color, each meshing with the other. The dark clouds had moved on, taking the stormy weather farther east, completely bypassing Dearborn.

"Want to take a walk before we head back to your place?" Hunter asked.

"A walk sounds nice."

She hesitated only a moment before she took his hand. Hunter whistled for Oxford and the threesome made their way through the orchard comprised of two dozen pear trees. Beyond the orchard lay what had once been cultivated farmland, but was now simply a green pasture. Hand-in-hand, they walked in silence, surrounded by nature—peaceful, yet vividly alive, just as they were.

"We've done a good job of avoiding two important subjects," Manda said, finally ending the solitude.

"And what two subjects would that be?"

"What happened between us last night and what is probably going to occur sometime before our wedding."

They stopped near the rickety fence that separated the pasture that had once been cultivated from the pasture that had once supported a small head of cattle. Hunter easily climbed over the fence, then reached out and helped Manda.

"What happened last night was bound to happen," he said. "I want you and you want me. That seems pretty simple. As long as neither of us expects more than sex, then I don't see any reason why our friendship can't include being lovers. But that's your call, Manda."

"I see." Her call. Take him on his terms or not at all. Friendship and sex. No love. No commitment. No forever after. What had she expected, a declaration of undying love? Of course not. But having him put the situation between them into words somehow diminished it, made it seem less than it was. But not less to him, only to her.

"Do you agree?" Taking her hand, he began walking again.

"I agree that we want each other, but I'll have to think about your conditions for an intimate relationship."

"You do that."

"No more discussion on that subject?" she asked.

"What else is there to say?"

"All right, then. So, on to the next subject. Our wedding is set for Saturday. Two days from now. If he's going to make an attempt on your life, then it has to be soon. Tonight. Tomorrow."

"I know."

Manda squeezed Hunter's hand, then stopped walking and looked at him. He turned to face her. There in the twilight shadows, they confronted the truth. The worst was yet to come. He ran his hands up her arms until he clutched her shoulders.

"I think the hit will come tomorrow evening, either before, during or after the rehearsal dinner. With so many people around—guests, musicians, caterers, deliverymen—it would be easy for a professional to become a part of the crowd."

"Oh, great. I'll be a nervous wreck, waiting and watching and wondering." The very thought that Hunter might be harmed made her question the sanity of their plan to capture a killer. "How can you protect yourself, if you have no idea who he is or how or when he'll strike?"

"Believe it or not, I've been in worse situations and I've survived."

"When you were a member of the Delta Force?"

"Mmm-hmm. And a couple of times since I've been working for the Dundee agency."

"Do you actually enjoy risking your life?"

"No, I don't enjoy it. But in each case, there was a job to be done and I was trained to do it." He lifted one hand to cup her chin, tilting it so that she looked up, directly at him. "Extra Dundee agents are coming in from Atlanta. One tonight and two more tomorrow evening."

Manda sighed. "That makes me feel a little bit better."

When he pulled her into his arms, she went willingly, quickly wrapping her arms around his waist and laying her head on his chest.

He stroked her back and nuzzled her temple.

Suddenly Oxford barked. Manda jumped. Hunter yanked her around to his side. Oxford kept barking. Hunter reached down and unsnapped his hip holster. Several yards away, the brush shivered as if someone or something was about to emerge. Oxford had treed either an animal or a person.

An adrenaline rush of pure fear shot through her. Had the killer tracked them to the Whitelaw farm? If so, what would happen next? Would he and Hunter take part in a gunfight? Another frightening thought occurred to her—what if there was more than one? What if her crazed admirer had hired two killers?

"Hunter?"

"Shh." He moved in front of her and whistled to Oxford, who stopped barking, but waited, his stance pointing at danger. "Stay behind me. And if there's any gunfire, hit the ground."

"Okay."

Hunter removed his Ruger from the holster. "If there's someone out there, show yourself. Now."

Manda's heart stopped for a split second as she held her breath.

Please, let it be an animal. A rabbit or a squirrel or even a skunk.

A tall, lean figure stepped out of the shadows. Manda gasped. In the murky twilight, she looked into the coldest, most dangerous green eyes she'd ever seen.

Chapter 11

"Damn, Wolfe, you scared the hell out of me!"

Hunter glowered at the somber man who moved toward them, then stopped, leaned over and petted Oxford.

"Sorry that I upset y'all," the man replied. "I thought you were expecting me."

"And I thought you were going straight to Manda's house when you arrived, supposedly at ten-thirty. You're early and you're at the wrong place."

"I got an early start," Wolfe said. "I should have phoned to let you know, but it was nearly dark when I arrived, so I assumed you would have left the farm by now. However, when I stopped at Ms. Munroe's house and y'all weren't there, I just came on out here." He focused his attention on Manda. "I'm truly sorry that I frightened you. I called out several times when I arrived at the farmhouse and I was fixing to call out again when your dog started barking."

"No harm done," Manda said.

"No, no harm done, unless you consider my heart failure," Hunter said, half joking.

He noted the way Manda was staring at David Wolfe, a strange fascination in her gaze. Women usually had that type of reaction to the man. As if they sensed he hid some deep, dark secret, one they would like to discover.

"Are you ready to head home?" Hunter asked Manda, his tone a little gruffer than he'd intended.

What was wrong with him? He was acting like a jealous lover. Idiot! He wasn't Manda's lover, not in the truest sense of the word. And he'd sworn off jealousy after he'd found Selina in bed with his Delta force comrade and came close to beating the man to death. In retrospect, he realized that his reaction had come more from his hurt pride than his love for his wife.

"Sure," Manda said. "It is almost dark. I suppose we should have left earlier, but it's such a nice spring night." She smiled at Wolfe. "Will you be staying at the house with us, Mr. Wolfe?"

"Just Wolfe, ma'am. And yes, I'll be staying with you and Hunter until—"

"Until we leave for our honeymoon Saturday night," Hunter said.

"If there is a honeymoon," Manda reminded him.

"We could catch our man tomorrow evening, Ms. Munroe," Wolfe said. "In that case there will be no need for y'all to follow through with the wedding."

"No reason whatsoever," Hunter said, then put his arm possessively around Manda's waist and whistled for Oxford.

Half an hour later Hunter showed Wolfe to Manda's guest room. Despite his moments of unwarranted jealousy out at the farm, Hunter was damn glad to have Wolfe in town.

"I hate to put you out of your bed," Wolfe said. "I'll be glad to bunk on the living room sofa."

"There's no need for that," Hunter said, then decided to be honest with Wolfe. The man acting as his backup needed to know the truth—that Manda was more than an assignment. "Look, I haven't been using this room. I'm sharing Manda's bed."

Wolfe's expression didn't alter, not by one iota. No rounded eyes. No lifted brow.

When Wolfe didn't respond, Hunter went on. "Our relationship is complicated. We go back a long way. We're friends and…and… I care about her. Manda's welfare is important to me for personal reasons."

"You don't owe me any explanations." Wolfe lifted his black vinyl bag onto the foot of the bed, unzipped it and pulled out a manila envelope. "Ellen sent you a condensed version of the information we've compiled on all the key players in Manda's life. I know she's given you a rundown over the phone, but we've gone over the facts several times and a few things don't add up."

"Like what?"

"Like the fact that fiancé number one's death seems to have been nothing more than an accident. The locals did a thorough investigation into the car crash and there was no evidence of any foul play. And before Dr. Austin's death, Manda didn't receive any warning letters. Other than the fact that Austin and Farrar were engaged to Manda Munroe, there was nothing similar in their lives or deaths."

"Perry has tried to convince Manda that Rodney Austin wasn't murdered, but she can't get it out of her head that whoever killed Mike also murdered Rodney."

"We're pretty sure that whoever killed Mike Farrar was a man. Either that or a woman strong enough to lift his hundred-and-seventy-five-pound body. The police report plainly states that Farrar wasn't shot down by the river. He was killed somewhere else and taken to the river."

"Which doesn't necessarily rule out my two female suspects," Hunter said. "Not if our killer hired an assassin."

"So, there doesn't seem to be any great revelations in these reports." Wolfe tapped the manila envelope. "You might want to read them over, anyway. Since you know the people involved, you might catch something we missed."

Hunter took the envelope. "Thanks. Sleep with one eye open, okay? There's always a chance our guy will show up tonight for one last scare tactic before he moves in for the kill."

Manda appeared in the doorway. "I wish you wouldn't talk like that. You sound as if you're fearless, as if the fact that someone is going to try to kill you doesn't bother you in the least."

"Manda, honey, I'm sorry. I didn't know you were listening." Hunter glanced at Wolfe, who remained silent. "See you in the morning, Wolfe."

Hunter cupped Manda's elbow and led her across the hall and into their bedroom. When he closed the door, Manda halted. She looked at the door, then at him.

"I'm not…we're not…not with Wolfe in the house," Manda said.

"I closed the door to give you privacy, not because I'm planning on ravishing you."

"Oh, I see."

"You sound disappointed."

"Of course I'm not disappointed." Manda strode

across the room, removed her robe, tossed it into a nearby chair, then got into bed.

"I'd be more than glad to accommodate you tonight," Hunter teased. "That is if you've changed your mind about waiting for our wedding night."

Just as Hunter entered the bathroom, Manda tossed a pillow in his direction. The goose down pillow hit the closed door and slid to the floor.

"I haven't changed my mind," Manda called to him.

Hunter suppressed a chuckle as he waited inside the bathroom. Within a minute, Manda banged on the door.

"What do you want?" he asked. "Can't a fellow even get a shower without—"

"When I said that I hadn't changed my mind, I didn't mean that I had agreed that—" she lowered her voice as if only now remembering that they weren't alone in the house "—we would become lovers on our wedding night."

He cracked open the door, just enough to exchange a glance with Manda. "Get in bed and try to rest. We have a busy day tomorrow. You'll need a good night's sleep."

"Hunter, I meant what I said. I haven't agreed to anything."

"Stop worrying about it. There's every chance things will come to a head tomorrow evening and there will be no need for us to go through with the wedding."

"I hope you're right."

"Yeah. Sure. Me, too."

Manda picked the pillow up off the floor and hugged it to her, then turned off all the lights in the bedroom, except Hunter's bedside lamp. She lay there listening to the shower running and couldn't stop her mind from rushing headlong into thoughts of a naked Hunter. If she were as adventuresome as she'd been at sixteen, she would strip off her gown and join him in the shower. Her body tingled with desire. If she asked him to, he would make love to her tonight.

She had waited twice before for a wedding night that never happened. If only she and Rodney hadn't waited. If only she and Mike had shared an intimate relationship. Her life was filled with *if onlys*. Once Hunter went back to Atlanta, would she add their unconsummated relationship to her list of *if onlys?*

But she had to remember one important thing—if this dangerous plan worked, then afterward she would be free to love and be loved, to find a wonderful man who wanted to share his life with her. Hunter Whitelaw wasn't that man. He was in her life on a temporary basis only. As soon as this assignment ended, he'd be long gone. He had given her no reason to believe otherwise. She'd be a fool to wish for more.

Manda tossed and turned, longing for sleep. Maybe she could pretend to be asleep when Hunter came to bed. If Hunter's predictions came true, she had to survive only one more night of sharing a bed with him. If the killer made his move tomorrow evening and they were able to catch him, this horror story she'd been living would come to an end.

The phone rang. Manda yelped and jumped. After taking a deep breath, she switched on the lamp then glanced at the caller ID and saw that it was Perry's cell phone. She grabbed the receiver.

"Hello, Perry?"

The recorded voice laughed. "How are you, Manda? All ready for the big day? Such a pity that once again, you won't have a groom. Call off your wedding or Hunter Whitelaw will die."

Hunter emerged from the bathroom, a towel draped around his hips.

"Was it him?"

Manda nodded. "He used Perry's cell phone. How did he get hold of Perry's phone? What if he's done something to Perry?" She grabbed the receiver, then dialed her brother's number.

"Here, let me talk to Perry," Hunter said as he motioned for Manda to move over. When she handed him the phone and scooted over, he sat on the edge of the bed.

"Ask him if he knows someone stole his cell phone." She leaned over against Hunter and tugged on the receiver. "I want to listen to what y'all say."

Hunter readjusted the phone so that they could both listen. The voice on the other end said, "Munroe residence."

"Perry?"

"Hunter, is that you?"

"Yeah. Listen, Manda just received a phone call and her caller ID showed your cell phone number," Hunter said.

"Damn! Look, I don't know where I lost the phone or if I lost it," Perry said. "On my way home from the office this evening, I went to take it out of my briefcase to give Gwen a call and the phone wasn't there. I have no idea if I misplaced the phone or if—"

"When was the last time you used it?" Hunter asked.

"Yesterday," Perry replied. "But I know it was still in my briefcase last night. When I put away a file I'd brought home from the office, the phone was still in my briefcase."

"Who had access to that briefcase last night and today?"

"I don't know. Hmm… Well, here at the house, Grams

and Gwen and Bobbie Rue, but they wouldn't have taken it. And at work, there's Grady, of course and Jennifer Waits, our paralegal and our secretaries, Erica and Tammy.''

Hunter made some mental calculations. Gwen. Grady. Two of his suspects. ''Anyone else? Anybody besides family at the house last night?''

''Only Boyd Gipson. He stopped by to see if Manda was here,'' Perry said. ''He'd gone by her house, hoping to check on her and see that she was all right after the bomb threat.''

''Could Boyd have gotten hold of your cell phone?''

''I don't see how— Hey, wait a minute. I left him in the den while I went in the kitchen and got some ice for our drinks. Bobbie Rue had forgotten to fill the ice bucket.''

''Okay, so that means Boyd could have stolen the phone,'' Hunter said.

Manda shook her head. Hunter placed his index finger over her lips as a suggestion for her to keep quiet.

''What about at the office today?'' Hunter probed again, seeking other possibilities. ''Anyone other than the people you work with? A client who might have—''

''Chris and Claire came by,'' Perry said. ''It seems that Claire was upset because Chief Burgess had questioned Chris about his Ferrari being downtown night before last around the same time Manda got that first warning phone call. Chris swears he was home, in bed, sleeping off a drunk. And Claire swears he was there. They just wanted to make sure that Chris wasn't in any legal trouble.''

''Was Chris, at any time, alone in your office? Could he have stolen your cell phone?''

''No, I don't think so.''

''What about Claire?''

"Claire?" Perry and Manda gasped the name simultaneously.

"Yes, Claire," Hunter said. "Is it possible she stole your phone?"

"Claire would never do such a thing," Manda said.

"I agree," Perry said. "But now that you mention it, when Chris and Claire first arrived at my office, I was in with Grady, so Tammy showed them into my office. Claire was there waiting for me. It seems Chris had gone to the bathroom and he came in a few minutes later."

"Thanks, Perry," Hunter said. "Don't worry too much about this. Manda is safe. I'm here with her and another Dundee agent arrived tonight. If we get another call, I'll contact the police and instigate procedures to trace any calls made on your phone."

"If there's anything I can do, let me know," Perry said. "And Manda, if you'd like for me to come over there, I—"

"No, Perry, there's no need for that," Manda told her brother. "I have two professional bodyguards here with me. I'll be fine."

Hunter replaced the receiver, then stood. Manda suddenly became very aware of the fact that beneath that towel, Hunter was naked. When he caught her staring at the towel, he grinned.

"Guess I'd better put on my pajama bottoms," he said.

"Yes, I guess you'd better." Manda slid her legs under the top sheet and bedspread, then placed her pillow against the headboard and leaned back in a sitting position. "Do you think he'll call again?"

Hunter paused in the bathroom doorway. "Maybe."

"Or maybe he'll just show up, unannounced, and do something crazy, like blow up the house or shatter all the windows with an Uzi."

"That's highly unlikely," Hunter said. "At this point, my guess is that our nutcase doesn't want to harm you. You're still unmarried and still a…still haven't had a wedding night."

"How would he know about…I mean I've never even told Perry that I was…" Manda had discussed her love life with Hunter more than she had with anyone else. He knew more about the intimate details of her relationships with Rodney and Mike than her own brother did.

"Is there anyone you confided in about the fact that you've never…that you're still a virgin?"

A warm flush spread up Manda's neck and colored her cheeks. "Grams and Claire."

"No one else?"

"Only you."

Just before Hunter closed the bathroom door, he said, "If the phone rings, wait and let me answer it."

She nodded. "Okay."

A couple of minutes later he returned to the bedroom wearing his black and tan-striped cotton pajama bottoms. She turned off her lamp, then eased down in bed to lie flat on her back. Hunter kept his back to her as he checked his gun, then he got into bed and turned off his lamp, throwing the room into darkness. She lay there, breathing quietly, staying very still, waiting for him to say something. He didn't. As her vision adjusted, she glanced his way and realized that Hunter was on his side, facing her.

"Are you looking at me?" she asked.

"Yes."

"He said that if I didn't call off the wedding, you would die."

"He's going to try to kill me," Hunter said. "But I'm not going to die."

"If anything happens to you…"

The phone rang.

Manda gasped loudly, then reached out to grab the phone. Hunter sat up and slid toward her side of the bed.

"Manda…Manda…Manda…"

Clutching the telephone, she listened to that low, grating voice repeating her name a dozen time over. No message. No warning. Just that weird, repetitive singsong. Manda, Manda, Manda.

The minute the caller hung up, Hunter switched on his bedside lamp. "I'm contacting Chief Burgess. Cell phone calls can be traced. If he makes another call, there's a good chance they can pinpoint his location."

They didn't get any sleep. After the third call ended around one-thirty, this one another dire warning message, Hunter and Manda got out of bed. She pulled on a robe, but he didn't bother searching through his bag for his pajama top. He wasn't even sure he'd packed it. On their way to the kitchen, they met Wolfe in the hall. He was still dressed in slacks and a pullover knit shirt, and still wore his gun holster. Obviously he hadn't been to bed yet.

"I'll fix some coffee," Manda said. "Is anyone hungry? I can scramble some eggs or fix some grilled-cheese sandwiches or—"

"Just coffee," Hunter said.

"Do you think the phone company will be able to pinpoint the location of Perry's phone?" Manda asked as she flipped on the overhead kitchen light.

"Probably." Hunter pulled out a chair and sat at the kitchen table.

Wolfe came into the room, his movements eerily quiet, as if his footsteps made no sound. Hunter had noted on more than one occasion that David Wolfe possessed the expertise of a trained warrior and the stealthy abilities of a person trained to kill.

"Would you like something to eat, Wolfe?" Manda asked hospitably as she prepared the coffeemaker.

"No, ma'am. Thank you."

Wolfe walked to the back door and looked through the glass, out into the dark night. As Hunter watched the intense way Wolfe stared into nothingness, he couldn't help wondering what the man saw. Something far beyond the obvious. If Hunter didn't know better, he would believe Wolfe possessed an innate sixth sense of some kind.

"I think I'll go outside," Wolfe said. "Maybe take a walk and check—"

Manda whirled around, her gaze nervously darting back and forth from Hunter to Wolfe. "Did you hear something? Do you think someone is outside?"

"No, ma'am, I didn't hear anything." Wolfe punched in the security code Hunter had shared with him earlier, then grasped the doorknob. Before he opened the door, he looked at Manda. "I'll probably stay outside for a while, so just leave the coffee and I'll pour myself a cup when I get back." He went out onto the porch, then quickly disappeared into the night.

"He's a strange man," Manda said. "What do you know about him? He seems so sad."

"Sad?" Hunter had never actually thought of Wolfe as sad, but then men didn't usually think in deeply emotional terms. Sadness was definitely a deep-gut emotion. Guys got pissed. They got rowdy. They got drunk. And they got laid. Men understood those kinds of things, but few would ever own up to being sad.

"He's been terribly hurt," Manda said. "You can see it in his eyes. They're so cold and filled with so much pain. Did he lose someone he desperately loved?"

"Hell, if I know. The guy's not exactly talkative, in case you haven't noticed."

"I thought all you macho men shared your exploits, about your dangerous assignments and about the women in your lives." Manda removed three mugs from an overhead cupboard and set them on the counter to the left of the coffee machine.

"Wolfe doesn't share anything with anybody," Hunter said. "Besides, a man doesn't share stories with other guys about a woman who's really important to him. By the way, you certainly seem interested in Wolfe. Does this mean that, here less than forty-eight hours before our wedding, I have competition for your affections."

Manda skewered him with a that's-not-very-funny glare.

Hunter shrugged. "Sorry. I was just trying to lighten the mood a bit. You seem awfully jumpy." He scooted back the chair and stood. "Wolfe is making sure everything is okay outside and I'm right here, safe and sound."

"I know. It's just I keep expecting the unexpected. I'm nervous and I'm going to stay nervous until this is all over." Manda removed a container of cream from the refrigerator and set it on the table beside the sugar bowl. "Do you know how Wolfe takes his coffee?"

"I'm not sure, but my bet would be black."

Manda poured the freshly brewed French roast coffee into two mugs, then brought the mugs to the table. "What's taking them so long to trace that call?"

"It hasn't been that long." He came up behind Manda and wrapped his arms around her waist.

Sighing, she closed her eyes, savoring the comfort and safety she felt in Hunter's arms. "I'm almost afraid to find out who he is," she admitted. "What if he really is someone I know?"

"We'll deal with that when it happens," Hunter said. His gut instincts told him that her harasser was someone she knew, someone she cared about and trusted. He only wished he knew which one of the suspects was the person determined to keep Manda unmarried for the rest of her life.

Just as Manda pulled away from Hunter and started to sit, the telephone rang. She froze to the spot.

"I'll get it," he told her, then headed for the wall phone. He lifted the receiver. "Whitelaw here."

"Mr. Whitelaw, this is Chief Burgess. We got a trace on Perry Munroe's cell phone."

"And?"

"We found the telephone. Someone had deliberately left it on. I can only assume they did this so it could be easily traced," the chief said. "Our man is playing games with us. We went straight to the phone, but he was long gone."

"Where did he leave it?" Hunter asked.

"In Perry Munroe's mailbox."

"Son of a bitch!" Hunter groaned. "Mighty nice of him to return the phone."

"We're checking it for prints, but my guess is it'll be clean." Burgess paused, then said, "I didn't see any point in waking up the Munroe household this time of night, but come morning I'll send someone over to ask a few questions. I doubt anyone there heard or saw a thing. I suppose you suspect what I do, don't you, Mr. White-law?"

"That we're dealing with someone who has done this sort of thing before. A hired killer."

Chapter 12

Manda had smiled so much that her jaws ached and she felt as if a nasty little gremlin was beating a drum inside her head. The rehearsal was supposed to have taken fifteen minutes—tops. But after thirty minutes Gwen still wasn't satisfied and requested that they go through the entire rigmarole again. If she had to make a grand entrance down the staircase one more time, Manda thought she would scream. The guests for the party were already arriving and Grams kept having to venture into the vestibule to greet them as Bobbie Rue answered the door. The last thing she wanted tonight was this ridiculous combination rehearsal dinner and engagement party. But Hunter and Perry had pointed out that if she put up a fuss about the gala celebration, Grams, Gwen and Claire might become suspicious that everything wasn't on the up-and-up.

Reverend Titus had been infinitely patient with Gwen's nitpicky attitude and had once, when she'd all but thrown a temper tantrum, taken her aside and spoken quietly to her. Manda suspected that the tense smile Gwen kept in place was for the minister's benefit.

"Enough already," Perry said. "Gwen, they're having a ten-minute ceremony, repeating traditional vows and ending with the customary *you may now kiss your bride.* You will precede Manda down the stairs, then Grams will be waiting at the foot of the stairs for Manda and she will walk her up the aisle to Hunter. I'll be at Hunter's side and you and I will provide the rings. We've gone through this three times. Everybody knows what they're supposed to do."

"Well, excuse me if I'm trying my best to make your sister's third attempt at matrimony come off without a hitch!" Gwen yelled.

"Your choice of words leave a great deal to be desired." Perry glared at his wife.

"I appreciate everything you've done," Manda told Gwen. "I know tomorrow will be perfect, in great part, thanks to you." She glanced at her brother. "And, Perry, I'm sure Gwen didn't mean anything unkind by what she said."

Gwen glowered at Manda and for the first time in years, Manda saw the anger and hurt that her sister-in-law usually kept hidden. "No, of course I didn't mean to be unkind. Everyone knows how terribly Manda has suffered. Few women have one fiancé killed right before their wedding, let alone two. I'm sure we'd all like to see Manda happily married at long last."

Grams scurried into the living room. "What's taking so long? People are arriving and I've had to steer them into the den. Finish up in here, so we can get on to the engagement party."

Grams to the rescue, Manda thought. Another couple

of minutes and Gwen might have told me what she really thinks of me.

"We're through with the rehearsal," Perry said. "Have the string quartet move out to the patio and start playing some mood music, then let everyone come on in and we'll start the party." He grabbed Gwen's arm and draped it over his. "Let's greet our guests, darling. And try to remember that you love Manda and are thrilled for her."

While Perry led his wife toward the wide pocket doors that opened to the foyer, Hunter came up beside Manda.

"Gwen despises you," Hunter said.

"Yes, she does. I don't think she's ever forgiven me for taking Rodney away from her."

Manda turned and glanced up at Hunter, who looked devastatingly handsome in his navy-blue suit, pale blue shirt and striped tie. She had watched him tugging on his collar and fidgeting with his tie all during the rehearsal and thought his nervousness made him seem all the more like a real bridegroom. And anyone seeing them together would never suspect them of subterfuge. Hunter had been attentive…almost to the extreme. But after she'd whispered what the others had assumed were sweet-nothings into his ear, he had toned down the adoration a bit. She had warned him that if he didn't stop touching her every two minutes, she was going to find a way to make him suffer. Didn't the man realize the effect he had on her, that it was difficult enough for her to act the part of the blushing bride without him keeping her in a perpetual state of arousal?

"Gwen really doesn't want to see you happy," Hunter said.

"Are you trying to imply that Gwen might be my stalker?" Manda asked.

"It's possible. Maybe she thinks you don't have a right

to be happy, since she's so miserable." Hunter shook his head. "I don't see how Perry stands being married to a woman who so obviously doesn't love him. Your brother deserves better."

"They seem content, if not happy. Gwen is the perfect wife for a man with political aspirations and you must know that Perry has big plans to run for congress."

"I think Perry has settled for less than he wants," Hunter said. "And regardless of his political aspirations, I'll bet he'd give up everything if the right woman ever came along."

"My, my, Mr. Whitelaw, I had no idea you were such a romantic."

He cleared his throat, then chuckled. "It's all this June, moon and spoon business associated with the wedding. I'm getting sentimental and—" he caressed her butt through the silk of her dress "—horny."

Manda laughed, then slapped his hand away from her derriere. "Behave yourself. We aren't alone in the house, you know. I swear, Hunter Whitelaw, you seem to have a one-track mind."

"Just contemplating our honeymoon."

"You should be contemplating keeping yourself alive," she told him, then wished the words back. If she hadn't spoken her thoughts out loud, then the danger wouldn't seem as real. "I've tried not to think about it, but how do you ignore a truth that's the size of an elephant?"

"I'm not ignoring anything." He draped his arm around her shoulders and pivoted her slowly. "Look over there at the waiter removing the lids from the heated chafing dishes. That's Matt O'Brien, a Dundee agent." He turned her to face the pocket doors. "See that photographer in the foyer snapping shots of your guests? Don't you recognize him?''

"It's Wolfe."

"Hmm. And outside posing as a valet is another Dundee agent, Jack Parker. All three men are armed and prepared for whatever might come down this evening."

"You say that so calmly, when we both know that what's going to come down this evening is an attempt on your life."

"Stop frowning," Hunter said. "Our guests are coming in and they'll wonder why the bride-to-be isn't smiling."

"God help me! I have a feeling that after tonight, I'll have a permanent smile on my face because my muscles will be stuck in grinning-like-an-idiot mode."

"Brace yourself, brat, here come your admirers."

"What?" She glanced across the room just as Grady, Boyd and Chris formed a charging trio. "I guess the least I can do is be nice and dance with each of them tonight."

"How gracious of you," Hunter teased. "A dance as a consolation prize. Believe me, if that's what you were offering me, I'd be damn disappointed."

"Shut up," she mouthed the words, then turned and held out her hand when Boyd approached first. "Thank you for coming tonight."

Boyd shook her hand and held it. She tugged. He tightened his hold. "I wish you every happiness." He abruptly released her and held out his hand to Hunter. "Congratulations. You're a very lucky man."

"Yes, I know."

Hunter shook hands with Boyd, who then walked away and immediately began talking to Gwen and Perry. Before she had a chance to catch her breath, Chris and Grady appeared in front of her.

"You look gorgeous, as always," Chris said.

"Manda, you're positively beaming," Grady told her. She kept her forced smile in place. "Thank you."

Chris held out his hand to Hunter, who accepted it.

"You're a brave man, Whitelaw," Chris said. "Or is it that you simply aren't afraid of the Manda Munroe Curse?"

Manda glared at Chris, not quite able to believe that he'd actually made such an unkind comment, tonight of all nights.

"Ignore him," Grady said. "The man's an idiot."

Hunter's gaze narrowed on Chris. His jaw tightened; his nostrils flared. She quickly draped her arm through Hunter's in an effort to calm his temper.

"I'm a man in love," Hunter said. "I'd risk anything to marry Manda. Wouldn't you?"

"Yes, I would," Chris replied, his tone quite serious. "But she's never wanted me, so I've never been in any danger of succumbing to the curse."

"All this business of a curse is ridiculous," Grady said. "It's hardly Manda's fault that some man is hopelessly in love with her and can't bear the thought of her marrying someone else." Grady looked point-blank at Chris. "If I were the police, I'd be investigating you, Austin. You seem to have more motive than anyone else."

"Gentlemen, if you'll excuse us," Hunter said, "Manda has other guests whom I hope will have the good manners not to bring up any unpleasant topics."

"I'm so sorry," Grady said.

"I'm sorry, too," Chris added. "You must forgive me, but you know what a sore loser I am."

Hunter led her through the room and around the patio, pausing here and there to talk to their guests and accept congratulations and good wishes. As the evening wore on, Manda's nerves became stretched almost to the breaking point. She had been waiting for an attack, expecting something to happen at any moment. Each loud noise unnerved her. When a waiter had dropped a tray on the patio, she barely managed to stifle a scream. She danced with several guests, but Hunter was never far away and no one thought it odd that he couldn't keep his eyes off her. Several of the ladies remarked about how Hunter seemed to simply worship her.

As Manda was forcing down a few bites of food, Claire came up to her and patted her on the arm. "Do you have a few minutes, dear girl? I'd like to speak to you alone."

Hunter was not going to approve of the idea of Manda being out of his sight, but he could hardly object to her sharing a few private moments with Claire, could he?

"Of course," Manda said. "Why don't we go into the den? Just let me just tell Hunter where I'll be."

When she told him, he shook his head. "You aren't going anywhere without me."

"Lower your voice. Claire might hear you and think you don't trust her. Besides, I thought you were the target tonight, not me."

"Give Claire any reason you like, but wherever you go, I go."

Manda huffed. "Very well."

When she and Hunter approached Claire, Manda said, "Do you mind terribly if Hunter goes with us? I'm afraid he's very protective and simply refuses to let me out of his sight."

Claire smiled faintly. "I don't mind at all if Hunter goes with us. I'm happy that you've found someone who cares so deeply for you. I'm sure Rodney would be pleased."

A sense of sadness wrapped itself around Manda as memories of another engagement party flashed through her mind. She had tried so hard not to think about Rodney or Mike, tried not to remember and compare her engagements to either man to her fake relationship with Hunter.

"That's very kind of you to say, Mrs. Austin," Hunter said.

"Please, let me steal y'all away for a few minutes." Claire took Manda's hand in hers, then whispered to Manda, "I have a little gift for you."

Once Manda and Claire entered the den, Hunter stood in the doorway, his back to them. "I'll stay here," he said. "That way y'all can have a little privacy."

"Thank you," Claire said, then reached inside the pocket of her beaded jacket and pulled out a small velvet box. "Manda, I love you as if you were my daughter and have since the day you and Rodney announced your engagement. More than anything I wanted you to be my daughter-in-law." Tears welled up in Claire's eyes.

"I wanted that, too. Very much." She glanced at Hunter's broad back and wondered if he cared at all that a part of her still loved Rodney Austin. *Of course he doesn't care,* an inner voice said.

"I bought a gift for you when you were engaged to Rodney. I had planned to give it to you at the rehearsal dinner the night before your wedding."

"Oh, Claire, you can't mean that this is—"

"Yes, dear girl, this is that gift." Claire lifted the lid to reveal a pair of diamond earrings. "Would you consider accepting these and wearing them tomorrow? It would mean so much to me."

"Yes, of course, I'll accept them and I'd love to wear them tomorrow." Manda wrapped her arms around Claire, who reciprocated. After they hugged, Manda took the box from Claire. "I will treasure these always."

Tears trickled down Claire's softly rouged cheeks. She

whispered to Manda, "I must admit that it won't be easy to watch you marry someone else, but..." She swallowed her tears.

"You will always be a part of my life," Manda assured Claire. "In my heart, you've always been my mother-in-law. That won't ever change."

Claire gave Manda another hug, kissed her cheek and then walked to the door, leaving Manda alone in the den. Hunter stepped aside and as Claire passed him, she laid her hand on his arm and patted him gently, then walked on until she disappeared down the hall.

"Are you all right?" Hunter asked as he came up behind Manda.

Tears lodged in her throat, so she simply nodded her head.

"That couldn't have been easy for you," he said.

Manda took a deep, calming breath. "It was much more difficult for Claire. Even though she wants me to be happy and wishes me well, I know it must make her very sad to know that I'm getting married tomorrow."

Hunter grasped her shoulders and pulled her back up against his chest. "When this is all over and you're free from your crazed admirer and free from your marriage to me, do you think you'll ever be able to love another man or will you spend the rest of your life in mourning for Rodney Austin?"

If Hunter hadn't been holding her so securely, she would have swung around and slapped him. How dare he say such a thing to her!

"You have no right to—"

Hunter whirled her around so quickly that she gasped with surprise. "If our engagement was real, I'd have every right to ask you that question. And someday, some man is going to have that right. What are you going to tell him?''

''The right man will accept the fact that a part of me will always love Rodney,'' she said, her voice quivering slightly despite her resolve to remain in control of her emotions. ''Mike and I could have had a good marriage. We understood each other and accepted the fact that we would both always love other people.''

''I wouldn't have a problem knowing that in some way you would always love Rodney, if you were able to put that love where it belonged—in the past. But I would have a major problem, sleeping three to a bed, knowing that you could never feel the passion for me that you had felt for him.''

''Then we wouldn't have a problem,'' she said, being totally honest. ''I feel more passion with you than I've ever felt with anyone. That's what our relationship is all about, isn't it? Physical attraction. A strong passion that overrides everything else, even common sense.'' She could never admit to Hunter that she loved him, that her love and passion for Rodney paled in comparison to the way she felt about him.

''If you can feel that strongly about me, then you can experience it again with a man you love.'' Hunter clutched the back of her neck and pulled her to him. ''And believe me, brat, I don't pity that guy, whoever he'll be. I envy him.''

Pleasure radiated through Manda. Pure, thankful pleasure. Perhaps Hunter didn't realize it, but he had just given her a gift with his words.

When he kissed her, she opened herself up to the sensuous enjoyment of the moment. She experienced the kiss with every fiber of her being. Sensations of joy and excitement burst inside her, warming her body and preparing it for the intimacy it craved. With Hunter. Only with Hunter.

Standing on tiptoe, she clung to him, her mound pressed against his sex. For several glorious moments she forgot where she was and what was happening all around her. But just as Hunter cupped her buttocks and deepened the kiss, a startled gasp reminded her that the door to the den stood wide open.

"You two are putting on quite a show for anyone who passes by," Gwen said. "I'm glad that Grams didn't see this vulgar display."

Hunter kept his hands on Manda's behind, refusing to release her as he glanced over his shoulder at Gwen. "Close the door, would you, Gwen? I'm going to ravish my fiancée and unless you want to watch…"

Gwen slammed the door. Hunter chuckled. Manda tried not to laugh, but couldn't stop the giggles that erupted from her throat.

"You're right," Manda said. "She hates me. And now, she envies me more than ever. She thinks I'm going to have it all—love and passion and a real happily-ever-after life."

"She's right. Someday you will have it all."

But not with you, Manda thought. The sad thing was that he didn't realize that with any other man it would never be the same. It could never be everything she wanted love to be. Love had been young and new and wonderful with Rodney. And it had been comfortable and consoling and sweet with Mike. But only with Hunter was it all that love should be—that earth-shattering, gut-clenching excitement that consumed a person body and soul.

"We really shouldn't stay in here much longer,"

Manda said. "We have guests. And after all, the party is in our honor."

Several hours later when most of the guests had left and the caterer's crew was cleaning up, Manda and Hunter said their good-nights to her family.

"You two must be here promptly at three," Grams said. "The photographer will be here then and can get the pictures done so that after the wedding there won't be any delay before the reception."

"We'll be here on time. I promise." Manda hugged her grandmother.

Despite the tension in the air, Gwen's hostility and Chris's rudeness, the evening had been somewhat enjoyable. She had almost forgotten that they had been expecting an attack all evening. Upon arriving. While they'd been out on the patio. Even inside the house.

As they waved goodbye and headed down the sidewalk, Manda noticed the Dundee agents were all outside. Matt O'Brien stood by the open doors of the catering truck. Wolfe stood off to the side, still snapping the occasional picture. And Jack Parker drove Hunter's Lexus into the drive, stepped out and opened both doors. Adrenaline rushed through Manda's body. For a couple of seconds her rapid heartbeat obliterated every other sound. Some strange sixth sense forewarned her of danger. She held tightly to Hunter's arm. Too tightly. He paused on the walkway and turned to her.

"What's wrong?" he asked.

She tried to smile, but failed. "I don't know. But I'm scared."

"Try to stay calm. If anything happens, remember that we've got the situation under control as much as possible."

Traffic on North Pine Street on a Friday night was always rather heavy, since the road led straight into town. The drone of vehicles several yards away on the street hummed inside Manda's head. Suddenly her feet seemed unnaturally heavy, as if her ankles carried lead weights. Her movements became sluggish. She glanced over her shoulder and saw Perry and Grams in the doorway. The moment suddenly became surreal.

As if in slow motion, she returned her gaze to Hunter, then heard the horrific sound of a gunshot. In her peripheral vision she noticed movement. The Dundee agents dispersing, jumping into action. Hunter threw her to the ground, but before he could cover her body with his, the first shot hit its mark and tossed Hunter backward and onto the sidewalk. Manda's scream echoed in her ears.

She crawled toward Hunter, but before she reached him, Jack Parker, gun in hand, came down over her, using his body as a shield. She fought him like a tigress, wild with the need to be with her mate.

"Hunter!" she cried. "Please, let me go to Hunter."

If Hunter was dead, she would die, too.

Chapter 13

Hunter felt as though he'd been kicked in the chest by a mule. The shooter must have been using a high-powered rifle, which confirmed their suspicion that Manda's crazed admirer had hired himself a hit man. With his chest aching and the wind knocked out of him, Hunter lay on the ground, thankful that the lightweight, tactical bulletproof vest he wore under his shirt gave protection up to Threat Level IV, which included all handguns, AK47s and .303 hunting rifles.

Manda's cries prompted him to action. The moment Hunter managed to stand, Jack released her and she came barreling toward him. He grabbed her arm and pulled her with him into the house. The front door stood wide open, apparently left that way by Perry and Grams, who hovered at the far end of the hallway. When he came inside, Jack slammed the door shut.

Manda clung to Hunter, her fingers caressing his face. "Are you really all right? The bullet didn't go through the vest? When I saw you fall, I wasn't sure. Oh, God, Hunter, if anything had happened to you. Please, tell me you're all right. Damn it, say something to me. I'm out of my mind—''

Hunter covered her mouth with his, adeptly silencing her manic tirade. The minute she stilled, he lifted his head and said, ''I'm okay. I've probably got a bruise the size of a grapefruit on my chest, but that should be the extend of the damage.''

Gwen came down the stairs, her eyes wide. ''What happened? I thought I heard—'' When she saw the man who had been parking the cars at the party standing by the front door with a gun in his hand, she stopped dead still halfway in her descent. ''My God, who...what are you—''

''It's all right, Gwen.'' Perry left Grams at the end of the hall and came forward so that his wife could see him. ''Don't be frightened. That man is a Dundee agent.'' He glanced at Jack. ''Is it safe for my wife to come downstairs?''

''It should be safe,'' Jack replied. ''Our shooter probably isn't anywhere on the grounds. Matt and Wolfe will be letting us know something soon.''

''Matt and Wolfe?'' Gwen remained glued to the spot in the middle of the staircase.

''More Dundee agents,'' Perry said. ''One posed as the photographer's assistant tonight and the other was one of the caterer's helpers.''

With his arm around Manda, Hunter urged her to come with him into the living room. When they passed in front of the stairs, Gwen gasped and her startled gaze met Hunter's. The woman looked surprised to see him alive. Had Gwen expected him to be dead?

''What's wrong?'' Hunter asked.

"When I heard the shot, I thought perhaps you'd been...that either you or Manda had been killed," Gwen said. "Thank God, you're both all right."

While Hunter led Manda into the living room, Perry hurried up the steps to Gwen. Grams walked down the hallway and when she passed Jack, she gave him a hasty upturned-nose perusal, then continued her regal strut into the living room.

"Would someone like to explain to me what's going on?" Barbara Munroe seated herself in a wing chair near the pocket doors. "There's been entirely too much excitement here tonight."

Manda clung to Hunter. They stood off to themselves, several feet away from Grams. Perry led his wife into the room and they sat together on the sofa.

"Someone tried to kill Hunter," Manda explained, her gaze never leaving his face. "Someone shot at him."

"So, it's happened again." Grams looked directly at Hunter. "How is it that you weren't killed? The man must have been a poor shot."

"Yes, ma'am, something like that," Hunter said.

A phone rang. Everyone either jumped, gasped or did both. Everyone except Hunter and Jack, who pulled a cellular phone from his pocket.

"Is that our telephone?" Grams asked. "Why isn't Bobbie Rue answering it?"

"Bobbie Rue went home for the night," Perry said. "And that's not our phone ringing."

Jack spoke so quietly that Hunter couldn't make out anything he said. After Jack returned the phone to his pocket, he holstered his pistol, then came into the living room, straight to Hunter.

"That was Matt," Jack said, his voice low. "The police that Chief Burgess posted across the street spotted a guy with a rifle. Before they could apprehend him, he sped away in a car alone. But they're chasing him down right now. Matt and Wolfe are right behind the police and as soon as the law apprehends our hit man, Matt will call back.''

''Once he's captured, he'll be able to tell us who hired him, won't he?'' Manda asked. ''Then the police can arrest whoever was behind Rodney and Mike's murders and—''

''Speak up, dear girl,'' Grams said. ''We can't hear what y'all are saying and it's terribly impolite to whisper like that.''

''Sorry, Grams.''

Manda gazed up at Hunter and he understood that she was asking his permission before giving the others any information.

''Mrs. Munroe, the police may soon be arresting the man who tried to shoot me,'' Hunter said. ''When they have him in custody, then Manda and I will go down to the police station.''

''Is that necessary?'' Grams asked. ''Manda shouldn't be exposed to such unpleasantness.''

Manda's lips twitched and Hunter knew she was as amused as he by her grandmother's comment. ''You don't understand,'' Manda said. ''This professional killer will be able to tell us who hired him.''

''Dear me.'' Gwen gasped. ''It's so unbelievable. Does this mean that the wedding tomorrow will be postponed? If so, then I have a great deal to do. I must contact Reverend Titus and the caterers and the florist and—''

Perry patted his wife on the back. ''Everything will be all right. I'll help you do whatever needs to be done.''

''We aren't postponing the wedding,'' Hunter said.

"We aren't?" Manda's eyes widened in surprise. "But if—"

Hunter whispered, "If the police captured the hit man, there will be time enough in the morning to cancel the wedding."

"If?" Manda asked, keeping her voice low. "Do you think he might get away?"

"Let's hope not."

Grams cleared her throat. "Y'all are doing it again. Whispering. I taught you better manners, Manda."

"Why don't I fix some coffee for all of us, while we're waiting to hear," Perry said. "I doubt we'll be getting any sleep tonight."

Forty-five minutes later, after Perry had served coffee in the living room and Grams had fallen asleep in the wing chair, Jack's cell phone rang again. He answered it after the first ring.

"Parker, here." Pause. "Yeah." Pause. "Damn!" Pause. "Okay, I'll tell them, and thanks, Matt. You and Wolfe come on back to the Munroe house and we'll discuss strategy with Hunter."

"What happened?" Hunter asked. "Did the police nab our hit man?"

"Not exactly."

"What do you mean, not exactly?" Manda asked.

"Three police cars were in on the chase," Jack said. "Matt and Wolfe kept out of their way, but stayed right with them. The guy was driving over a hundred miles an hour. They were closing in on him when he lost control of the car and careened over an embankment, flipped over twice and flew headlong into a tree."

"Don't tell me." Hunter clenched his jaw.

"Yeah, our hit man is dead. Matt said it looks like his

neck is broken. So this guy isn't going to be telling us anything.''

Manda slumped against Hunter. ''We still don't know who hired him…don't know who's behind the threats.''

''This means that our maniac might have to act on his own, if he's going to stop the wedding tomorrow.''

Manda looked at herself in the cherry cheval mirror in her old bedroom in the Munroe house. Despite the fact that she'd gotten only a few hours' sleep in the wee hours of the morning, Grams and Gwen kept assuring her that she looked lovely. The off-the-rack wedding dress fit her perfectly. She had decided to wear her hair down because that was the way Hunter liked it. She lifted the beaded headband out of the box and set it in place. Her fingers slipped down to caress the diamond earrings Claire had given her.

She took one final look in the mirror. There, she was ready. Ready to enter into a marriage that was doomed for a quickie divorce. She wondered if Hunter was as nervous as she was. Probably not. After all, he didn't have the emotional investment in their relationship that she did. To him this farce of a marriage was just part of his job. And if they lived through the ceremony and the reception, and they actually went on a honeymoon, then sex with his temporary bride would simply be a bonus for Hunter.

A knock sounded outside her room. ''Yes?''

Grams cracked open the door and peeped inside. ''May I come in? I have something that I'd like for you to wear today.''

''Please, Grams, come in.'' What could it be? Manda wondered. Something borrowed or something blue? Claire had provided the something new, so perhaps Grams thought she should contribute the something old.

As Grams entered the bedroom, Manda noticed the sheer lace and tulle veil in her hands. Oh, no, please, no. She recognized the item. The veil her mother had worn on her wedding day.

"I know you didn't order a veil, dear, and had all your pre-wedding pictures taken without one," Grams said. "But I thought surely you would like to wear this one for the ceremony. It's your mother's veil. It's not quite as white as it was forty-two years ago, but…" Grams swallowed her tears. "You look like your mother. She was a lovely woman. I know she would be so pleased if you wore her veil today."

Oh, Grams, don't do this to me. You have no idea how difficult today will be for me. And for so many reasons. I'm marrying a man I've loved since I was just a kid, but he doesn't love me and this marriage is nothing more than part of an elaborate scheme to catch a madman. And then there's that madman—he's still out there, without his hired killer to do his dirty work. She knew that Hunter expected her secret admirer to make his move at the wedding, to expose himself in a fit of rage and jealousy.

"May I help you put this on?" Grams asked.

What could she say other than, "Yes, of course."

After Manda removed her headband, Grams held up the large, beaded headpiece to which the veil was attached. Manda had seen her parents' wedding pictures and her mother had looked like a princess in her elaborate gown and veil. While Grams helped her station the headpiece and veil just right, Gwen rushed into the room carrying Manda's bouquet. A lush arrangement of cream roses, pale pink tulips, white French lilac, yellow narcissus, hyacinth and white irises, tied together with white satin ribbon.

"You left your bouquet downstairs," Gwen said.

"Thank you for bringing it upstairs to me." Manda had chosen the floral arrangement herself, one of the few things she had personally selected for the wedding. It had been so much easier to allow Grams and Gwen and Claire to take care of all the details.

"I start down the stairs in five minutes." Gwen wore a simple, floor-length, pale pink gown and looked every inch the elegant wife of a wealthy lawyer. Holding her own bouquet of pink tulips and cream roses in one hand, she handed Manda the bridal bouquet. "Grams, don't you think you should head downstairs so you can take your place?"

"I may be seventy-seven years old, Gwen, but I'm perfectly capable of getting down the stairs in less than five minutes." Grams kissed Manda on both cheeks. "You're a beautiful bride. Be happy, my dearest child."

Manda hugged Grams, who quickly wiped the tears from the corners of her eyes and marched out of the room, shoulders back and head held high. Forever the regal grande dame.

"You're a brave woman," Gwen said the minute Grams was out of earshot. "I wouldn't have the nerve to go through with the wedding, not if my fiancé had been nearly killed last night."

"Hunter refuses to allow some maniac to stop us from getting married," Manda said. "If I'm brave, if I'm daring, then I owe my newfound courage to him."

"You've finally gotten what you want, haven't you?" Gwen glared at Manda. "You may actually get married this time, but I'm wondering how long it will be before you're a widow."

Manda barely stifled a gasp. Why should she be surprised by her sister-in-law's brutal honesty? It wasn't as if she believed that Gwen actually cared for her, as a sister or as a friend. Whatever friendship they had once shared had ended when Rodney Austin fell in love with Manda. Over the years, Gwen had simply faked affection for Manda in front of others and had maintained an icy indifference to her in private.

"Gwen, you're a heartless bitch and I hope one of these days my brother realizes that he can do a lot better than you."

"Perhaps I'll be the one to find someone better," Gwen said.

"You'll never find a better man than Perry, but maybe you can find a man more suited to you."

The string quartet ended their final tune and the harpist began her first song. Heavenly music drifted upstairs and signaled them that it was time for the bride and her attendant to make a grand entrance.

Gwen smiled, then laughed softly. "There's our musical cue. Time for me to go. Count to twenty, then follow me down the stairs. And while you're making your way to your groom, remember that someone might shoot him in the middle of the ceremony."

As she glided down the staircase and took Gram's arm, Manda tried not to think about what Gwen had said, but she couldn't erase the frightening thought from her mind. Although she kept a fragile smile in place, she felt as if her heart would beat its way out of her chest. Only close friends and family surrounded her, but what if one of those trusted people was the person determined to destroy her happiness?

When she reached her groom, Grams placed her hand in his and Reverend Titus began the ceremony. Hunter wore a bulletproof vest under his tux, but that didn't protect him from a head shot. While she made all the right responses and repeated all the right words, she prayed a constant prayer that God would keep Hunter safe.

"I now pronounce you husband and wife," Reverend Titus said. "You may kiss your bride," he added in a low voice.

Hunter lifted the veil and gazed into her eyes. And in that one brief moment, Manda's imagination played a cruel trick on her, making her think that she actually saw love in Hunter's expression. The kiss was passionate, but short. Then he slipped his arm around her and they turned to face their guests.

"Ladies and gentlemen, may I present Mr. and Mrs. Hunter Whitelaw," Reverend Titus said.

The harpist and the string quartet played the recessional as the bride and groom walked down the aisle created by the two sections of folding chairs filling the living room. Hunter escorted her through the French doors and out onto the patio where the reception was being held. As they had been instructed, they went straight to the table where the large, elaborate Victorian wedding cake had been placed. Wolfe appeared out of nowhere, camera in hand and snapped pictures while they cut the cake and took turns feeding bites to each other. In her peripheral vision Manda saw Matt O'Brien once again acting as a member of the catering staff. And she knew that Jack was out front, with the other guys doing the valet parking.

Grams had insisted on a receiving line, so the moment Perry and Gwen escorted Grams onto the patio, Hunter and Manda joined them. Claire and Chris were first through the line and although both wished them well, Manda understood the sad look in Claire's eyes and the hostility in Chris's attitude. Grady had brought a date, an attractive woman Manda didn't know, someone named Constance. And Boyd had escorted Lisa, although Lisa whispered to Manda that she wasn't dating Boyd, but they had decided to come together since neither had had a date for the wedding.

A loud bang stopped everyone dead in their tracks. Manda held her breath; every nerve in her body screamed. Hunter leaned over and whispered, ''Relax. That wasn't a gunshot. Someone opened a bottle of champagne.''

Mandy laughed nervously and turned to the next person in line. She didn't recognize the woman. A voluptuous blonde in a stunning, street-length dress of hot-pink silk that clung to all the woman's well-rounded curves. Her short, straight platinum hair should have made her look less feminine, but it didn't. Nothing could diminish the raw sexual appeal the woman possessed.

''My very best wishes,'' the woman said to Manda, then reached over to kiss Hunter's cheek. ''Congratulations.''

''Thank you, ma'am.''

When the gorgeous woman moved on, Manda punched Hunter in the ribs. ''Who is she?''

''My boss,'' Hunter said. ''The CEO of the Dundee agency, Ellen Denby.''

''She's the head of a security agency?''

''Don't let her looks fool you. Ellen can kick butt with the best of 'em.''

''I'll just bet she can.'' Manda shoved the green-eyed monster back into its dark hole and breathed a sigh of relief that Ellen Denby was Hunter's boss and not an ex-girlfriend.

Music wafted through the air, a springtime breeze fluttered through the treetops, champagne flowed and a good time was had by all. Or almost all. By eight-thirty, when she changed into her traveling suit, the bride was almost

out of her mind with fear. The attack she had been expecting for the past two and a half hours hadn't happened.
But they weren't out of harm's way. Not yet.

"A few more minutes and we'll be in the limo headed
to the airport," Hunter said. "Once we get in the helicopter and fly off, there's no way anyone will be able to
follow us."

"I think you could at least tell me where we're going."

"We're going somewhere quiet and peaceful and secluded. Somewhere we'll be safe."

"I don't see how following through with the honeymoon will do us any good in trapping the person who
hired that hit man to kill you."

"If our nutcase doesn't strike before we leave today,
then while we're away, he's going to spend the week plot-
ting our demise and building up the courage to carry out
his plans," Hunter said.

"Oh, gee, something to look forward to when we come
home."

He kissed her forehead. "I'm glad to see that you
haven't lost your sense of humor."

The crowd awaited them when they walked down the
stairs. She carried her bouquet because Grams had said
she simply must follow through with tradition, even
though she had refused to wear a garter for Hunter to pitch
to the bachelors in the crowd. When she was halfway
down the stairs, Manda stopped to give the single women
a chance to gather up front and prepare for the big production.

Manda turned her back, lifted the flowers above her
head and threw the bouquet down into the bevy of gig-
gling females. She turned around just in time to see Lisa
jump into the air, catch the bouquet and then lose her
balance. She fell backward, straight into Perry, who

opened his arms and grabbed Lisa to prevent her from hitting the floor. Lisa turned in Perry's arms and smiled.

Hunter led Manda down the stairs, through the foyer and out onto the porch. As they began their march down the sidewalk, well-wishers tossed birdseed at them and in the distance church bells rang, an announcement to the town of Dearborn that Manda Munroe was married.

When they reached the white limousine, Jack Parker opened the door. She noticed that he wore a chauffeur's uniform. After she and Hunter were secure in the back seat, she wasn't surprised in the least when Jack got behind the wheel. Nor was she surprised to see Wolfe riding shotgun.

"I'd say we have plenty of protection." Manda relaxed for the first time all day.

"Look behind us," Hunter said.

Manda did. A dark sedan followed them. "More Dundee agents?"

"Matt and Ellen. All four agents will stay with us until we reach the airport, then Matt will pilot the helicopter which will take us to our honeymoon destination."

"Can't you tell me now where we're going?"

"Want to venture a guess?"

She and Rodney had planned on a Paris honeymoon. Mike had booked a honeymoon in Hawaii. "The Caribbean? Since we're going by helicopter, it can't be Europe or the South Pacific."

"Nothing so exotic," he said. "But somewhere much safer, where we can be alone."

Manda wished that this was a true honeymoon and not one planned and executed to convince the killer that her marriage was real. But they had come this far—had actually gotten married—so they had no choice but to continue the farce. Regardless of the reason for their honeymoon, the fact remained that she would be alone with Hunter for an entire week. Together without danger and fear plaguing them. If only this were a real marriage, she would be looking forward to these days secluded with her husband.

Her husband. Hunter Whitelaw *was* her husband.

Was it possible that during a week alone with him, she could make him love her, make him want to stay married to her for the rest of their lives? She didn't know if that dream could become a reality, but she had seven days to seduce, entice and persuade. And she intended to make good use of her time. Even if she didn't win his heart, she could make enough beautiful memories to last a lifetime.

Chapter 14

When Matt set the helicopter down on a lighted landing strip, Hunter opened the door and hopped out, then reached up to help Manda. Slightly unbalanced, she fell against him as she emerged, but he caught her shoulders to steady her. Matt tossed their luggage out to Hunter, who caught each item and placed it on the dirt runway.

Manda had no idea where they were. All she could see from where she stood was the small well-lit airstrip and utter darkness beyond that point. Even though it was mid-May, there was a chill in the air that made Manda suspect they were in the mountains somewhere, probably the north Georgia or eastern Tennessee mountains since their trip from Dearborn had been relatively brief.

Hunter handed Manda the overnight case, then lifted the other bags and nudged her into motion. They hurried to the edge of the airstrip. The minute Matt lifted off, a black Jeep appeared as if out of nowhere.

"There's our ride," Hunter said.

"Our ride to where?" Manda asked.

"To our honeymoon hideaway."

Hunter opened the Jeep's back hatch and tossed their luggage inside, then opened the door and lifted Manda up and into the back seat. The minute he got in and slammed the door, the driver turned to them and smiled.

"Hi, I'm Elizabeth Landry." She looked first at Manda and then focused her gaze on Hunter. "Reece went down to the cottage to build y'all a fire in the fireplace. It's a bit chilly tonight."

The incredibly beautiful brunette introduced herself as if Manda should know who she was, but she didn't have the foggiest notion of who their hostess was or where they were. "Nice to meet you. I'm Manda Munroe."

"Manda Munroe Whitelaw," Hunter corrected.

Elizabeth laughed as she turned around and headed the Jeep Cherokee up a winding gravel road. "You'll get used to the new name and all that goes with it soon enough."

Manda knew better. She and Hunter wouldn't be married long enough for her to become accustomed to being Mrs. Whitelaw.

"I hope Sam explained that the only way to the cottage is on foot," Elizabeth said. "And there's no electricity."

"No electricity!" Manda gasped. "Where are we, in the wilderness?"

"Didn't your husband tell you anything about his honeymoon plans for y'all?" Elizabeth asked.

"No, ma'am, I didn't," Hunter said. "I wanted it to be a surprise."

"I see. So, Manda, do you have any idea where you are or who I am?" Elizabeth kept the Jeep on the narrow road that wove and twisted around the side of the mountain, taking them higher and higher.

"I'm afraid I don't," Manda replied.

"Well, you're in the mountains of northern Georgia and my uncle arranged this honeymoon for you. And before you ask, my uncle is Sam Dundee, the owner of Dundee's Private Security and Investigation."

"Hunter's boss," Manda said.

"Our place is off the beaten path, totally secluded and very private," Elizabeth said. "My great-grandfather built the honeymoon cottage as a wedding present for his bride. They spent their wedding night there and every anniversary for the rest of their lives. Reece and I are doing the same."

"Then you don't live out here, you just come for your anniversary every year?" Manda tried to assimilate all the information as quickly as Elizabeth gave it to her, but she still had a dozen or more questions.

"Oh, no, we live here. That's our cabin up ahead. The honeymoon cottage sits in the middle of the woods and is a ten-minute walk from our place. I've stocked the cottage with essentials and if y'all need anything, all you have to do is let us know."

When Manda glanced through the windshield she saw an enormous, sprawling, two-story log cabin with lights shining in every window and illuminating the huge wrap-around porch. A tall, dark-haired man stood on the steps, a large German shepherd at his side. Manda assumed this was Reece, Elizabeth's husband. When the Jeep stopped, Reece came forward and opened the door, the dog at his heels.

"Hello, there," he said. "Would y'all like to come in for a while or do you want to go straight to the cottage?"

Before either Manda or Hunter could reply, Elizabeth said, "This is their wedding night. I'm sure they want to go straight to the cottage. Why don't you help Hunter with the luggage?"

Laughing heartily, Reece undid the hatch and lifted out the suitcase, overnight case and leather bag. ''Want me to carry these for you or do you want to take them yourself?''

Once they were outside, Hunter met Reece at the back of the Jeep.

''I think I can manage. Thanks.''

''I can take one of them,'' Reece said. ''I'll have to guide y'all down to the cottage since it's nighttime. We don't want our guests getting lost.''

''Thanks.'' Hunter handed Reece Manda's suitcase.

''You and your wife just enjoy your honeymoon and don't worry about a thing,'' Reece said.

Elizabeth petted the German shepherd who leaned against her leg. ''This big baby is MacDatho. He's getting to be an old man. He'll be ten soon.''

''I have a one-year-old springer spaniel,'' Manda said. ''My brother is taking care of him while we're gone.''

Suddenly, without a prelude, without a warning, Elizabeth reached out and took Manda's hands into hers. The woman's actions startled Manda so that she couldn't disguise her surprise.

''It's all right. Don't be frightened,'' Elizabeth said. ''I know that you've loved and lost, that your heart has been broken and you think there is no happiness for you. But you are wrong. Great happiness lies ahead for you and Hunter. You must not give up hope.''

''Did your uncle...did Mr. Dundee tell you about why Hunter and I married, about—''

''I know that Hunter has brought you to our cottage for more than one reason. You will find what your heart has longed for and what your soul desperately needs. ''

''I don't understand.'' Manda stared into the woman's

deep, pure blue eyes and a shudder of awareness passed between them.

"You will find happiness, Manda. Someday you will have children. Strong, healthy children." Elizabeth pulled Manda closer and whispered, "But first you must free yourself of the obsession that a loved one feels for you. This person means you and Hunter great harm. You must not trust those closest to you, for among them is your enemy."

Manda jerked free. She stood there and stared at her hostess. "Who are you really? And what are you?"

"I'm a clairvoyant, with strong psychic abilities. My powers are my curse and my blessing. They are the reason we live secluded in these mountains."

Hunter came up to Manda. "Are you ready to head out?"

With her breath caught in her throat after hearing Elizabeth's admission, Manda managed to only nod.

"Just follow me," Reece said.

"Let me know if you have any problems," Elizabeth said. "And don't worry about the children coming down there to bother y'all. I keep a tight rein on my brood."

"You have children?" Manda asked.

Elizabeth beamed with pride. "We have three. Boys, six and three. And a girl, one."

"How wonderful." Manda sighed, a tinge of envy in her heart.

Ten minutes later Reece left Hunter and Manda on the porch of a small Victorian cottage that seemed totally out of place in the middle of the woods. Remembering distinctly that Elizabeth had said the cottage had no electricity, Hunter wondered if there were a hundred candles burning inside the house. The cottage shimmered with light and warmth, each window afire with a golden glow.

Hunter swept Manda up into his arms, opened the door and carried her across the threshold. She kept her arm around his neck as they entered the cottage. Two kerosene lamps burned on either side of the wooden mantel and another gave off more light from its position in the center of a green wicker table. Floral cushions rested in the seats of the antique wicker furniture. A crackling fire heated the room.

Getting his bearings, Hunter realized that there were four rooms—living room, kitchen and two bedrooms— and probably only one bath. He had to guess which bedroom their hosts had prepared for them, but since only one door stood wide open, he figured that was it. He strode straight to the open door, stopping only when they were inside the chosen room. One kerosene lamp cast a shadowy, gilded radiance over the cream walls, the moss-green iron bedstead and antique mahogany armoire in the corner. The bed had been turned down for the night and flower petals covered the pillows and sheets, as if they had cascaded down from the sky and landed haphazardly over the soft cream linens.

"Does this meet with your approval?" Hunter asked.

"It's beautiful," Manda said.

"The bed looks sturdy."

"Hmm."

He sensed the tension radiating from her and wished he could ease all her fears and give her a few days of peace and contentment—before putting his plan into action. He wouldn't tell her tonight, maybe not even tomorrow. Not until it became absolutely necessary. When he and the Dundee agents had devised the "honeymoon plan" to trap Manda's maniac, Perry had reluctantly agreed, but only after Hunter assured him that Manda would be protected at all times. No matter what came down when the killer showed up, Hunter would guard Manda, keep her safe, even if it meant sacrificing his own life. But for now, for a few brief, idyllic days, they would both be completely safe because no one except the Dundee agency knew where they were.

He wanted to give Manda an unforgettable honeymoon. But did he have the right? Their marriage was destined to end and when that happened, she would be free to find a real husband, a man she could build a future with, have children with and love forever. But regardless of what the future held for her, Manda wanted him now. He knew that as surely as he knew the sun would rise in the east tomorrow morning. But he also knew that if they shared a real wedding night, nothing would ever be the same again. Not for Manda. And certainly not for him.

Hunter eased Manda to her feet, inch by slow torturous inch, his body aching everywhere she touched him. He was hard and hurting, wanting this one particular woman in a way he had never wanted another. No matter what lies he told himself about his relationship with Manda, one truth could not be ignored—she was his fantasy and he was hers. He had judged every woman he'd ever met by Manda. Had she done the same, comparing all the men in her life to him?

"Hunter?"

He gazed down into her blue eyes and saw both longing and uncertainty. And in that one moment he knew that whatever happened between them tonight, and the following nights while they were secluded in this mountain cottage, would be Manda's decision. He was prepared to protect her, to make sure there were no unwanted consequences so that when their marriage ended, they could go their separate ways with no regrets. For him, there could be no regrets. What man would ever regret being Manda's lover? *Her first lover,* an inner voice reminded him. But could an emotionally fragile woman like Manda, with a romantic heart, give herself completely to a man who would be only a temporary fixture in her life?

"It's all right." Hunter kissed her forehead, then released her and walked away, but paused in the doorway. "I'll get our luggage off the porch.

She smiled. "Good idea. I'd like to get out of this suit. And I'd love a bath."

"Why don't you go ahead and get started on that bath," he suggested. "I can bring your overnight case in to you, if you'd like."

"I can wait. But while you're bringing in our things, I'll check out the bathroom and start my bathwater."

"Sure."

The minute Hunter disappeared into the living room, Manda opened the door to the bathroom that obviously had been added to the cottage by taking off several feet from each bedroom and enclosing it with bead board. Another kerosene lamp had been placed on the back of the commode. The bathroom fixtures—the commode and sink—were old, dating back a good fifty years. The tub was a true antique, a large brass container with no faucets.

Oh, great. How did you take a bath without water in the tub? It would have to be taken from the sink in a bucket and dumped into the tub. Then she remembered that there was no electricity. But surely there was a gas cookstove and a gas water heater, right? She turned on the sink faucets. Cold water came out of both. Damn! What was she supposed to do, take a cold bath?

"Here's your luggage, madam," Hunter called from the bedroom.

"There's no hot water," Manda said. "And this tub is

ancient. Looks like we'll be taking cold sponge baths while we're here.''

Hunter came into the bathroom, glanced around and grinned. ''This place is pretty rustic, isn't it? Sorry, if you're disappointed. But we can heat some water in the kitchen and fill the tub.''

''Have you checked out the kitchen?'' she asked. ''If there's no gas water heater, then there's probably no gas stove and there's no electricity, so how do you propose to heat water?''

''I don't know. Maybe there's a wood-burning stove.''

''Maybe I'll skip a bath tonight and just sponge off.''

''I'll take a look at the kitchen and give you a little privacy.''

''Thanks.''

A stack of towels and washcloths rested on a wall shelf in the corner. When Manda lifted the top cloth, a piece of paper fell off the cloth and drifted to the floor. Manda reached down to pick it up, all the while her heart beat erratically. Had her crazed admirer somehow found out where they were and had left a note? That's impossible! Stop this unreasonable thinking, she warned herself. She picked up the note and read it.

You can heat water for the tub on the woodstove in kitchen. Or you can bathe in the creek if the weather's warm. There's a path in front of the house that leads to the creek and the waterfall. But if it's too cool for that, try the hot spring. Go out the kitchen door and follow that path straight to the spring.

A hot spring? Wouldn't that be something like soaking in a hot tub, only one that was nature made? she thought.

Manda rushed out of the bathroom and into the bedroom. She immediately noticed that Hunter had placed her luggage on the floor, but his bag was missing. Did that mean he had put his things in the other bedroom? Had all his teasing about waiting for their wedding night to make love been just that—teasing?

She hurried into the living room and ran smack-dab into Hunter.

"The stove is wood-burning," he said. "But there's plenty of wood in the kitchen and it wouldn't take long to get a fire started, so if—"

"There's a hot spring behind the house," Manda said. "I found a note from Elizabeth."

"Honey, it's dark out there. Maybe in the morning we can find it."

"Tonight would be better," she told him. "This has been a nerve-racking day and I'm exhausted. I'd love to soak in some nice hot water and try to relax. Is that too much to ask?"

"I always knew you were a high-maintenance lady."

"Is that a yes?"

"Why not?"

She threw her arms around his neck and squealed with delight. "You're so good to me."

"Yeah, and you'd better not forget it."

Hunter had insisted on checking out the hot spring first. He'd taken a kerosene lantern with him to light the way. When he returned she'd already undressed, pinned up her hair and put on her white robe.

"Give me a second to get out of this suit," Hunter said, then disappeared into the other bedroom.

When he came out to join her, he was wearing his matching white robe. "Ready?" he asked.

"More than ready."

"You carry the towels and I'll carry the lantern."

The night was pitch-black, except for a quarter moon and distant twinkling stars. The light from the lantern illuminated a stepping-stone path that led through the woods and into a small clearing. Manda gasped the moment she saw the hot spring. A dozen kerosene lanterns circled the small spring-fed pond, bubbling with warm mineral water. A large silver tray sat on a huge rock that was the size of a tabletop and almost as smooth. A bottle of red wine and two glasses graced the center of the tray.

"How did you…when did—?"

"When I spoke to Elizabeth on the phone several days ago, she told me about the hot spring, so I asked if she'd leave you a note in the bathroom and prepare this place for tonight."

Manda socked Hunter's arm playfully. "You beast! This is so lovely." Tears gathered in her eyes and glistened on her eyelashes.

Hunter kissed away the tears. "I hope those are tears of happiness."

"They are. It's just that these past twenty-four hours have been hell and I really didn't know what to expect on this honeymoon," she admitted, then dropped the towels she carried onto the flat rock.

"Expect to get whatever your heart desires," Hunter told her.

Her heart stopped beating for a split second when she gazed up at him and once again thought she saw the look of love in his eyes. Was it simply her own foolish imagination? Perhaps so, but whether it was love she saw in his eyes or simply lust, one thing was clear—Hunter Whitelaw wanted her.

"Who goes first?" he asked.

"You."

"All right."

Without the least bit of modesty, he shucked off his robe, tossed it on the flat rock and stood before her gloriously nude. The very sight of him took away her breath. He was devastating. A prime male specimen. Big. Perfectly formed. Unabashedly aroused. He stepped down and into the hot spring, the lower half of his body slowly disappearing beneath the gurgling water. He moved around in the small pond, sank his body into the depths, up to his chin, then rose to stand on the shallow bottom. The churning water hit him at the waist.

"Coming in?" he asked, as he offered her his hand.

Manda hesitated, wondering if she'd been reckless in doing as he'd done by wearing nothing under her robe. The moment of doubt faded quickly and with a courage born of desire, she untied the belt and leisurely removed the robe, letting it circle her feet. She stepped out of the fabric puddle and stood at the edge of the pond. Hunter let out a long, low whistle, then extended his hand to help her into the burbling pool. She took his hand and held it to steady herself as she walked into the hot spring and straight into Hunter's arms. The water was warm, almost hot, but with the cool nighttime breeze caressing her face and shoulders, the spring's heat felt heavenly. But the crush of her body against Hunter's created the real heat.

"Do you like it?" he asked.

She lifted her arms and draped them around his shoulders, interlocking her fingers behind his neck. "I like it all. The hot spring. The lanterns. The wine. But most of all, I like being here with you."

"Good. My aim is to please you. Tonight. Tomorrow. Tomorrow night."

"Then let's not think about what's waiting for us when

we leave here at the end of the week. Let's live only for the moment. For right now. Tonight.''

He spanned her waist with his hands, then lifted her just enough to bring her face into alignment with his. When he kissed her, he cupped her buttocks, bouncing her upward until she spread apart her thighs and wrapped her legs around his hips. His sex pulsated against her, the feel of him sending a tingling awareness from the core of her femininity throughout her body.

Cocooned in their private heated lagoon, she gave herself over to Hunter's ravishing kiss. He showed her how truly intimate a mating of mouths and tongues can be. Each moment enticed her. Aroused her. Pleasured her and yet left her wanting more. So much more.

Chapter 15

Manda surrendered to her heart's desire and to her body's needs. Even if this glorious freedom to give and take, to share the intimate joys of lovemaking was no more than stolen moments from her life, she didn't care. No matter what next week or next month or next year brought, she would always have these days to remember. And even if someday she married again and found the happiness that Elizabeth Landry predicted, she would never forget Hunter. He would be a part of her forever. And she would love him to her dying day.

They kissed and laughed and played in the pond fed by the hot spring, their time together a mixture of fun and teasing and seduction. They sipped the wine, each from their own glass and then with arms twined, from each other's crystal flute. But with each passing minute, the sexual yearnings within them grew stronger and the frolicking became sensually bolder. Deep, tongue-thrusting kisses. Love bites. Hands and fingers and tongues exploring above and below the water level. Bodies entwined, rubbing, undulating, advancing and retreating.

Hunter rose from the pond, rivulets of water dripping from his big body, droplets clinging to his hair, glistening on his broad chest and long legs. He picked up his robe and slipped into it, then lifted her robe and held it open. As she emerged from the hot spring, the cool night air chilled her. She slid her arms into the robe and Hunter quickly wrapped it around her. When he swung her off her feet and into his arms, she laughed, enjoying the feeling of being abducted, of being stolen away by a man intent upon claiming her for his own. She clung to him as he lifted one of the lanterns to light their way. Within minutes, he kicked open the back door and carried her through the cottage kitchen and into the living room, setting the lantern on the hearth as he passed by.

"Your first time should be in a soft, warm bed covered with rose petals," Hunter said as he carried her into their room and laid her sideways atop the cream sheets. "I promise I will make this first time good for you. And then, I'll do my best to make the times that come after even better."

The pleasure of his promise filled her, heating her within and without. When he spread the robe apart, she lifted up just enough so that he could remove it. Then he withdrew a condom from his pocket before quickly taking off the matching robe. He stood over her, looking at her, visually caressing her so powerfully that she could feel his touch. Her nipples puckered and peaked. Her femininity clenched and unclenched. Tingling sensation flooded her body with hot moisture. She watched while he removed the condom from its wrappings and then eased it into place over his erection.

As he put his knees on the bed, on either side of her

thighs, his big hands came down to her face and his fingers traced the outline of her facial bones, as if he were trying to memorize their structure. He gazed at her with adoration and longing, then lowered his head and kissed her. A feather-light brush of lips. She opened her mouth on an indrawn sigh, expecting his invasion, but instead he showered her face and neck with kisses, then moved over her shoulders, down her arms and upward across her belly until he reached the underside of her breasts. When she tried to touch him, he grabbed first one hand and then the other and lifted them over her head.

"You can touch me later," he told her, his voice ragged with desire. "Right now, just concentrate on feeling and sensing and enjoying the pleasure I want to give you."

She simply smiled at him, then closed her eyes, loving the idea of being pleasured by Hunter Whitelaw. He kissed and licked and caressed her body. Her arms. Her legs. Her neck, shoulders, back, belly and buttocks. Arousing her to the point of pleading frustration. Her breasts ached. Her nipples tightened painfully. The feminine folds of her body gushed with moisture and her core throbbed. But he avoided touching her nipples or stroking her intimately and the longer he made her wait, the more desperate she became.

When he had her primed and ready, he flicked his tongue over one nipple and then the other, eliciting a cry of arousal from her lips. She reached up for him, unable to keep her hands off him any longer.

"Please, Hunter. Please."

"Please, what?"

"Please, make love to me."

"That's what I've been doing," he said, his voice a rasped whisper.

She touched him, surrounded his sex and pumped him gently. "I want you inside me."

"You know it's going to hurt," he said, a strained expression on his face, as if the thought of inflicting even a minute amount of pain was intolerable.

"I'm already hurting and only you can take away that pain."

He cupped her buttocks, lifting her as he sank down, bringing their bodies together. His sex probed and found what it sought, then eased inside slowly. She shuddered, longing, spiraling out of control within her. And then with one forceful lunge, he took her, thrusting deep, imbedding himself completely. She cried out as searing pain burned throughout her femininity and her body stretched to accommodate his size.

He kissed her. Wild and hot. Devouring her mouth as he began to move inside her, retreating and then advancing, repeating the process until her pain lessened and finally vanished. While he made love to her, she felt totally possessed, as if with each hard, urgent lunge he claimed her as his own, branding her with his mark. Her body tightened around him, holding him, milking him. She felt the stirrings of completion and knew she was on the verge of fulfillment.

Suddenly Hunter tensed, then stopped and took several deep breaths. She moved against him, urging him to action. She opened her eyes and looked up at him. His face was wet with perspiration, his eyes hooded, his jaw clenched.

"Hunter?"

"I'm losing it fast. I've got to take a minute."

"I don't need a minute." She moved against him, showing him that the time was now.

"Oh, Manda…"

He pumped into her with frantic need. Within seconds she climaxed. An earth-shattering completion that shook her to the core. Shards of pleasure exploded inside her and just as she shivered uncontrollably, Hunter roared like the beast he had become at that primal moment.

As the aftershocks of their lovemaking fluttered through her, Manda sighed contentedly and curled up against Hunter when he eased off her and onto his back. He lay there for several minutes, breathing hard, his heart thumping loudly. Manda inched her fingers across his chest to play in his damp, curling hair. He captured her hand, brought it to his mouth, turned it palm up and planted a hot, wet kiss in the center.

She wanted to confess her love, to shout it from the rooftops, to tell Hunter that he was the love of her life, the man she had been born for, but she remained silent. Anything she said might jeopardize this indescribable bliss. She was happier than she'd ever been. And she wanted to hold on to that happiness and make it last as long as possible. For tonight and tomorrow and the rest of the week.

"I knew it would be good," Hunter said. "I just never thought it would be that good."

Manda smiled when he caressed her naked hip. She had known that being Hunter's lover would surpass anything that came before or afterward. "Being with you was everything that I dreamed it would be."

"It's not always that powerful, you know. Sometimes it's lazy and easy and sweet. And sometimes it's wild and crazy and so hot you think you'll burn up alive."

"I want to experience everything." She lifted herself up so that she could gaze down into his face. "With you."

He clutched the back of her neck. She trembled.

"Give me a little time to recuperate and we'll see what

happens the second time around.'' He met her lips in a
languid kiss that lasted a good long while. "Now, lay
down and be a good girl. Get some rest because later on
I'm going to wear you out."

"I'm looking forward to that."

Her last thought was how satisfied and content she felt
lying in Hunter's arms. And how safe.

Seconds became minutes and minutes hours and time
began to blur into one long, continuous pleasure. They
made love, then slept. They made love, then soaked in
the hot spring. They made love, then fed each other fruit
and berries and fresh-baked bread left on their doorstep
by their hosts. They made love and swam in the creek,
beneath the waterfall. And with each mating, the bond of
possession grew stronger until Manda thought of Hunter
as her husband, her mate for life. And she suspected that
he was beginning to think of her in the same way. Sunday
passed. Monday came and went in a sensual haze. When
Tuesday brought thunderstorms, they stayed indoors all
day, leaving their bed only when absolutely necessary.

At twilight they stood together on the porch, his arms
holding her close, and watched the sunset. At dawn they
woke to the birth of a new day and the renewed passion
that had only hours earlier been temporarily satisfied.

They talked about their childhoods, each sharing the
heartbreak of having lost loved ones. He, his mother,
whom he'd barely known, and his devoted grandparents.
She, her mother and father, as well as Rodney and Mike.
They had laughed about Manda's teenage crush on Hunter
and the amount of willpower it had taken him to resist
her. She told him more about Rodney, feeling comfortable
sharing her memories with Hunter. And he vented his

frustration about his disappointing marriage to Selina and his inability to trust another woman. Until Manda.

They spoke of liking each other, of caring deeply. Of enjoying lovemaking almost beyond reason. But love was never mentioned, although Manda didn't see how Hunter could miss the look of love in her eyes every time their gazes met.

She didn't press for more, didn't ask for anything beyond this fantasy honeymoon. Soon enough reality would destroy the fantasy. The demon who had plagued her for so long was yet to be destroyed.

Wednesday evening Manda and Hunter finished off a dinner of delicious chicken stew and cornbread, left by their hosts in a box on the front porch. And a batch of chocolate brownies had been wrapped in a red-and-white-checked kitchen towel and placed atop the other items. Hunter had built a fire in the cookstove and made coffee. After their meal, they took their cups out onto the porch and sat side-by-side in the wicker rocking chairs. Yesterday's rain had nourished the verdant woods and new life sprang up all around them. The scent of honeysuckle wafted on the evening breeze, blending with the subtle sweetness emitted by the flowers on the climbing rosebush that curled around the lattice attached to the side of the porch.

He would prefer to postpone this moment forever. Had rather face a firing squad than destroy Manda's peace of mind. But she had known that this honeymoon couldn't last, that their mission was yet to be accomplished. What real difference would it make if tonight or tomorrow or this coming weekend brought that ending? They had no choice but to face a harsh reality. The person who had manipulated Manda's life for his or her own needs was still out there, waiting to strike, preparing to kill.

While Manda had napped this afternoon, Hunter had walked up to the Landry's cabin and made a couple of telephone calls. Perry would leak the information, to Gwen and Claire and Chris tonight. And then to Boyd and Grady tomorrow morning. Matt O'Brien would bring the Dundee agents in by helicopter tonight and the Landry family would head down to Dover's Mill, the closet town to Sequana Falls. Sequana Falls, named for the nearby waterfall, was the surrounding area, including the land on which the Landry cabin had been built. The agents would form an unseen guard and lie in wait for an uninvited guest. Unless Hunter had calculated wrong, Manda's crazed admirer had probably built up a big head of steam by now and wouldn't be thinking straight. All the better. An irrational attacker would be more vulnerable and thus easier to catch.

"Manda?"

"What?"

When she looked at him and smiled, he felt like the biggest heel in the world. She trusted him. How would she react when he told her that he had kept the truth from her? The plan to entrap Manda's harasser had been worked out in detail before their wedding day. Would she understand that he had chosen not to tell her until the last minute because he hadn't wanted her to spend days and nights worrying about what was going to happen?

He cleared his throat. "There's something I have to tell you and I'm afraid you're not going to like it."

She set her coffee mug on the porch floor, then turned to him. "What's wrong?"

"Nothing's wrong. Not exactly. It's just that something is going to happen…probably…and you need to be prepared for it.'' He downed the last drops of coffee and placed his mug beside Manda's on the floor. ''I guess I should have told you before now, but I didn't want to—''

''Tell me,'' she said. ''Whatever it is, just tell me.''

''All right.'' He stood, walked across the porch to the edge and gazed out over the slopping land that dropped gradually to a clearing that overlooked the valley below the cottage. With his back to her, he said, ''The night before our wedding, actually in the hours before dawn, after you finally went to sleep, the other Dundee agents and I formed a plan to capture this maniac.''

''What sort of plan?'' Manda got up and walked over to stand by Hunter. She didn't touch him, didn't look at him, simply stayed at his side.

''Tonight Perry is going to let Gwen and Claire and Chris overhear him telling Grams where we went on our honeymoon. And in the morning, he's going to reveal the same information in a similar manner to Boyd and Grady.'' Hunter waited for her response; there was none. He went on, ''If my guess is right, our nutcase should be in a frenzy by now, knowing that not only are we married, but that we've made love. He's not going to wait for us to come back to Dearborn, not when he can sneak up here while we're all alone and kill us.''

''You've known about this plan the whole time. Every day. Every night. All the while we've been... You knew this was coming, knew that our honeymoon would be cut short.''

Hunter grasped the porch railing, his big hands manacling the wooden rounds so tightly that his knuckles turned white. Manda laid her hand over his.

''It's all right,'' she said. ''I'm glad I didn't know, glad that you waited until tonight to tell me.''

He turned to her then, and when she smiled at him, he

breathed a heartfelt sigh of relief. "Thank God you don't hate me. I was afraid that you wouldn't understand."

She reached up and caressed his cheek. "You're in the right business, do you know that? You're a man who instinctively protects those he cares about, whether they want to be protected or not."

He pulled her into his arms. "Are you saying that in the future, you'd prefer for me to be totally honest with you up front and not keep any secrets?"

She slipped her arms around his waist, tilted her chin and stood on tiptoe. "That's a good idea. But, no, actually I'm saying that I am an old-fashioned woman who likes having a big, strong man around to protect me."

"Manda, Manda, you are definitely my kind of woman."

"I'm glad." She lifted her face to his, inviting his kiss.

"Because you're my kind of man," she whispered against his lips.

He loved the sweet softness of her mouth, the eagerness with which she responded to him. She held back nothing, giving herself completely to every moment as if it might be their last. The very thought of losing her, of having to give her up and walk away once all this was over, made him want her all the more. She had become as addictive as any drug, her power over him growing stronger each day.

He had meant the kiss to be reassuring, but it quickly got out of hand. His tongue plunged and swirled, seeking, discovering, awakening the desire he couldn't control. Not when Manda was in his arms, her breasts against his chest, his sex pulsing against her mound. He eased his hand between them and undid the buttons on her blouse, then reached inside to cover her bare flesh. Her breast filled his hand. When he massaged the nipple, she keened quietly, deep in her throat and hurriedly ran her hands beneath his loose shirt to splay them on his back.

He picked her up and set her on the wide banister railing, all the while kissing her lips, her cheek, her ear and then her neck. When he lowered his head to her breast, she clung to him to balance herself and then reached out to unzip his jeans. His sex sprang free.

Accepting the invitation she offered, he shoved her skirt up to her hips, then spread her legs and lifted her just enough to position her so that he could fit himself into her. She whimpered when he rammed into her hot, wet depths and she held on to him as he pumped her hips back and forth, creating a grinding rhythm that soon had them both panting. As the tension tightened, the pace accelerated. She moaned and sighed. He grunted and growled. And they came apart simultaneously.

When they regained control of their senses, Hunter helped her down and onto her feet, then cupped her chin and ran his thumb across her lips.

"I didn't use any protection," he said. "I'm sorry, Manda. I let things get out of control."

She licked his thumb. "It's all right. I enjoyed it even more without the barrier between us. I loved feeling that part of you inside me."

"Damn, Manda, you keep talking dirty like that I'm going to lose my head all over again."

She took his hand and led him into the house, into their room and straight to their unmade bed. The sheets were rumpled, the pillows at odd angles and the quilts hung halfway on the floor.

"If this is our last night, then let's make the most of it," Manda said. "I want to go to sleep in your arms tonight and wake up in your arms tomorrow morning."

They shed their clothes, then Manda sat on the edge of the bed and held open her arms. Hunter went to her, wanting what she wanted, needing what she needed and praying that tonight would never end.

Chapter 16

Morning came too soon, the mountain wrapped in mist before the sun broke through the clouds and brought another beautiful spring day to Sequana Falls. Manda and Hunter made love one last time, each knowing what lay ahead. Their mating ended in a frenzy and when it was over they held fast, lingering, reluctant to let the moment pass. But no matter how much they wanted it, time would not stand still. The day progressed, each tick of the mantel clock like a nail hammered into a coffin. Hunter tried to keep her occupied, playing checkers, playing poker, sharing his plans with her for his retirement.

"You know, I really am serious about moving back to Dearborn, into the old farmhouse. I'd like to raise fruit and cattle and become a gentleman farmer," he'd said.

Unbidden thoughts of living on the farm with him came to mind. Thoughts of her being his wife, of bearing his children and raising those sons and daughters out in the country, in the sunshine and fresh air. *Strong, healthy chil-*

dren, Elizabeth Landry had predicted. More than any-thing, she wanted those children to be Hunter's. If dreams came true, they could build a life together. Side-by-side, day and night, year after year.

Manda struggled to stay calm and sane and not run from the cottage screaming. The pressure built as they waited, not knowing when or if her crazed admirer would show up. If Mr. Maniac wasn't one of Hunter's suspects, then no one would come to the cottage today or tonight and all this waiting and worrying would have been for nothing. And they would have to face the moment of truth when they returned to Dearborn. Manda didn't know which scenario would be worse. Of course, it really didn't matter. Now or later, the confrontation was inevitable.

Although she had neither seen nor heard the Dundee agents, she knew they were out there, strategically posi-tioned to guard the cottage. Jack Parker. Matt O'Brien. Wolfe. And another agent she hadn't met by the name of Domingo Shea. They lay in wait, silent and deadly. A force to be reckoned with. Professional guardians of souls in trouble. Each man prepared to lay down his life in the line of duty.

Afternoon slipped by, one slow torturous moment at a time. No visitors came to their door, not even a squirrel or a field mouse. She had forced herself to eat a sandwich for lunch, but when dinnertime came, she refused to taste even a bite. Her stomach was tied in knots. Her head throbbed. And her nerves rioted. Every noise upset her. Even the rustle of tree limbs scraping across the roof of the cottage when the breeze grew stronger.

"I'm sorry you have to go through this," Hunter said as he came up beside her while she paced in the living room. "If I had the power, I'd spare you every minute of this waiting."

She paused and offered him a weak smile. "I know." Although she felt the tears coming, she willed them to stop. Now was not the time to cry, to give in to weakness. She had to stay strong and in control. Hunter didn't need to deal with her hysteria while he was preparing to bring down a madman.

"This will all be over soon." Hunter reached for her.

She practically fell into his arms, thankful for his strong embrace. "If something doesn't happen soon, I'm going to lose my mind."

He kissed her forehead, then captured her face with his hands and gazed into her eyes. "Just hang in there, brat." He swallowed hard. "My sweet, beautiful, little brat."

His mouth devoured hers, telling her without words how much he cared, and oddly enough the kiss also told her that he was scared. Afraid for her, not himself.

"I'll be all right," she promised when he allowed her to come up for air. "I won't fall apart on you. Whatever happens, I'll hold it together."

He caressed her face, tenderly, with the utmost gentleness. "I know you will. You're a lot stronger than you think you are. What you've been forced to live through would have destroyed a lesser woman."

She took his words into her heart, storing them there where they could comfort her in the future.

The mantel clock struck five-thirty. Manda jumped. Hunter ran his hands up and down her arms in a soothing gesture. If something didn't happen soon, sometime in the next couple of hours, night would fall and the tension would continue to increase. Fear thrived and grew stronger in darkness.

Suddenly Hunter heard the signal. Wolfe's birdlike

warning call. Someone was coming, heading straight for the cottage. But who? God, who?

"Manda?" He clutched her shoulders.

"Yes?"

"There's someone coming."

"How do you know?"

"Listen. Did you hear that?" he asked.

"Are you talking about the bird chirping?"

"Yes, but that's not a bird. It's Wolfe alerting us of danger."

Manda's face paled, but she didn't cry out, didn't even gasp.

"I'm going to put myself in the line of fire," he told her. "I want you in the room so you can be seen, but not directly in front of a window." He lifted her sweater and checked her bulletproof vest, then kissed her and led her to the far corner of the room. "We need to be talking and acting as natural as possible."

"What if the Dundee agents can't shoot him before he—"

"They will get him before he gets me," Hunter assured her. "Once he pulls a gun and aims, they'll take him down. They'll try not to kill him, but if they have no other choice, they will."

The mantel clock's ticking hammered inside her head. She began talking, jabbering about the weather, then changing the subject to discuss first one thing and another. Hunter replied and commented, helping her keep the conversation going at a fairly normal pace.

Suddenly, unexpectedly, she heard footsteps on the porch. Whoever was out there, he wasn't doing a very good job of sneaking up on them. Loud, pounding bangs hit the front door repeatedly.

"Manda, dear God, if you're in there, come to the door!" a male voice called.

She knew that voice. Regret welled up inside her. She hadn't wanted it to be him. It would break his mother's heart.

"You're in danger, damn it. Please, for pity sake, let me in!" Chris Austin begged as he kept beating on the door.

"Stay where you are," Hunter whispered to Manda. "I'm going to open the door."

"No!" Manda gasped the word, fear and uncertainty overriding every other emotion.

"If he pulls a gun, Wolfe will take him out with one shot."

When Hunter walked to the door, Manda held her breath. He grasped the knob. Her heartbeat went wild. He opened the door. Her nerves shrieked.

Hunter's big body blocked her view so she couldn't see the man who stood on the porch, but she could hear him.

"Have you seen her? Is she here? Please, Manda's life is in danger. And so is yours."

Moving lightning-fast, Hunter grabbed Chris Austin and jerked him into the living room, then twisted Chris's arm behind him in a painful maneuver to subdue him. Chris yelped.

"You've got to listen to me," Chris said. "I came to warn y'all."

"Warn us about what?" Manda asked. "Warn us that you killed your own brother and then Mike. Warn us that you've made my life a living hell."

"Damn it, Manda, it wasn't me." Chris looked at her pleadingly. "You've got to believe me. I know the truth now. I've suspected it for some time, but I wouldn't let myself believe it."

"What the hell are you talking about?" Hunter asked.

"He's talking about me." The female voice came from the porch.

Hunter whirled around, using Chris as a shield when he faced Claire Austin. She stood just outside the open door, a 9 mm Smith & Wesson in her hand. He glanced at the gun hurriedly. Then he studied the woman's face. Pure hatred radiated from her, an emotion so strong that it seemed to take on a life of its own.

"Claire?" Manda gasped.

"Yes, dear girl, it's me."

"Don't move," Hunter warned. "She has a gun."

Manda's mind simply could not assimilate all the information that was bombarding her. Confusion reigned supreme. Chris was her crazed admirer, wasn't he? He had come here to kill Hunter and her, hadn't he? So what was Claire doing here? Had she found out that her own son was a murderer and had come to try to stop him from killing again?

"Mother, please, don't do this," Chris said. "You're sick. You don't know what you're doing. You don't want to hurt Manda. You love her. Remember how much she means to you."

A startling truth began to break through the cloud of confusion inside Manda's brain, but she couldn't bear to face that truth because it was so hideously ugly.

"Mrs. Austin, why don't you put down the gun?" Hunter retained his hold on Chris, continuing to use his body as a shield. "Chris is right. You don't want to hurt Manda."

"I didn't want to harm her," Claire said. "Not until she defied me and married you. I warned her. She knew the risk she took by being unfaithful to Rodney. She was my son's bride. You must see that I couldn't allow her to be with another man.''

"Claire, please..." Manda took a tentative step. "I don't understand. I know you didn't kill Rodney. You would never—"

"Rodney's death was an accident," Chris said. "She went a little loopy after it happened, don't you remember?''

"Why don't you shut up, Chris?" Claire said. "Of course, I didn't kill Rodney, but it was in my best interest to allow you to believe that the person responsible for Mike's death had also killed Rodney."

"Did you kill Mike?" Hunter asked.

"I paid someone to do it," Claire admitted. "Just as I hired someone to kill you."

"Mother, you can't do this," Chris said. "There are three of us. You can't kill all three of us before one of us stops you."

"Don't get in my way," Claire warned her son. "If you interfere in what I must do, then I will shoot you, too."

Everything happened all at once. Manda came forward, her hands outstretched in a pleading gesture. Hunter yelled for her to stay back. Claire Austin aimed her pistol. Chris broke free while Hunter was preoccupied with Manda's safety. The gun in Claire's hand went off simultaneously with another gun, a rifle shot from outside in the woods. Chris yelped, grabbed his shoulder and fell backward while his mother's eyes widened in shock. Claire dropped to the floor as blood oozed profusely from the gaping wound in her chest.

Manda screamed and screamed and screamed. Somewhere inside her mind, she knew what had happened. Saw Chris lying wounded on the living room floor. Saw Claire crumpled on the porch, the exit wound from a rifle shot no longer bleeding. Saw Matt, Domingo and Jack storming the cottage. And saw Wolfe hold back, staying out in the yard, pointing his rifle toward the ground.

The moment Hunter touched her, she stopped screaming, then sucked in a deep, hard breath.

"It's all over," he told her. "You're safe and I'm safe."

"How is Chris?" Manda trembled uncontrollably.

Hunter glanced over at the man. Jack and Matt carried him to the sofa.

"How is he?" Hunter asked the Dundee agents.

"Shoulder wound," Jack replied. "Doesn't look too bad. I think he'll make it."

"What about Claire?" Manda asked.

Without hesitation, Hunter said, "She's dead."

"Oh, God, I never dreamed that Claire…that she was capable of murder. I thought I knew her. I believed she loved me." Manda tried to hold back the tears, but the flood of emotion that she had held in check was about to break free. "You remember that promise I made to you not to fall apart? Well, I'm fixing to break that promise."

She burst into tears. Painful, gasping sobs. Hunter slipped his arm around her waist and led her through the kitchen and out the back door, away from the scene of both shootings. While she cried, he held her, his hands soothing her, his words comforting her.

Hunter had accompanied Manda to Claire Austin's funeral. She had been buried next to her late husband and in the same plot as her eldest son Rodney. Chris had attended, his arm in a sling and his shoulder still bandaged. Odd thing was that Hunter actually felt sorry for Chris, despite the fact that he didn't like the man and never would. But Chris had cared enough about Manda to try to warn her against his own mother. Hunter had to give him credit for that.

"Mother had been restless and edgy ever since Manda's wedding," Chris had told them. "Then after we overheard Perry telling Mrs. Munroe where y'all went on your honeymoon, she stayed up the whole night roaming around the house like a madwoman. I tried to talk to her, but she kept putting me off. So when she left the house the next afternoon, I followed her, making sure I kept far enough behind so that she wouldn't see my car and know what I was doing."

Manda had insisted on visiting Chris while he'd been in the hospital and Hunter had to admit that when she kissed the guy, albeit only on the cheek, a surge of jealousy had ripped his gut apart. Any way you looked at it, he was as possessive as hell when it came to Manda. His wife. But not for long. It was only a matter of time until Perry began divorce proceedings and their brief marriage would come to an end.

They had stayed at the Munroe house after they returned from Sequana Falls and had shared a bedroom that first night, although all they had done was sleep together. But the minute Grams had found out that the marriage had been a farce, a lie perpetrated to apprehend Manda's harasser, she had insisted Manda and Hunter have separate bedrooms. When Manda hadn't protested, he'd known that not only was the honeymoon over, but so was the marriage.

Today would be his last day in Dearborn. He had made plans to return to Atlanta first thing in the morning. He'd told Manda that Perry could mail him the divorce papers to sign, and she had simply nodded. What the hell had he expected, that she would put up a fight? Did he really

think that she would want to stay married to him? He had
served his purpose, now it was time for him to get the
hell out of Dodge. Manda no longer needed him. She had
her brother and her grandmother to comfort her. And one
day in the not too distant future she would find another
husband, one she wanted to spend the rest of her life with.

Today he had the Munroe house all to himself. The
morning after Claire Austin's funeral, Gwen had made
reservations at a spa and left for the week. Perry had gone
back to work yesterday, after taking time off to be with
Manda. Grams was spending the afternoon playing bridge
with her cronies. And Manda had told him that she had
some errands to run and wouldn't be back until later.

Passing the time alone, he watched TV for a while, but
soon realized that he was too restless and on edge to relax.
Maybe he should take a swim in the pool and work off
some energy. He went outside and found a pair of Perry's
swim trunks in the pool house, then quickly changed into
them and dove into the pool. He made several laps and
soon began to feel the tension inside him easing up some.
He swam the length of the Olympic-size pool two more
times, then hauled himself out and dried off. The sun was
warm and bright, almost straight overhead, announcing
the high-noon hour.

Hunter lay in the wicker chaise longue, closed his eyes
and tried not to remember the last time he'd sat beside
this pool. Seventeen years ago. But he could not stop himself from remembering. His vision was of Manda parading
around in front of him wearing that skimpy red bikini. He
had been torn between wanting to shake her until her teeth
rattled and wishing that she wasn't sixteen.

When he heard movement nearby, he opened his eyes.
There stood Manda. In a bikini. A skimpy red bikini. He

blinked several times, wondering if he had fallen asleep and was dreaming.

She sat beside him, then held out a bottle of sunscreen. "Do you mind doing my back?" she asked. "I can't reach my back and with this fair skin, I burn easily."

He had to be dreaming. This wasn't really happening. His mind was playing tricks on him, reliving a moment from the past.

"Sure, I'll do your back. Turn around."

The minute he took the bottle of sunscreen and felt the container in his hand, he realized this was no dream, that this was happening, that this was real.

Manda undid the string that held her bikini top in place and removed the scrap of red material, then tossed it aside. "There, that'll make it easier for you."

"Easier for what?" he asked, then swallowed the huge lump in his throat.

"Easier for you to apply the lotion," she replied, then turned around so that he could see her naked breasts.

"I thought you wanted me to put this stuff on your back."

She snatched the unopened bottle out of his hand and threw it on the table between them, then stood and came over to him. "Don't you want to protect my front, too?"

"Brat, I want to protect every delicious inch of you."

She leaned over him and when she did, he grabbed her and dragged her down on top of him. She giggled with pure delight.

"You've already made so many of my fantasies come true, I was wondering if you'd mind fulfilling one more," Manda said.

"One more for the road?" he asked, wondering if this was her way of saying goodbye.

She kissed him playfully. "Are you going somewhere?"

"Back to Atlanta tomorrow," he replied. "But you already knew that."

"You can't leave," she said.

"Why not?"

"What if I'm pregnant?"

Every muscle in his body tensed. Pregnant? It was possible. He had made love to her that one time without using a condom. What the hell would they do if she was pregnant? They damn well wouldn't get a divorce.

"If you're pregnant—"

"I'm probably not," she said. "Not yet. But if we keep practicing, it's bound to happen sooner or later."

"If we keep practicing?"

She rubbed herself against him and laughed when his sex pulsed against her mound. "We could do some practicing right here, right now. And who knows, by the time we celebrate our first anniversary, you might be a daddy."

"A daddy." Hunter almost choked on the word. What sort of game was Manda playing? *Pregnant. First anniversary. Daddy.* "How do you propose we share a first anniversary when we're going to get a divorce?"

"We're not getting a divorce," Manda said.

"We're not?" His heartbeat roared in his ears.

"I've lost too many people I love. I have no intention of losing you. So, Hunter Whitelaw, you'd better get used to the idea of being married to me because I'm never going to give you up."

"You're not?" He found the string ties of her bikini bottom and hurriedly undid them.

"Don't you think it's time for us to be honest with each other? Time to confess." She gasped when he peeled her bikini bottom off her buttocks and caressed her naked flesh. "I'll go first. I love you, Hunter. I've loved you since I was just a kid and I'll love you to my dying day."

Her words wrapped themselves around his heart, filling him with a happiness he had never known. Manda was all that he wanted, everything he had ever dreamed of in a woman. And more. And she was his. His wife. His· lover. His friend. And someday she would be the mother of his children.

"I've never loved anyone else," he told her. "Not the way I love you, Manda. You're everything to me."

"That's what I wanted to hear." She kissed him again, this time a little less playfully. "Now, how about making that fantasy of mine come true."

"Would that fantasy have anything to do with my making love to you out here by the pool?" he asked.

"Mmm-hmm. But we'd better hurry," she told him. "Grams will be back from Mrs. Anderson's in about an hour."

"Oh, brat, what I can do to you in a hour."

And much to her enjoyment, he proceeded to show her.

Epilogue

Manda buzzed around in her big country kitchen, the first room she and Hunter had remodeled in the old White-law farmhouse. In the thirteen years they had lived there, they had completely restored the house, the barns and added peach and apple trees to the orchard. Hunter raised prime Angus cattle and kept the pond stocked with fish for the delight of their children and guests alike. She had worked part-time at the Hickory Hills Clinic until two years ago when their youngest child started kindergarten, then she returned full-time. Her life was all that she had ever dreamed it could be—and more. Being Hunter's wife and the mother of his children brought her complete happiness.

"They're coming!" Twelve-year-old Dalton, her first-born, announced as he came rushing through the back door. "Daddy said that he saw Uncle Perry's car coming around the bend by the pond, so you'd better round up the girls and get out on the front porch, pronto."

Oxford raised his head from the floor, where he lay by his feeding dishes in the corner, then roused up and padded over to Dalton, who rubbed the old dog's ears.

"You get your sisters and take them with you," Manda said. "I've got to put the cover on this cake to hide it and check the pot roast in the oven."

"Sure thing." Dalton smiled, then raced out of the kitchen.

Her son's smile was so like his father's. Although he was blond like her, he resembled Hunter a great deal. At twelve, Dalton was already five-ten, which was a good indication that he would probably reach his father's six-four height by adulthood.

She hurriedly covered the birthday cake, then opened the oven to check on the pot roast and vegetables. After testing and finding the meat cooked to perfection, she put the lid back on the pan and turned the oven down to the warming temperature. Everything was ready. All they needed was their guest of honor. As she darted up the hall, Manda glanced to the left and then to the right to give the living and dining rooms one final visual check. She wanted everything to be perfect today.

Just as she walked out onto the porch, Congressman Perry Munroe parked his SUV in the driveway. Hunter came over and put his arm around her waist and within minutes both girls attached themselves to either side of their parents. Nine-year-old Barbara, named for Grams, was her mother's look-alike, except for her dark brown hair. But little Miss Rebba, their seven-year-old named for Hunter's grandmother, was the spitting image of her father and was already as tall as her older sister. Sometimes people mistook the girls for fraternal twins.

Perry emerged from the SUV, then ran around to the passenger side to help Grams. While her brother lifted

their grandmother to her feet, Lisa and the kids got out
and Perry's children came rushing toward their cousins.
Zeda was eight and her younger brother Zack was six. His
children were the joy of Perry's life, but Lisa was his heart
and soul. The day his divorce from Gwen became final
twelve years ago, Perry had phoned Manda and asked her
to fix him up on a date with Lisa. His request had surprised Manda, but delighted her. Within a year Manda had
been helping Grams plan another Munroe wedding.

Using a walking cane to aide her, Grams held on to
Perry's arm as he helped her up the steps and onto the
porch.

"Well, I hope y'all have a big celebration planned for
me today," Barbara Munroe said. "After all, it isn't every
day an old lady turns ninety."

"We've got you lots of presents," Rebba said. "And
Mama baked you a birthday cake."

"Rebba, you weren't suppose to tell," young Barbara
scolded her sister. "It's supposed to be a surprise."

"That's quite all right, dear girl," Grams said. "I'd be
surprised only if y'all forgot my birthday."

Dalton came forward and held out his arm to his great-
grandmother. "Would you like to see the trophy I won
for being the most valued player on our Little League
baseball team?"

Grams released Perry's arm and took her great-
grandson's. "You know that your uncle Perry and your
father were very good athletes. They were stars of their
football team."

When Grams passed Hunter, she paused and glanced
up at him. "Don't I get a birthday kiss from my favorite
grandson-in-law?"

Hunter dutifully kissed her. "Happy birthday, Grams."

The other children followed Dalton and Grams into the

house. They could hear Grams chatting away, telling the kids about when Perry and Manda were youngsters.

Perry and Lisa exchanged hugs with Manda and Hunter and the foursome lingered on the porch.

"She's amazing, isn't she?" Lisa said. "If I didn't know it was true, I'd never believe she was ninety. She still plays bridge three times a week, never misses a church service, swims in the pool with the kids and manages to keep Bobbie Rue in line."

"Let's face it, honey," Perry said, "Grams manages to keep all of us in line."

"Oh, Grams has never had a problem with voicing her opinion or issuing orders," Manda said. "But when she's wrong, she likes to forget about it and pretend otherwise. She would never admit now that she was opposed to my marrying Hunter."

"She had her doubts about me up to the day Dalton was born," Hunter said. "Then suddenly I could do no wrong because I was her first great-grandchild's father."

Lisa laughed. "Same with me. Remember how she reacted when Perry told her that he was marrying me, a secretary at the Hickory Hills Clinic? But the minute I got pregnant with Zeda, I suddenly became the most wonderful wife and mother-to-be in the world."

Young Barbara cracked open the front door and called, "Grams says would everyone please come inside."

The adults obeyed instantly. They found Grams seated on the sofa in the living room, flanked by Dalton and Zack. Rebba and Zeda sat on the floor on either side of Gram's feet.

"The queen and her subjects," Perry said.

While Perry and Lisa went into the living room, Hunter pulled Manda aside and down the hallway, just far enough so that they couldn't be seen by the others. When he slid his arms around her waist, she lifted her arms to circle his neck.

"Happy, Mrs. Whitelaw?"

"Deliriously happy, Mr. Whitelaw."

"I don't think I've told you lately how much I love you," Hunter said, lowering his head so that his lips almost touched hers.

"Not since we got out of bed this morning."

"Then let me rectify that error immediately." With his lips brushing hers, he said, "I love you, Manda. More than life itself."

"And I love you."

The moment he kissed her, they became the only two people in the world, lost in a passionate love that only grew stronger and deeper with each passing year.

Suddenly Manda felt a tug on her skirt and heard Rebba's little voice saying, "Mama, Grams says for you and Daddy to behave yourselves and get in the living room right now. She's ready for her birthday party."

*   *   *   *   *

THE PROTECTORS
continues next month
with a brand-new,
longer length, single title release,

THE PROTECTORS:
SWEET CAROLINE'S KEEPER

Only from
Beverly Barton
and
Silhouette Books!
Available in June at your
favorite retail outlets.
Here's a sneak preview...

Chapter 1

She wasn't quite sure what she'd been expecting, but the man standing on her front porch wasn't it. He was tall, broad-shouldered and lean, with a bronze tan, thick dark blond hair and tinted aviator glasses that hid his eyes. He wore a cream-colored sport coat and a teal-blue shirt, casually elegant attire for a man with money who wanted to project a fashionable and yet masculine image. He wasn't handsome, but he was devastatingly attractive, in a self-assured way that professed to the world he was a man to be reckoned with. A shiver of apprehension fluttered in Caroline's stomach.

"I'm Wolfe," the man said, his voice dark and rich and distinctively Southern.

"Won't you come in, Mr. Wolfe? We've been expecting you. I'm Caroline McGuire."

When she held out her hand, he simply stared at it for endless seconds, then encompassed it within his own huge hand. The moment they touched, a current passed between them. A shocking sensation of awareness.

''Hello, Caroline,'' he said.

Startled by her reaction to the stranger, Caroline snatched her hand away, but couldn't stop looking directly at him in the same way he continued staring at her. Did he feel it, too? she wondered. That odd sense of recognition, as if she had known this stranger all her life, perhaps even in a dozen other lifetimes.

He couldn't take his eyes off her. She was more lovely than any picture he'd ever seen of her. This was Caroline—his Caroline. He wasn't sure exactly when he'd begun to think of her that way. It had been a gradual thing, taking place so imperceptibly that he had no way of pinpointing the precise moment that his thoughts of her had become obsessively possessive. Perhaps if he'd had a family of his own, his feelings for Caroline wouldn't have taken on such monumental proportions. Aidan Colbert had had a few distant relatives, but no real family to speak of, and David Wolfe had no one. There were no parents, no siblings, no wife and no children. Only Caroline.

When he noticed the flush on her cheeks and the way she suddenly broke eye contact, Wolfe realized he had been staring at her for longer than was socially acceptable. In the future he would have to be careful and take advantage of unguarded moments, when no one else was around, to drink his fill of her. He wondered if a thousand lifetimes would be enough.

Then he remembered why he was here, what had brought him into her world. And he realized he had no rights where she was concerned. None whatsoever. He could never be more to her than a bodyguard, an intruder into her private world....

In July 2001

New York Times bestselling author

TESS GERRITSEN

joins

ANNETTE BROADRICK

&

Mary Lynn Baxter

in

TAKE5

Volume 4

These five riveting love stories are quick reads, great escapes and guarantee five times the suspense.

Plus

With $5.00 worth of coupons inside, this is one *exciting* deal!

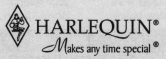

HARLEQUIN®
Makes any time special ®

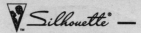

where love comes alive—online...

eHARLEQUIN.com

your romantic
books

- 🌷 Shop online! Visit Shop eHarlequin and discover a wide selection of new releases and classic favorites at great discounted prices.

- 🌷 Read our daily and weekly Internet exclusive serials, and participate in our interactive novel in the reading room.

- 🌷 Ever dreamed of being a writer? Enter your chapter for a chance to become a featured author in our Writing Round Robin novel.

• • • • • •

your romantic
life

- 🌷 Check out our feature articles on dating, flirting and other important romance topics and get your daily love dose with tips on how to keep the romance alive every day.

• • • • • •

your
community

- 🌷 Have a Heart-to-Heart with other members about the latest books and meet your favorite authors.

- 🌷 Discuss your romantic dilemma in the Tales from the Heart message board.

your romantic
escapes

- 🌷 Learn what the stars have in store for you with our daily Passionscopes and weekly Erotiscopes.

- 🌷 Get the latest scoop on your favorite royals in Royal Romance.

All this and more available at
www.eHarlequin.com
on Women.com Networks

SINTA1R

SILHOUETTE® MAKES YOU A STAR!

Look in the back pages of
all June Silhouette series books to find an
exciting new contest with fabulous prizes!
Available exclusively through Silhouette.

Don't miss it!

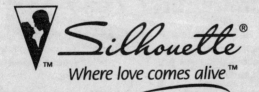

Silhouette®
Where love comes alive™

P.S. Watch for details on how you can meet
your favorite Silhouette author.